M&B Literary Creations

Copyright © 2013 by M. E. May

Library of Congress Control Number
2013917614

Cover Art by Julie Kukreja, Pen and Mouse Design

Quote used with the permission of Ashleigh Brilliant©

Printed in the United States of America
10 9 8 7 6 5 4 3 2

Books by M. E. May

Circle City Mystery Series:
Inconspicuous
Perfidy

Dedication

In loving memory of two people who were very dear to me, my sister-in-law, JoNell Magee, and my brother-in-law, Dorsel White. Their lives were an inspiration to many and they are sorely missed.

Acknowledgements

The *Circle City Mystery Series* would be nothing without those who serve and protect the great city of Indianapolis—the men and women of the Indianapolis Metropolitan Police Department. I am especially grateful to those in the department who have been willing to answer my technical questions about the IMPD's policies and procedures.

I also want to acknowledge those in the Indianapolis Fire Department for assisting me with water recovery procedures. They also advised me on the difficulties of recovering remains that have been in the water for a long period of time. Thank you for helping me be as accurate as possible.

Thanks to Matt Aston, President of GPRS, who sent me a wonderfully detailed description on how to use a Ground Penetrating Radar device. He not only gave me details on its use, he also described how weather, soil composition, and soil depth can affect the device's accuracy.

To those who work with the dogs at Indiana K9 Search and Recovery, I am most grateful for the information on how these amazing dogs are trained, and how they are able to find remains even under the most impossible circumstances. A special thanks goes to Leah for reading and critiquing the chapters where the dogs are working. In my research with this group, I learned that this organization is totally funded through donations, so the work they do is free to those who need them. A portion of the net sales from this novel will be donated to this organization. If readers would like to know more about Indiana K9 Search and Recovery, please take a look at their website at: http://indianak9sar.org/ .

Thanks go out to my critique partners and authors, Sue Myers and Lisa Mork, for reading my first drafts and providing honest, helpful guidance. To my faithful friend and fellow author, Tricia Zoeller, who has been reading my prose since the day I started writing, I give my thanks.

Of course, I wouldn't be able to get through all the publishing highs and lows without my family—my husband, Paul; my children, Brian and Marie; and my four wonderful grandchildren, Kodey, Kaleb, Kameron and Gustin. Their encouragement and support mean the world to me.

"Please don't lie to me unless you're absolutely sure I'll never find out the truth."

–Ashleigh Brilliant©

Chapter 1

Tommy Sturgen was about to experience the perfect fishing day. Pulling his vehicle into the parking lot near the boat docks, he saw the brilliant colors of a sunrise about to peak over the dam. This third Sunday of June started out at an unseasonably cool temperature of sixty-eight degrees. He knew the fish would bite like crazy on a day like this.

Eighteen-year-old Tommy and his younger brother, Bobby, pulled their fishing gear from the trunk of the car and headed for their dad's fishing boat. This was the first time his father had entrusted Tommy to take the boat out on his own with his brother in tow.

The two of them loaded their gear and a couple of small coolers onto the boat. They climbed in; Tommy started the engine, and headed out onto the still blue waters of the reservoir. After finding a spot in the newly opened fishing area, Tommy stopped the boat, cut the engine, and dropped the anchor. They prepared their lines with flies, weights, and bait.

Tommy frowned at Bobby. "Ain't that the fly Grandpa made and gave to you for Christmas?"

Bobby nodded.

"I thought you said you wasn't gonna use it 'cause it's special."

"Changed my mind," stated Bobby.

"Okay," Tommy sighed. "It's your loss if it gets tangled up."

"Don't worry about it," Bobby retorted, scowling.

"You've got too many weights on there. The line will go too deep."

"Shut up, Tommy! I've been fishin' long enough to know what I'm doin'."

"Shh! Keep your voice down," Tommy whispered. "You'll scare off the fish."

Bobby sneered at his brother, gave him the finger then cast his line. It didn't take long for Tommy's prediction to come true. After casting it a third time, Bobby's line caught on something and he couldn't get it loose.

Bobby tugged on the line. "Shit!"

"Watch your mouth."

"Yeah, Tommy. Like you've never said *that* word or worse

before. My fucking line is caught!"

"I told you that would happen." Tommy couldn't believe his brother's defiant attitude. "Cut the line."

"No! I'm not losing Grandpa's fly. That's the last one he made for me before he died. I'm going in after it."

"You lookin' to join him?"

"No," Bobby said, angry tears forming in his eyes. "I can't lose it, Tommy. I'm a good swimmer." He looked around the floor of the boat. "This rope, tie it around me. If I get in trouble, I'll tug it and you can pull me up."

"I don't know, Bobby," Tommy said his face lined with worry.

"Come on, Tommy. I can't lose Grandpa's fly."

"Okay, okay. Give me a minute to pull up anchor and start the engine. I'll go slowly while you reel in your line so we can get closer to where it is."

Bobby reeled the line in slowly, raising the rod above his head. It appeared to be at least five feet out.

"You make sure you keep reelin' in the line as we move closer to it. If it gets tangled up in the motor blade, it'll snap and we'll have to forget it. Understand?"

Bobby nodded.

Tommy proceeded slowly while Bobby kept his line as taut as possible without snapping it. When they reached the spot where the line appeared to be nearly straight down, Tommy stopped and cut the engine. He dropped the anchor again to keep the boat from drifting.

"Okay, Bobby. You know if you go and drown yourself I'll be joining you and Grandpa shortly."

Bobby gave him a baffled look.

"Mom and Dad will kill me."

"I won't drown." Bobby put the pole in the rod holder locking the reel. Then he stripped down to his t-shirt and boxers, shivering in the nippy air. "Tie the rope around me. Oh, and get my goggles out of my backpack."

Tommy retrieved Bobby's goggles. "You ready Aquaman?"

"You're so lame. I'm fifteen. I don't like cartoons anymore."

"Whatever, jack off. Let's just get this over with."

Tommy tied the other end of the rope to one of the seats and steadied the boat as Bobby entered the cold dark water. Bobby gave him a thumbs-up, breathed in deeply then dove. Tommy held onto the rope loosely in case Bobby tugged it.

Tommy noted Bobby had been down there for almost a minute when he felt a hard tug from the rope. He tried to pull it up, but it wouldn't budge. Tommy stripped off his shoes and jacket and dove into the water. He opened his eyes which burned in the lake water. Following the rope, he searched desperately for his brother.

Finally, he saw Bobby still yanking on the rope, a portion of it caught on something. Tommy could see the panic stricken Bobby wasn't trying to untie it from around his waist. He reached his brother and concentrated on loosening the knot. It wouldn't come loose. He dove further down to the source of their plight, admonishing himself for not thinking to untie the rope from the other end. Tommy found the rope hooked around a car bumper. He pushed it with his feet and pulled at the rope, which finally broke loose of its grip.

Swimming toward his brother, he grabbed Bobby's arm and pulled him toward the surface. Once Bobby realized he was free, he pulled away and swam upward. Seconds later, both boys emerged splashing, coughing, and spitting.

"Tommy, did you see that?" Bobby spat.

Tommy nodded and coughed. "Get in the boat, Bobby."

They swam to the boat. Bobby tossed his precious fly in, and Tommy helped him hoist himself into the boat. Then Bobby held it steady while Tommy pulled himself in.

"What the hell?" Tommy retrieved a towel from the floor of the boat and threw it at Bobby. Then grabbed one for himself. His cold soaked clothing made him shake.

"L...l...looks like there's a...a...a... car d...d...down there," Bobby said through chattering teeth.

"No shit!"

"Watch *your* mouth!"

"Okay, smart ass," said Tommy, glaring at Bobby's pale face and blue lips. "Just tell me what *you* saw."

"It's got a lot of gunk on it, but I could see the bumper and part of a license plate."

"That how you got stuck, idiot? You decide to take a closer look."

Bobby frowned. "What difference does it make? I'm fine."

"There's only one reason I'm not tellin' Mom and Dad how stupid you are. If they find out you nearly drowned tryin' to get that fly, they'll never let us take the boat out again. Right now, we have to call the police. We've scared all the fish away from here by now so we may as well go ashore to wait for them."

Tommy pulled up anchor, cranked up the engine again and headed for shore. He pulled his cell phone out of his backpack and called 911.

Chapter 2

"All right my brothers and sisters! I've got these very tasty *It's a Girl* candy bars for y'all." Detective Tyrone Mayhew entered the sea of desks in the Missing Person Department smiling as if he'd won the lottery.

Today, he beamed with pride. Nine days ago, he and his wife had danced at Mandy Stevenson's wedding reception where a very pregnant Jada's water broke. Two hours later, their fourth child and only daughter came into the world. Tyrone insisted they name her Adanne, which means 'resembling the mother'. In his eyes, this child definitely inherited her mother's beauty.

"What happened to good old cigars, Mayhew?" shouted Detective Warren Hill.

"The wife won't have anything to do with those *nasty things*. Bad enough you smoke them smelly cigarettes, Hill."

Tyrone grinned broadly, as he tossed a bar to each of his colleagues receiving their congratulations as he made his way to his desk. There at the next desk with stacks of files between them, Tyrone found Sergeant Benjamin Jacobs working on his computer and looking sullen.

"What's goin' on jackass? Don't you want to share in the joy of my newly born daughter?"

Jacobs glanced up at Tyrone. "Oh, it's you. Congratulations. I would've come by the hospital, but they let her out so fast I didn't get the chance."

"Yeah, these days they barely get in there before they're sendin' them home. Her mama's here for a couple more days." Tyrone tossed a candy bar to Jacobs, which hit his jacket sleeve and then skimmed across his keyboard. Jacobs looked up at him with his best *I'm the jackass?* stare.

"So what'd I miss this past week?"

Jacobs pushed back in his chair in a more relaxed position. "Captain Melrose decided to retire. He never fully recovered from the bullet he took a couple of years ago. He's still having memory issues, so he took early retirement."

"That's a shame," said Tyrone. "You said *took*. Is he already gone?"

"Yep, he left the department last week. They announced Lieutenant Terhune as interim commander. I bet they make it permanent."

"Yeah, well, he's a good man." Tyrone lowered his voice and watched Hill devour his candy bar. "Better Terhune than Hill, the cocky S.O.B."

"I couldn't agree more," said Jacobs. "I'm glad you're back because we've been assigned a cold case."

"What's up?"

"You made it back just in time to help me reinvestigate the Wendy Matherson case."

"Wendy Matherson?" Tyrone crinkled his nose in thought. "Why does that case sound familiar?"

"It's a case from ten years ago, when I was still on the streets. You and Percy Grimes investigated this one the first time around."

"Oh, now I remember. I'd just started in Missing Persons. Wendy Matherson. Early 40's, dark hair and blue eyes. Last seen havin' dinner with a friend on a Saturday, sometime in July."

"July second."

"Husband said she never came home Saturday night. There'd been some tension in the marriage, so we looked at Mr. Matherson first. They had three boys who I believe were sixteen, thirteen, and nine at the time."

"Good memory." Jacobs raised an eyebrow.

"You never forget your first." He watched Jacobs roll his eyes.

"Anyway, yesterday a couple of teenagers were fishing in Eagle Creek Reservoir and snagged a line on something, so the one kid jumps in to see what's going on. He spots something which looks like part of a vehicle. The other kid calls it in on his cell. Sheriff's Department asked for a couple of fire department divers to take a look. When they'd cleared off some of the sludge, they found a red 2002 Dodge Intrepid. They had a hell of a time pulling it out of there. Car's in the lot waiting for Forensics to go over it. The plates on the car belong to Mrs. Matherson so they called us in on it."

"Interestin'," said Tyrone. "Was she in it?"

"Nope, no remains were in or around the car. Fire Department's going out again today."

Tyrone leafed through the case file. "Does the husband know?"

"Lieutenant Terhune informed Reid Matherson yesterday afternoon. We've been able to keep the car's owner out of the news so far, but you know how it is."

Tyrone nodded and paced, rubbing his chin. "Her kids would all be adults now. Are they still living in the area?"

"I checked." Jacobs pulled out his notebook. "The oldest boy, Tanner, now twenty-six, went to Ohio State University, completed his Pre-Pharmacy degree three years ago. He's in the OSU Doctor of Pharmacy graduate program now."

Jacobs turned the page. "Son number two, Ryan age 23, attended Rose-Hulman. He graduated from the Aerospace Studies program a year ago. He's now a lieutenant in the Air Force stationed in Fort Sill, Oklahoma."

"The youngest son, Jared, just turned nineteen. He seems to be the troubled one. He has a sealed juvenile record, so his problems started a long time ago. He went to Purdue University in Lafayette for a semester. According to Purdue's records, he got into a couple of fights in his dorm. They told him to make other living arrangements, so he dropped out. He was failing anyway. Rarely made it to class, etcetera."

"So where's the kid now?"

"I'm getting there," said Jacobs, eyebrows knitting together. "Seems he decided to come back to town and live with Dad. The Indiana University side of IUPUI accepted him. He tried his hand at a degree in Liberal Studies. He squeezed out a 2.8 GPA his first semester; however, the next semester he started cutting class again, missing tests and assignments. He flunked out. Current employer is a garage door place in Carmel. Called there this morning, they said he called in sick. I thought you and I could go have a little chat with him."

"Sounds like a plan." Tyrone tossed the case file on his desk. "I'd like to stop at the park to see where they found the car first. We can see if the divers have anything new."

Jacobs furrowed his brow. "We can go, but there's not much to see."

"I know, but sometimes it helps me get a feel for somethin'. Like, why there?"

"It's hard to buy the idea Mrs. Matherson would have bothered putting her car there in an attempt to make it look like she'd disappeared," said Jacobs.

Tyrone saw Jacobs eyeing the pink wrapped candy bar, which had slid between his keyboard and telephone. "No breakfast again this mornin'? Grab your candy bar and you can eat it on the way to the dump site."

Jacobs grabbed his notepad and slipped it in his pocket. The candy bar was out of its wrapper and half eaten before they even got to the elevator.

"I've missed you, Sarge," said Tyrone as they entered the elevator.

"I told you not to call me that," said Jacobs, his words muffled by the gooey, melting chocolate.

Tyrone simply smiled.

Chapter 3

"So, this is where they found the car." Tyrone peered at the still water from his place on the bank. He could see crime scene tape draped from trees and posts for several feet along both shorelines. The fire fighters had aligned buoys with crime scene tape in the water prohibiting boat traffic, squaring off the crime scene area.

He and Jacobs turned to see a red fire department SUV approaching. It must be the divers from the Indianapolis Fire Department. Tyrone recognized Lieutenant Marvin Clark as he climbed out of the vehicle.

"Hey, Clark!" Tyrone approached the lieutenant and extended his hand.

Clark grabbed Tyrone's hand, shaking it vigorously. "Mayhew, you son-of-a-gun, it's been a long time. Where you been keeping yourself?"

"Producing offspring," said Jacobs.

"I heard," said Clark. "Congratulations. Heard you and Jada had a girl this time."

"Finally, and she's a beauty." Tyrone beamed, nearly forgetting his purpose.

"Must look like her mother then," quipped Clark.

"Definitely," Jacobs agreed.

Tyrone gave Jacobs a dirty look then spotted a thin woman with bright orange hair pulled back in a ponytail. She was wearing a wet suit and pulling diving equipment from the vehicle.

Clark gestured toward her. "That's Kelly McPhearson. She's been with us for two years now. Kelly's great at finding the little things."

"What's she looking for?" Jacobs said, frowning.

"She'll search the area where we found the car to see if there's any debris we missed the first time around. The car was pretty rusty and we're sure we lost parts when we pulled it out of the water yesterday."

"Is there a crew looking for the owner's remains?" Tyrone pointed to the reservoir.

"We didn't find her in the immediate area. After ten years, it becomes very difficult for us to find human remains. The skeletal bones become darker and covered with silt so they blend in.

Depending on how much the water is moving, it's hard to see the bottom. Luckily, the reservoir is pretty still unless they open the dam. We checked and they don't plan to do that any time soon."

Jacobs paced a couple of times, gazing at the water. "Could she have floated away from this site?"

"I doubt it; otherwise, she, or pieces of her, would have been found a long time ago," said Clark. "As a body decomposes, it can come apart. The only way she's down there is if someone sealed her in something and weighted her down. I have a second team coming who will do a wider search. There comes one of our recovery teams now."

Clark pointed up the road at the oncoming vehicle. "If we don't find anything today, we may want to ask for a water recovery dog. At least the dog could tell us where to search. Doesn't matter how long a body's been in the water, those dogs can find it."

Three more fire department personnel exited the dual cab truck. The driver positioned the truck so he could back up and put the boat into the water. Two of the newcomers guided him and in a short time, the boat was in the water and the driver was parking his truck. Lieutenant Clark and Kelly McPhearson put their equipment in the boat and prepared to head out.

"You can stick around if you like," called the lieutenant.

"We'll be here for a while," said Tyrone. "I want to check out the area."

Tyrone watched as Lieutenant Clark guided the boat to a spot about 1,000 feet away. Dropping anchor, Clark helped McPhearson with her gear. Once fully equipped, McPhearson sat on the edge and dropped into the water scuba tank first. Two of the four men who'd come in with the boat had put on gear and were walking out to the area nearest the shore.

Tyrone scanned the area where forests of lush green trees, many of them maples, grew. Turning, he saw a large picnic shelter containing at least twenty tables and parking area behind him. What was it like here ten years ago? How had the car wound up so far away from shore?

"What's going through your bald little head?" asked Jacobs.

"Did you ask the Parks and Recreation people what this area was like ten years ago?"

"*No.* They just found the car yesterday," answered Jacobs testily. "It's only 9:30 on a Monday morning. When was I supposed to get around to talking to them?"

"Okay," said Tyrone. "I've been off a while. I forgot they just found the car yesterday."

"Alright then," said Jacobs, who then turned and walked towards their car in a bit of a huff.

As he watched his partner walk away, he said to himself, "If any man needs the love of a good woman, that one does. I sure hope he and Erica make up soon. I don't know how much longer I can take this bitchy attitude."

Then, he followed Jacobs to the car and they headed for the Parks and Recreation office.

Chapter 4

Leaving the site in the capable hands of the fire department crew, Jacobs and Mayhew headed out. It took about fifteen minutes for them to reach the Parks and Recreation offices. The Planning Office was the place to go to find the changes made in the past ten years.

"May I help you?" asked a middle-aged woman from behind the counter.

"Yes, please," said Jacobs. He introduced himself and Tyrone to the woman and told her what they needed.

"Certainly, I'll be very happy to find those records for you. Just have a seat at the tables over there and I'll be right back with the plans from ten years ago and our current plans so you can compare."

Tyrone and Jacobs waited at a tall, long, waist high table for her. Leaning forward and resting his elbows on the table, Tyrone stood in silence as he looked at the bland décor that only the photos of wild game could save.

"Here we go," said the clerk. "Let's spread these out and take a look. Point out the area where you found the car on the most recent map."

Tyrone checked the map scanning down the road they'd taken. "Here it is. The car was found approximately 1,000 feet from this shoreline."

"Okay," she said, placing a small ruler on the spot. "Let's compare this map."

Tyrone spotted the area marked in the same block on the older map. "Is this the same area? The reservoir looks bigger in the newer map."

"You're correct, Detective Mayhew," she said, smiling. He felt like he was in elementary school again. "As you can see, it's a good 1,000 feet wider. At some point, the planning commission must have decided to allow more water into the reservoir. I can look up those records if you like."

"Thanks," said Jacobs. "That would give us a timeline to follow."

"I'll check my computer and be right back," she said, her enthusiasm palpable.

"She must not get many visitors," Jacobs noted.

"She is a bit over-the-top, isn't she?" said Tyrone. He hadn't seen anyone so anxious to please in a very long time.

"This answers our question though, doesn't it?"

"It should make even more sense once we find out when it happened," said Tyrone. "It would definitely explain why no one found the car right away."

"Here we go, gentlemen," the clerk announced upon her return. "I've made a print out of the information for you. You'll see that ten years ago on July first the planning committee decided there needed to be more water released into the reservoir. The plans I showed you from ten years ago would have been created months before the decision was made."

"Thank you so much," said Jacobs. "You've been very helpful. This is precisely what we needed."

She beamed at him and scurried over to the table to roll up the maps.

As they walked out the door, Tyrone nudged Jacobs with his elbow. "And I thought *she* was over-the-top."

"I just wanted to make her feel good about her job," said Jacobs. "Besides, this is big. I just wonder how much press it got. This could be the reason why the person who dumped the car was assured it wouldn't be found right away."

"I expect you're right," said Tyrone. "So what's next?"

"We'd better go talk to the family. See what they have to say. We'll start with Jared."

Chapter 5

"I'm back, Pop." Erica Barnes gave her dad a quick peck on the cheek handing him the car magazine she'd just purchased at the grocery store. "What do you want for lunch?"

"Depends." He looked over at her with one eyebrow cocked. "I don't want any of that rabbit food you've been feedin' me."

"You need your veggies," she said, giving him a toothy grin and setting her bags on the counter.

"I didn't see you eatin' any of it. If it's so good for me, maybe you should start eatin' it now so you don't have a heart attack later." She could see a cantankerous mood brewing. This wasn't going to be an easy afternoon.

"So what's got your feathers all riled up?"

"I'm tired of bein' cooped up in this house all the time. The only time I see daylight's when you take me to the doc. It's been a month; when's this damn elbow going to heal up?"

"I know it's hard to lose your independence, Pop, but you know it takes older bones longer to heal."

"How could somebody your age know what it's like to lose your independence?" he snapped.

Erica turned away from him, a pain radiating through her chest. She most certainly did know what it was like. She'd used her father's injury as an excuse to stay with him these past few weeks. After what had happened in her apartment a month ago, the idea of moving back terrified her.

"Whatever you say, Pop. Now what about lunch?"

"I'll compromise," he said. "How about some turkey bacon, lettuce and tomato sandwiches? With light mayonnaise, of course. That'll get my rabbit food in."

"Comin' right up." She smiled as she pulled out a pan. Her dad was just as scared as she was right now. He'd taken a fall, which knocked him unconscious and he'd suffered a broken elbow. The doctor told them it would take six to eight weeks to heal because of his age. She could tell the incident shook him. He probably felt as frightened as she did about being alone.

"So, how's Ben? Heard from him lately?"

"I've talked to him a couple of times." She and Ben Jacobs had been an item for over a year now, but her near death experience had put a wedge between them. She'd met someone on her last case that made her feel things that only confused her. She loved Ben, but she needed time to sort out her feelings. Another good reason to stay with Pop.

"You need to sit down and talk to the boy," he said, giving her his famous squinty-eyed glare.

"I don't have time for dating right now...."

He slammed his fist on the table and Erica jumped.

"You look here young lady; men like Sergeant Benjamin Jacobs don't grow on trees. You knew exactly where things stood before all that mess with the Emerson case and that FBI jerk. Don't look at me like that. That guy's a player. Believe me, I know the type."

"You've made your point. I'll invite Ben over for dinner sometime soon, okay?"

"That's more like it. Now when you goin' back to work. You're gettin' on my nerves."

"And here I thought you loved having someone around to cook your meals and wait on you hand and foot." She looked into his eyes and watched them soften. He'd had his little tantrum and now he was going into loving father mode.

"Kitten, I've been where you've been. I know you're not stayin' here just to take care of me and make sure I behave myself." He got out of his chair and touched her shoulder. "It's hard to be a cop and worse to be in homicide. Seein' the horrible things people do to one another for the craziest reasons messes with your mind. However, your case is solved and he won't be botherin' you anymore. You're young. You need to get your life back on track."

She knew he was right. "I'm seeing the department shrink. We're making progress. He suggested I get a different apartment, you know, kind of a fresh start."

"You know I don't put much stock in those head doctors, but he may be right. Maybe you should buy a condo or a small house. Invest in something that won't suck all your money into somebody else's pocket. Call Ben and go out to dinner or have him over here. I want you to be happy, Kitten, and staying here lookin' after your dear old dad isn't cuttin' it."

She grabbed her father and hugged him tight. He squeezed her with his good arm and kissed her cheek.

"Thanks, Pop. I love you, ya know."

"I love you too, Kitten." He pulled back from her and gave her a faux frown. "Now where's my lunch?"

Chapter 6

"This is the house they lived in when Mrs. Matherson disappeared?" asked Jacobs. "Looks sort of run down."

"Sure does," responded Mayhew. "Not as many flowers around. Looks like Mr. Matherson let those rose bushes turn into hedges. It definitely needs a woman's touch."

Jacobs rang the doorbell twice before a tall lanky young man with the dark stubble of a beard, dark brown hair, and blue sleepy eyes appeared.

"Yeah," he said, yawning.

Tyrone figured they'd woken him. "Are you Jared Matherson?"

"Who wants to know?"

The detectives showed him their badges. "This is Sergeant Jacobs. I'm Detective Mayhew. We're from Missing Persons."

"Who's missing?" he asked, yawning again and rubbing his right eye with the heel of his hand.

"We found new evidence in your mother's case," said Tyrone.

"You're shittin' me," he said, eyes opening wider. Then his face fell. "Did you find her?"

"No," said Jacobs. "Is it all right if we come in and talk to you?"

"Oh…sure…sorry." He stepped aside, allowing the detectives to enter. "By the way, I *am* Jared. Can I get you some coffee or something?"

"None for me, thanks," Jacobs answered while Tyrone shook his head. "Why aren't you at work?"

"Oh, it's not working out," said Jared. "They get a little pissed when you're late once in a while, so I called in sick. I'm gonna quit before I wind up getting fired."

Tyrone glanced around the living room. On the mantle, he saw photos of the children when they were young, a couple of candlesticks, and a set of books. However, he saw no photos of Wendy Matherson there or anywhere else in the room.

"Okay, then," Jared said as he quickly grabbed blankets off the couch, making room for them to sit. "What new evidence did you find?"

Tyrone looked over at Jacobs who shrugged. Obviously, Reid Matherson hadn't told his son about the discovery of his wife's car.

From the photos Tyrone had seen of her during the initial investigation, he couldn't help but see Wendy Matherson's face behind the young man's beard. Jared definitely had her clear blue eyes.

"I was one of the detectives originally assigned to the case," said Tyrone. "Do you remember me?"

"Detective Mayhew, I have a hard time remembering anything from the night Mom didn't come home. My dad said I went to bed at 10:00 p.m. and didn't wake up until 6:00 a.m. I remember Dad said he'd take us to buy fireworks, because the Fourth of July was coming up. When I asked him where Mom was, he told me he didn't know. She hadn't come home Saturday night. I remember arguing with him, because I thought she had, but he said I must have dreamed it."

"So you didn't wake up in the middle of the night? You didn't even get up to use the bathroom?" asked Tyrone.

"I don't remember," said Jared. "I know the bad dreams started shortly after Mom disappeared, but I can only remember pieces of them."

"Like what?" Jacobs asked.

"Stuff like a monster trying to get me, blood, being scared. Then later, graves and dying."

"Who died?" asked Mayhew.

"Me," Jared answered. "So, are you going to tell me about the new evidence?"

"A couple of fishermen found her car in Eagle Creek Reservoir," said Jacobs. "There was no one in the car, but diving teams are out there looking for more evidence."

"Could she have escaped?" Jared asked, jumping to his feet. "Maybe she got out. That's it!"

Jared surprised Tyrone with his sudden manic behavior. He was pacing and excited like someone who'd just made a great scientific discovery.

"She probably hit her head or something and couldn't remember who she was," said Jared waving his arms. "That's why she didn't come home."

"Whoa there, Jared," said Tyrone. "There isn't any indication anyone was in the car when it went into the water."

Jared turned abruptly, staring into Tyrone's eyes. "This doesn't make sense."

"Since we found no remains in the vehicle, it's hard to tell how or who put it there," explained Jacobs. "When they pulled the car from the reservoir, parts of it fell off and there are divers looking for them as we speak. A lot of damage occurs after ten years of submersion. It will be very difficult to prove whether or not she was in the car when it went into the water."

"It could have been placed in neutral and pushed in, or something could've been wedged on the accelerator to make it move forward," said Tyrone, trying not to give Jared any false hopes. "Truth is no one really knows much at this point. The lab's goin' over the car very carefully. If there's a clue to be found, they'll find it."

"I know," Jared responded. "I keep hoping she'll miss me enough to come back. Maybe then the nightmares will go away."

"I hope you get your wish, son," Tyrone said, his heart heavy with sympathy for the boy. Tyrone's own father had died when he was only eight. There were five kids. His mama and three older brothers worked hard to keep the family together and to provide for him and his little sister. His mama taught him everything about being a good man—respecting his elders and the ladies.

"Here's my card," Jacobs said, handing one of his business cards to Jared. "Let your father know we stopped by and need to talk to him."

"He's not going to like it," Jared said, shaking his head. "Some of the kids made fun of me at school, saying the cops thought Dad had killed Mom. Dad was really upset when that was going on. He didn't think the police investigated other suspects thoroughly enough."

"Spouses are generally the first suspects," said Tyrone. "Assure him we're not accusing him of anything. I know we checked out some leads in the initial investigation, but we had no concrete evidence of foul play or a viable suspect. Even now, all we have is the car and it's been in the water so long any DNA evidence will be gone."

"I know, but Dad doesn't feel the police did their job the first time around. I don't think he'll trust you now."

"Just make sure he knows we need to talk to him," said Tyrone. "If he doesn't contact us by tomorrow afternoon, we'll come back or we'll stop by his office."

"I'll tell him," Jared said, grinning. He showed the detectives to the door. Tyrone thanked him for his time saying they'd stay in touch.

"Last time I saw Jared he was the same age as my oldest son is now," said Tyrone opening his car door. "Ten years of nightmares. Lordy."

"Before you came in this morning, I looked over the old files. Mr.

Matherson wouldn't let you or Grimes interview Jared or his brothers back then. At only nine, nobody thought it was necessary. If he's been having bad dreams all these years, maybe he *did* see something."

"That's what I'm thinking," said Mayhew. "We'll see what Dad says now that he can't keep Jared or his brothers from talkin' to us. I'm hungry. Let's grab some lunch."

"Always thinking about your stomach, aren't you?"

"I need my strength. I not only have to put up with your sorry ass, I've got four kids to deal with."

"Whatever. Shapiro's is right around the corner. How about I treat the new daddy to a Reuben?"

"You're on!"

Chapter 7

"Fill me in on the Matherson case," said Lieutenant Terhune as soon as Tyrone and Jacobs returned from lunch. "Did you get a chance to speak with any of her family yet?"

"We went over to the house today and talked to the youngest son, Jared," said Jacobs. "It seems his father hadn't told him about the car. Jared was excited to hear we'd found it, but didn't think his father would be very happy about talking to us."

"He's probably right," said Terhune. "Reid Matherson didn't seem pleased with me when I called him on Sunday afternoon to inform him of the find." Terhune fixed his gaze on Mayhew. "So what's your take on Jared?"

"He seems genuinely excited to finally have a clue in his mother's disappearance, but doesn't remember much. This is the first time I've spoken to him. He was only nine when this all happened and daddy dearest wouldn't let us interview him."

"From looking at the files, it appears that this kid's been pretty messed up," commented the lieutenant. "Did you get a line on the others?"

"I called and spoke with the eldest son, Tanner," answered Jacobs. "He didn't want to discuss it on the phone. He's on break from school and said he'll be in town tomorrow. Ryan was able to convince his superiors this was a family emergency, so he should be in sometime tomorrow."

"You should talk to Mrs. Matherson's family as well," said Terhune. "I take it they've been notified about the car?"

"Yes, I spoke with them by phone," answered Jacobs. "We didn't want them to hear it from the news media. Her brother and sister were ecstatic to hear we've reopened the case."

"Of course, we never close cases until they're solved," said Lieutenant Terhune.

"They always maintained their sister wouldn't leave so abruptly," said Tyrone. "They insisted she'd never leave her boys behind."

Jacobs pulled out his notebook. "The sister, Cindy Woods, is a stay-at-home mom. Got her address right here if you want us to go interview her."

"Sounds like a good idea, Sarge," Mayhew said with an impish grin.

"Stop calling me Sarge," Jacobs growled under his breath.

"Just tryin' to give you the respect you deserve."

Lieutenant Terhune frowned at them. "Okay, *children,* what else do you have for me?"

"We stopped off at the Parks Department this mornin'," said Tyrone. "We talked to the Public Information Officer about the configuration of the crime scene area ten years ago."

"She looked up their old records and discovered the shoreline there was about 1,000 feet farther in than it is now," said Jacobs. "That explains how the car could be so far away from the current shoreline. They'd dredged the current shoreline a month after Mrs. Matherson disappeared, giving the car enough time to sink and be unnoticed. When they opened up the dam to fill it in to the current shoreline, the force could have shifted it even further until it settled into the position where we found it."

The lieutenant rubbed his chin. "Which means it could have been placed in the water somewhere closer to the dam."

"Yeah, that's possible, but not probable. We also stopped by the crime scene before we came back here to check on our divers," stated Tyrone. "We told Lieutenant Clark about the shore line change. He's thinkin' about usin' water recovery dogs to try to locate remains, if there are any. The only things they've found in the current location are the front bumper, a windshield wiper and one of the side view mirrors."

"No signs of clothing, jewelry, or anything else which might have belonged to Wendy Matherson?"

"No, sir," answered Tyrone. "Lieutenant Clark said they'd just about covered a radius which went shore-to-shore and 1,000 feet in both directions. There's nothing to indicate Miss Matherson was in the water."

"We're still waiting on Forensics to process the car," said Jacobs. "I checked with Impound before this meeting. Sergeant Fisch says they have three other cars ahead of ours. It'll be at least a couple of days before they can get to it."

Lieutenant Terhune tapped his right index finger on the desk. "Is there anything else?"

"No, sir," said the detectives simultaneously.

"Then you'd better get going. I'm sure Mrs. Woods will be anxious to give you her viewpoint again. Maybe she'll come up with something we don't have in the reports."

"You got it, Lieutenant," said Tyrone.

Chapter 8

After the meeting with Lieutenant Terhune, Tyrone drove to the far northwest side of the city with Jacobs to interview Cindy Woods. Cindy lived in a blond, brick ranch house in one of the older, well-established neighborhoods with her husband and two daughters. Tyrone remembered how Cindy had championed her sister's cause by convincing the media to come to their annual "Don't Forget Wendy" vigils. Her brother, Kevin Saunders, was supportive, but not quite as vocal as Cindy was. As Tyrone pulled up to the house, he saw her emerging from a blue Honda Civic.

Cindy turned when Tyrone's car pulled into her driveway. When he exited the vehicle, she said, "I wondered if you might be back on the case, Detective Mayhew."

"Believe me, Miss Woods; I want to find out what happened to your sister almost as badly as you do."

"I doubt it, but thanks for saying so."

"This is Sergeant Jacobs. He's our shift supervisor and will be working on your sister's case with me."

"I believe we spoke on the phone." She extended her hand. "Nice to meet you, Sergeant Jacobs. What happened to the detective who worked with you originally?"

"Detective Grimes' wife wanted to live closer to her family in Cincinnati. He moved there about five years ago. The last I heard, he's workin' for the Cincinnati P. D."

"No offense, but I'm glad he's gone," she said. "He never seemed to believe my sister might be in trouble or dead. I didn't feel he took as great an interest in finding her as you did."

"We all had our opinions. I just couldn't buy a dedicated mother leaving her kids," said Tyrone. "Not for this long."

"Oh, gosh! I'm so rude," she exclaimed. "Please come in and sit down so we can talk."

Cindy unlocked her front door, set her purse and keys on a table in the foyer, and then guided them to the kitchen. Honey brown cabinets, white counter tops, and bright yellow eyelet curtains made the room warm and inviting. She gestured for the detectives to take seats at the round maple table.

"Would you like some coffee, a soda, or water?" she asked.

"Coffee, please," said Jacobs.

"Coming right up. You too, Detective Mayhew?"

"Yes, thank you."

"I know I may come across as way too happy about this," she said, as she measured the coffee. "It's just that no real effort has been afforded this case for a long time. I've accepted the fact something awful happened to Wendy. I've grieved for her already. Now, I just want to find her and give her a proper burial."

"So *you* think she was murdered?" Jacobs pulled out his notepad, pen poised for her answer.

"I believed it back then for a variety of reasons. Now that you've found her car dumped in the reservoir—yes, you bet I do." Cindy's reaction to his question brought a harsher tone to her voice and a red tinge to her cheeks. "Of course, I've always said there was no way my sister would have gone away without trying to contact her sons. She loved them more than life itself. No matter what went on between her and Reid, she wouldn't have left those boys."

"I'm sure you've answered a lot of these questions before," said Tyrone. "I hope you don't mind answering them again. Since Sergeant Jacobs wasn't involved in the case from the beginning, he may catch something Detective Grimes and I didn't."

"I understand, and I'll answer questions a hundred times over if necessary. All I want is justice for my sister."

"We know she had problems in her marriage," Jacobs began. "I saw in our files her husband thought she was having an affair."

"Hmph! If she was, she didn't say anything to me. We were very close. She would have told me if she was involved with someone. I think Reid tried to deflect suspicion onto someone else." She turned as the coffee maker finished brewing. "Do you gentleman take anything in your coffee?"

"A teaspoon of sugar, please," said Jacobs.

"Black's fine," said Tyrone.

She poured the coffee, set the sugar bowl and a spoon in front of Jacobs, and then brought them each a cup. After adding cream and artificial sweetener to her cup, she joined them at the table and continued.

"I don't hate my brother-in-law. I just don't feel he's telling us everything he knows."

Jacobs had just taken a sip of coffee, so Tyrone took over. "Can you be more specific?"

"He absolutely refused to let his sons talk to anyone about their mother, especially the police. He claims they were all in bed and sound asleep, so he saw no reason for the police to harass them."

"He can't keep us from talking to them now," said Tyrone. "Matter of fact, we talked to Jared early this mornin'."

Cindy leaned forward. "Did he tell you anything?"

"He doesn't remember much," said Tyrone. "He remembers goin' to bed, wakin' up the next day and being told his mama didn't come home."

"What a crock," she exclaimed, stomping her foot. "From what I've heard, Jared's a mess."

"We know he had a hard time in school and barely made it into college only to flunk out," said Jacobs. "When we talked to him today, he mentioned nightmares he's been having ever since his mother disappeared."

"I didn't know." Her eyes welled with tears. "Poor, sweet Jared."

"Have you ever tried to contact him?" asked Jacobs.

"Reid refused to allow any of our family to talk to them. He said if we weren't going to support him, the boys were off limits. I don't know how he expected to get our support when he kept acting like he was hiding something."

"I see what you mean," said Tyrone.

"It's a shame, too," said Cindy. "Jared and my eldest daughter are the same age and were very close. It was tough to tell her she might never see her cousin again. I can only imagine what Reid told Jared. His mother disappears for no apparent reason and then he has her family stripped away from him. He must feel so alone."

Tyrone needed to get the focus back on Wendy Matherson. "Miss Woods, can you think of anyone else Miss Matherson had problems with? Co-workers? Boss?"

"The only significant problems I knew about involved Reid."

"So she had problems with someone else?" Tyrone watched her facial expression change. "Miss Woods, even if you think it trivial, you need to tell us about anyone who might have been upset with her."

"About six months before she disappeared, she'd had a confrontation with one of the vets where she took her cat."

"Tell us about the argument," said Jacobs.

"Pansy, their cat, had been ill for a while. She'd been very lethargic, vomiting from time-to-time. When Wendy took the cat to the clinic, the only vet who could see her was one with whom she wasn't familiar."

"Go on," said Tyrone.

"The veterinarian misdiagnosed Pansy's illness," said Cindy. "When the cat died, her regular vet told Wendy about the misdiagnosis. She was so upset. She'd nursed Pansy from birth because the mother had rejected her."

"So she confronted the guy," said Jacobs.

"Oh, yes," said Cindy. "Wendy told me she'd asked to speak with him while she was there and they ended up in a shouting match."

"Did anything else come of this?" Tyrone didn't recall this coming up in the initial investigation.

"After she had Reid pick up Pansy's ashes, she talked to the corporate office about the incident. She told them if they didn't do something about the guy she'd contact her lawyer and file a lawsuit. Apparently, this wasn't the first complaint against the vet so they fired him."

Jacobs stopped his note taking. "Did your sister ever hear from him after he was fired?"

"I'm not sure," said Cindy. "For a few months after the incident, Wendy did receive a lot of prank calls at the house where no one spoke to her when she answered the phone. I tried to convince her to ask the phone company to put a trace on it, but she thought it was silly."

"Do you remember the vet's name?" asked Tyrone.

"No, but I have a business card for the clinic. We took our cats there for years. They specialize in cats only." She got up and found the card and gave it to Tyrone.

"This will be helpful, Miss Woods," said Tyrone. "I'm sure they can at least provide a name. Business owners usually don't forget former employees who brought them close to gettin' sued."

Jacobs pulled out his card, giving it to Cindy. "Please give us a call if you think of anything else helpful. Remember, even the slightest confrontation might set a person off."

"I'll keep it in mind," she said as she turned. They followed her out of the kitchen.

"By the way, when will we know about the car?" she asked as they walked out the door. "If there's any evidence found."

"Wish we could give you a definitive answer," said Tyrone, feeling a twinge of guilt. It was hard to tell someone who'd already waited ten years they'd have to be patient and wait a little longer. "Lab's backed up right now and there aren't any funds for overtime.

Could be several days before they can look it over and test results can take months."

"Finding the car is big," said Jacobs. "Just the fact it's been found puts us a step closer to finding out what happened. Having the opportunity to talk to her sons without their father's permission or interference is also a new advantage. They may know something they were afraid to tell us before."

"I can tell you this," said Tyrone, "Jared seemed real anxious to figure things out. We're hopin' our conversations will help him remember. He wants to understand his nightmares. Sounds like his daddy might have fed him a story he accepted as the truth."

"Thank you," said Cindy. "Please tell Jared I'd love to see him if he wants to come by some time."

"I sure will, Miss Woods," said Tyrone.

As he and Jacobs walked out the door, Tyrone contemplated how different Jared's life would have been had he continued the relationship with his aunt, uncle, and cousins.

Cindy Woods waved at them as Tyrone and Jacobs reached their car then shut the door. Tyrone slid into the driver's seat, slipped the keys into the ignition then glanced over at his partner. "How do families get so screwed up?"

"Don't know," responded Jacobs. "I've only got the one brother. We argued a lot when we were kids, but Mom and Dad taught us we're the closest blood two people can be. They always said someday we might be all we have. I think we turned out pretty good."

"Well, at least one of you did," said Tyrone, glancing at his partner.

"Shut up and drive."

Tyrone grinned as he cranked the engine to life.

Chapter 9

Tyrone pulled into the parking lot of the Cats-R-Us Clinic at 4:25 p.m. The lobby contained a huge reception area with three women in attendance. Several chairs lined the walls for patrons waiting for their turn, but only three customers waited at this late hour. One woman had an orange tabby so big it looked like a tiger cub. A man sitting with a small boy watched as the youngster struggled to hold onto a gray kitten with white paws. The cage in the corner held four black and white kittens up for adoption.

Sergeant Jacobs approached the receptionist who'd just finished with a customer and showed her his credentials. "Hello, I'm Sergeant Jacobs and this is Detective Mayhew. We'd like to speak with someone regarding a former employee."

"You would need to talk to Carrie. She's our office manager. I'll go get her for you."

Jacobs turned to Tyrone. "Have you ever seen so many cats in one place?"

"Can't say I have," said Tyrone. "I keep tryin' to talk Jada into gettin' a dog for the boys, but she keeps sayin' no."

"Dogs are a lot of work. The kids and husbands who want them never wind up taking care of them, no matter how many promises they make. I don't blame her for telling you no."

"I guess." What Jacobs said made sense. He remembered his mama giving in and letting them have a dog. He and his brothers were so excited. They'd promised to take care of it, but after about a month their mama was doing it all.

The receptionist returned with a short, plump middle-aged woman who smiled pleasantly at them as she approached. "Hello, Detectives. I'm Carrie Tims. What can I do for you?"

"We need the name and a possible forwarding address for a former employee of yours," stated Jacobs.

"What's the employee's name?"

Tyrone lowered his voice. "Do you have an office where we can talk, Miss Tims?"

"Sure, right this way." She came around the counter and took them to one of the exam rooms. The detectives sat on the bench while she stood near the exam table. "Sorry, but this is much bigger than my closet-sized office."

"Not a problem," said Tyrone.

"Mrs. Tims, did you work here ten years ago?" asked Jacobs.

"Yes, I've been with the clinic for fifteen years."

Jacobs pulled out his notebook. "Do you recall a veterinarian being fired after losing too many *patients*?"

Her pleasant smile turned into a frown. "Oh, yes, you must be looking for Kirk Golden. We had five complaints on him when we let him go. After the first three cats died under suspicious circumstances, Dr. Spade, the head veterinarian, decided to start doing autopsies. He found incorrectly administered medications in the next two deaths and a misdiagnosed condition for which the feline wasn't getting proper treatment."

"How did Golden react to his termination?" asked Tyrone.

"That's the really funny part. Not funny, ha ha, but ridiculous," she said. "He was really ticked off. Claimed none of the women told the truth. Don't get me wrong, we usually lose an average of ten patients a year, but this guy lost six within a four month period of time." She rolled her eyes and shifted her weight.

"He sounds like quite the narcissist," said Jacobs. "He's always right, everyone else is wrong, the tests were wrong, that sort of attitude."

"Exactly," she said. "It wasn't *his* fault. The lab must have sent back the wrong test results. The owner wasn't following prescribed doses of medications."

Tyrone knew this type too well. "Do you remember him sayin' anything specific? Was he the type who might retaliate against any of these pet owners?"

"I remember he was very focused on Wendy Matherson. Her complaint was the last straw for the company. Wait. Didn't she go missing around that time? Do you think he had something to do with her disappearance?"

"We're reinvestigating her case due to new evidence," said Tyrone. "This Kirk Golden didn't come up in the original investigation. We're talkin' to everyone who had a beef with her."

"He's definitely someone who might seek revenge," she said. "We found road kill by the employee entrance several mornings after his dismissal. Then someone made calls to our office, hanging up. Sometimes he'd give the girls bogus names and make appointments then not show up."

"When did it stop?" asked Jacobs.

"It went on for a couple of months," she replied. "We asked the police to put extra patrols in the area, so we think it must have scared him off. We also told the caller we planned to ask the phone company to trace his calls if it didn't stop. The calls stopped after that."

"Can you provide us with his last known address?" asked Jacobs.

"You bet I can. Wait here while I get it for you."

Tyrone leaned forward, forearms on his thighs. He looked around at the shiny metal exam table, the jars of cotton swabs, cotton balls, and gauze.

The door opened and Carrie came back in the exam room. "Here you go, Detective Mayhew." Carrie gave him a message note with Golden's address written on it. "Of course, this is the address he gave us ten years ago, so it may not be current."

"Thank you, Miss Tims," said Tyrone. "Having his name is a good start. If he moved, we'll trace him through forwarding addresses or DMV records. We'll find him sooner or later."

"Well, if he had anything to do with what happened to Mrs. Matherson, I hope you nail him to the wall."

"Thank you for your help," said Jacobs. "We'll see ourselves out."

Once they reached the car, Tyrone settled into the driver's seat and grimaced. "By the time we get back to the office and write this one up, it'll be six. I hope those boys have been helpin' their mama out today or there'll be hell to pay."

"They're three boys under age ten, what do you expect?"

"Oh, I don't mean they'll be payin'," said Tyrone. "Jada will have my head on a platter for comin' in so late."

Jacobs rolled his eyes and sighed. "Okay, drop me off at the station and I'll type up our report."

"You're a life saver, my man. Her mama wants to go out tonight, so I promised to pick up the slack. Tomorrow lunch is on me."

"I'll hold you to it," said Jacobs.

"I have no doubt," said Tyrone. He always gave Ben Jacobs a hard time, but he knew who had his back. He hated seeing Ben so miserable over his shaky romance with Erica. Even though their relationship had been sorely tested since the conclusion of the Emerson case, Tyrone had a gut feeling they'd find their way back together.

Chapter 10

Sergeant Jacobs hit the save key on his report. As he was about to log off, his cell phone rang. Checking the caller ID, his breath caught as he realized it was Erica.

Since she'd been on leave, he'd been doing all the calling. He'd been disappointed by her many refusals to spend time with him. His patience had nearly worn out on several occasions, but somehow he found the desire to keep trying.

As he heard the fourth ring, he also heard Mayhew's voice in his head. *Answer it before it goes to voicemail, jackass.*

"Hello, Erica?"

"Surprised to hear from me?"

"No, of course not. I just finished a report so I hadn't shifted gears yet. You okay?"

"I get better every day."

He heard the lie in her voice, but declined to point it out to her. Ben didn't want to jinx the conversation.

"Ben, I had a talk with Pop today and he's getting kind of sick of my hovering." She paused and it took all of Ben's strength not to interject.

"I wondered if you'd like to grab some fast food and a movie tonight."

His heart leapt with hope, but he needed to stay cool. Erica was his first really serious relationship and he didn't want to scare her off by acting too over anxious.

"Sounds great," he said. "What movie did you want to see?"

"There's a new romantic comedy just came out."

He knew exactly what movie she meant. A chick flick, but if that's what it took to get a chance to spend time with her, so be it. "A comedy sounds great after the depressing crap I've dealt with all day."

"Great. Are you ready to leave the office?"

"I should be there within a half hour."

"I'll be ready."

He took in a deep breath, not realizing how tense he'd been during that five-minute conversation. Again, he heard Mayhew's voice. *Don't blow this, Jacobs. Relax. Go with it.*

* * *

Near the end of the movie, Ben could hear Erica sniffing as Faye and Joey finally realized they were in love. He decided to take a chance and reached over for her hand. To Ben's delight, she responded by squeezing his hand.

The credits ran and the lights came up. Ben smiled at her.

Erica wiped her last tear away. "Sorry about the blubbering."

"You weren't the only one." He lowered his voice and pointed. "That guy two rows up cried like a baby."

She laughed—a welcome sound to his ears. It had been a while. Maybe things were finally getting back to normal.

Confidence up, Ben ventured another request. "Want to go somewhere for a late night dessert? Have some coffee and talk for a while?"

When she let her gaze fall to the floor, he knew the answer would be no.

"This is the first time I've been out of the house since Pop came home from the hospital. I really need to get back there. No telling what sort of trouble he's getting in to."

Ben knew she was using her dad as an excuse, but at least this was progress. "That's okay, next time."

She lifted her eyes to his and smiled. "Next time, I promise."

Chapter 11

"Oh, Lord, if that sweet child of mine don't start sleepin' through the night soon I don't know what I'm gonna do," said Tyrone, yawning with a cup of coffee in his hand.

"Maybe you and Mama should've found an African name meaning *up all night*," said six-year old Reggie.

His three-year-old brother, Malcolm, giggled as he watched his mother pour corn flakes into his bowl. "You funny, Reggie," he said.

"Never mind," said Jada. "Adanne is the perfect name for your little sister. All this waking up in the middle of the night will pass. She's not even two weeks old yet."

"Your mama's right, as usual," said Tyrone, winking at his wife.

She raised an eyebrow at him. "Would you like some scrambled eggs this morning?"

"Yes, please," said Tyrone in his sweetest voice. He knew he always scored points when he said please. "Where's Darryl?"

"Sleeping," said Reggie.

"It's school break," said Jada. "He can sleep in until 9:00 then I'll roust his behind out of bed. Once my mother goes home, he'll have to step up."

"Where's your mother?" asked Tyrone.

"She's rockin' Adanne, Daddy," said Malcolm, milk and cereal running down his chin. "Just like she rocked me when I was a baby."

"You're still a baby," said Reggie. "You can't even keep your food in your mouth."

"No I'm not," squealed Malcolm.

"Cut it out, Reg," Tyrone said, staring at his second born. "So what are you havin' for breakfast, my man?"

"Mama, may I have some scrambled eggs like Daddy?" asked Reggie.

Tyrone nudged the boy and mouthed the word please at him.

"Please, Mama."

"I guess, since you said please." Jada smiled at Tyrone.

Jada served up the eggs with toast and bacon on the side, and then took a seat next to him. "So last night you started to tell me a little about this cold case you're working on."

"It's the one I was workin' the year we got married. It's the missing woman who had the three sons. Her brother and sister were convinced of foul play, but we had no solid evidence. The investigation must have been hard on those kids, yet the older two boys turned out pretty good. I'm worried about the youngest boy, Jared. He's been havin' bad dreams since it happened. I'm wondering if he saw something and can't remember because it was such a shock."

"It's a good possibility," said Jada. "Like you said last night, if his father's been pounding a story into his head for all these years, he's probably convinced himself his father's version is the truth. His subconscious will fight to reveal what really happened and at the same time try to protect him from the horror of the event."

"Have I told you lately how brilliant you are?" Tyrone took her hand and kissed it.

"Yuck!" said Reggie, and Malcolm followed suit.

"Someday you won't find this so yucky," said Tyrone.

Reggie and Malcolm looked at one another, scrunching up their faces as though they'd just taken a bite of a particularly sour lemon. Then they looked at their father and burst into laughter.

Tyrone took his last bite of breakfast and gulped down his coffee. He took his dishes to the sink then hugged his sons and kissed his wife. "Better hit the road. Lots of work to do today."

"Bye, Daddy," said Malcolm. "Love you!"

"Love you, too, big guy. Love you, Reg. You too, Jada." He grabbed his keys from the counter on the way to the garage. He felt like the luckiest man in the world.

Chapter 12

Tyrone no sooner entered the Missing Person Department than Lieutenant Terhune was at his side. "Reid Matherson's here and he's hot. Jacobs is waiting for us outside of the interrogation room."

"What's he all worked up about?"

"Not sure," said Terhune as they approached Jacobs. "He's ranting about your visit to his house yesterday."

"Just took a look at him from the observation room," said Jacobs as the lieutenant and Tyrone arrived. "He's pacing like a caged animal."

"You two get in there and I'll observe," said the lieutenant. "Just calmly tell him our investigations never close until they're solved."

"Yes sir," said Jacobs.

Upon their entering the interrogation room, Reid Matherson abruptly stopped pacing and stared angrily into Tyrone's face. Tyrone stood his ground and waited for Matherson to speak first.

"What the hell's going on, Detective Mayhew," Matherson shouted. "How dare you come to my home without contacting me first."

"Mr. Matherson," Tyrone said in his most professional voice. "Please sit down and we will explain…."

Before Tyrone could finish his sentence, Reid Matherson took a menacing step toward him, continuing to shout even louder. "I don't want to sit down! You didn't have permission to come to my home and question my son!"

"Mr. Matherson," Tyrone said as calmly as he could, given Reid Matherson's aggressive stance. "You will sit down and you will do it now. If you don't, Sergeant Jacobs and I will be forced to handcuff you to the table. Do I make myself clear?"

Matherson looked from one detective to the other. He must have decided he couldn't take both of them on, because he turned and took his seat without further defiance.

"Since the rules are understood, Sergeant Jacobs and I will tell you what's goin' on," stated Tyrone. "Number one, we came to your house to talk to you and Jared about your wife's case. Your *adult* son invited us in."

"As you know from the phone call you received on Sunday

morning, two fishermen found your wife's car in Eagle Creek Reservoir," said Jacobs.

"Yes, I know all of this already." Reid's face grew redder. "My son told me about your visit. It took me years to convince him she wasn't coming back. In less than twenty minutes, you two have him all worked up and hopeful."

"I will repeat. Your son is an adult now. He's capable of making his own decisions," said Tyrone. "You said your wife ran off. If you're right, she might come back. Of course, I'm not so sure she left of her own free will or that she's still alive."

"People usually don't hide their cars in a reservoir when they *plan* to disappear," said Jacobs. "They leave them in a bad neighborhood with the keys in them or in a parking garage at the airport."

"I'm telling you for the last time, my wife took off with her lover. She decided she didn't want to live with us any longer," said Reid, his eyes flashing.

"I do remember your story, Mr. Matherson," said Tyrone, leaning forward with his arms on the table. "But I've been working in the Missing Person Department long enough to know that people who leave don't completely cut themselves off from family members or close friends. Your wife hasn't contacted anyone for ten years. There's no trace of her obtaining another job or havin' a bank account *anywhere* in the United States."

"I want you to stay away from my family," interjected Matherson pointing his finger at Tyrone. "We're finally past the pain and want to be left alone."

"Jared didn't give us that impression." Tyrone glared into Matherson's eyes. "In fact, he seemed thrilled at the prospect of us continuing to look for his mother."

"Jared doesn't know what he wants. This won't help him get on with his life."

Tyrone could see pain in the man's face. He just couldn't quite figure out where it was coming from. Was Matherson hiding something? Did he kill his wife and Jared witnessed it?

"Mr. Matherson, Jared hasn't moved on," said Jacobs. "I'm sure you're aware of the nightmares. He needs closure."

"Don't tell me what he needs," shouted Matherson slamming his hand on the table. "He's my son."

"Again, Mr. Matherson," said Jacobs more sternly. "You need to calm down and stop presenting yourself in this threatening manner. If you've nothing to hide, our investigation shouldn't be a problem. You do want us to find her, don't you?"

"You find Wendy and then what? How's she going to explain being gone for ten years and deserting her children?"

"She won't if she's dead." Tyrone couldn't believe this guy was so angry. You'd think he'd want some closure for himself and his boys. "One thing I can't figure out is why you're so sure she left town with someone, but you can't tell us who it was. There are no men missing from that time period who were associated with your wife."

Reid Matherson appeared at a loss for words. He sat there looking to one detective and then the other. He finally said, "I know she was seeing someone. The last six months before she left us, she would go out every Friday and Saturday night. I followed her a few times and never caught her with anyone, so I can't tell you who it was, but I know she wouldn't have left unless she had someone to take care of her."

Jacobs looked at Tyrone, and then pulled his notebook and pen out of his jacket pocket.

"So you don't think she'd tell a friend or her sister about a lover?" Tyrone leaned in. "In my experience as a police officer, I can't remember a missing person who left on their own who hadn't confided their plans to at least one other person."

"It doesn't mean it didn't happen," said Reid.

Tyrone glanced at Jacobs and sighed, and then turned back to Reid. "Okay. Your son told us there were people you suspected had something to do with your wife's disappearance during our initial investigation. Jared said you don't believe we interviewed or investigated these people thoroughly. Your sister-in-law gave us some information on a veterinarian who was fired after your wife complained and we're tryin' to locate him. Was there anyone else?"

"There was a Drew Blake at the company where she worked," Reid responded. "She told me about him because she was thinking about filing a sexual harassment suit against him. You might want to talk to Portia Graves. She and Wendy hung out together after work a lot. She probably even witnessed some of what happened."

"Anyone else?" Jacobs asked as he made notes.

"No. The veterinarian was the only other person I knew of who had it in for Wendy," said Reid.

"Just so you know, we'll be talkin' to your other two sons when they arrive in town," said Tyrone. "It could be they heard or saw something earlier in the day. If your wife was having an affair, they may have overheard a telephone conversation or seen someone come by the house to talk to her who wasn't familiar to them."

"My boys were in bed fast asleep." Anger subsiding, Reid's insistence nearly sounded like begging.

"Mr. Matherson," said Jacobs. "You can't be sure they were sleeping unless you had all of their rooms on spy cam monitors where you could sit and watch all of them at once all night. Jared doesn't remember anything except what you told him. Maybe the other boys will think of something they couldn't tell the police ten years ago."

"May I go now?" Matherson glared at them and shook with renewed rage. From his beet red face, Tyrone guessed Matherson's blood pressure must be sky high.

"Yes," said Jacobs. "We'll let you know when the car is processed. Of course, we'll also call if we find any further evidence of Mrs. Matherson's whereabouts."

Tyrone opened the door and Reid Matherson stood and quickly walked out.

"He's definitely hidin' something," said Tyrone. "His concern for Jared's well being is non-existent. Did you see how he was shakin'?"

"Shaking with anger because we're reinvestigating the case," answered Jacobs. "Well, I guess we'd better concentrate on finding Kirk Golden, DVM. And, we need to talk to this Portia Graves before we question the sexual harasser to get her side of the story first."

"I'll look in the file, but it seems to me I remember talking to Drew Blake. But you're right; maybe Portia Graves can put a different slant on what went on."

Chapter 13

Tyrone discovered Portia Graves was now Mrs. Portia Brennan. She no longer worked for the insurance company, but had become a stay-at-home mom with two daughters aged five and three. He and Jacobs arrived at her home in Zionsville at 2:00 p.m.

Portia answered the door before Jacobs had a chance to ring the bell. Tyrone guessed her height at about five-foot-two, and she was slightly overweight. She had a white toothy smile which made him feel welcome, despite the gravity of their visit.

"Come in, Detectives. Hope I didn't startle you by opening the door so abruptly. My girls are napping and I didn't want the bell to wake them."

"Not a problem, Miss Brennan," said Tyrone quietly. With double her crew, he knew naptime was a precious thing.

She guided them to her bright and cheery living room which was a little too white for Tyrone's taste. How did she keep it so clean with two kids? Was this the difference between having boys and girls? He couldn't imagine any of this furniture remaining white once his boys got through with it.

"I saw the news this morning," she said. "Was it really Wendy's car?"

"Yes," said Jacobs. "But we didn't find any remains in the car."

"I see," she said letting go of a breath perhaps held for the worst of news.

"Our lab will be going over it for evidence later in the week," Jacobs continued. "Unfortunately, it's been in the water for a long time. Any evidence she was in the car before it went into the water is most likely destroyed."

"Wendy was a really good person," she said. "She treated everyone with respect and she was so much fun. I always wondered if she was…." Portia couldn't finish her sentence, and appeared to choke on the last unspoken word.

She looked away from them for a moment, wiped her face with her hand and continued. "I know you've probably talked to Cindy already. I've always agreed with her in respect to that runaway theory of Reid's. Wendy loved her boys. If she left with someone, she'd have taken them, too."

"To your knowledge, was she having an affair?" asked Tyrone.

"No," she answered, vigorously shaking her head.

"How can you be sure?" asked Jacobs.

"Because Wendy was very honest with me. She told me all about her marital problems. She told me about the vet who killed her cat. Of course, I knew everything about Drew. I assume that's why you're here."

"So if she was having an extramarital affair, you're positive she would have told you about it?" asked Jacobs.

"Absolutely," said Portia. "She didn't have time for an affair. Her boys were sixteen, thirteen and nine at the time. One or all of them had something going on all the time with after school activities. Every now and then she'd take some time to go out with me after work or meet me on a Saturday night for dinner."

"Her husband claims she went out every Friday and Saturday night," said Jacobs.

"Bull shit," she exclaimed. Then Portia gasped and her hand went directly to her mouth. "I'm so sorry for the language, but he's lying. I know she wasn't doing any such thing. Wendy was a good self-sacrificing woman. She wouldn't miss Tanner playing basketball, or Ryan playing soccer. She went to every school performance, PTA meeting, and field trip for those boys. I just hope I'm half as good a mother as Wendy Matherson."

Portia grimaced, her face flushed with anger. Even after all these years, Tyrone could see Portia was angry with Reid Matherson.

"Miss Brennan," said Tyrone, "what did Miss Matherson tell you about her marriage?"

"She told me he was a cold fish. The marriage was good at first, but she was young and stupid. However, she had no intention of getting a divorce before her sons were grown. *That's* what I meant by self-sacrificing and *that's* why I don't believe she ran off with somebody."

This definitely put a new twist on things. Now all Tyrone needed was to find out more about Drew Blake.

"I see your point," said Tyrone. "Let's talk about Drew Blake. Did you witness his advances towards Miss Matherson?"

"Drew hit on everybody, married or not. He's the owner's nephew and thought he had free reign. He was particularly obsessed with Wendy. He'd overheard some of our conversations about her marital troubles and thought she was fair game."

"So what'd he do?" asked Jacobs.

"He'd ask her out, she'd say no and he'd go off to pout. However, the Friday before she disappeared, he overheard us talking about going out for drinks and dinner Saturday night. He showed up at the restaurant while we waited for a table in the bar and insisted on sitting with us. Wendy got mad and told him straight out his ploy wasn't going to work. She was married and there was no way she'd be going out with him, now or ever."

"What was his reaction?" asked Tyrone.

"Totally pissed. He slammed his hand on the table and told her she'd regret it and stomped out of the bar."

"Was he still there when you left?" asked Tyrone.

"I didn't see him. We'd parked only a few cars apart, so I saw her get into her vehicle at about 9:00 p.m. and that's the last time I saw her."

"Was Mr. Blake back to work the following Monday?" asked Jacobs.

"Yes." Then, her facial expression changed.

"What is it, Miss Brennan?" asked Tyrone.

"I remember him having this long scratch along the left side of his neck," she recalled. "I asked him if he'd gotten into a fight with a tiger and he told me to mind my own business." She stood and paced with her hand to her mouth. She turned with terror on her face. "You don't think he followed her and she's the one who scratched him, do you? Why didn't I think of that before?"

"I don't believe anyone interviewed you before," said Tyrone. His blood began to boil as he realized his and Grimes' mistake. Portia should have been one of the first people they interviewed since she was so close to the victim.

"I didn't talk to you, but I talked to another detective. His last name started with a G, Gray or Grind or...."

"Grimes?" Tyrone's mind began to whirl. What the hell? Why hadn't Grimes discussed this with him? He didn't recall this interview being part of the file.

"Yeah, sounds right. White guy, little shorter than you, salt and pepper hair? I remember him because he was so rude."

Tyrone gave Jacobs a look indicating her description fit his ex-partner. Jacobs wrote it down in his notes. Tyrone had every intention of calling Grimes as soon as he had the chance.

"Is Drew Blake still working for the insurance company?" asked

Jacobs.

"As far as I know, he is. I only stayed with the company for about a year after I got married. I resigned after I had my first baby."

"Thank you for your time, Miss Brennan," said Tyrone. "You've been very helpful."

"I don't expect you to find Wendy alive, but I do hope you find her," she said. "Her boys deserve to know their mother didn't intentionally desert them."

Tyrone nodded in agreement.

After Portia showed them to the door, Tyrone walked towards the car so quickly Jacobs could barely keep up with him. He got in and slammed the door so hard it nearly fell off its hinges.

"Hold on there, Tyrone," said Jacobs taking his seat. "Calm down before you start the engine."

"Damn it, Ben. I know I was new to the department and I was young, but I'd been a patrol cop for five years. How could I have been so stupid? And, why the hell didn't I see Grimes wasn't doin' his job?"

"Becoming a detective is like being a rookie all over again," said Jacobs. "It's a whole different thing. The seasoned veteran is supposed to mentor us. We trust them to know what they're doing."

"Well, apparently I shouldn't have trusted Percy Grimes," Tyrone said, his head pounding with frustration and confusion. "Was he really so incompetent? Now I'm wondering if he went to Cincinnati because of his wife's family or because IMPD was catchin' on to his ineptitude."

"There's only one way to find out. Ask some of the higher ups who knew him back then."

"As long as I get to call the son-of-a-bitch myself," said Tyrone.

"He's all yours."

Chapter 14

"Damn it." Tyrone slammed the phone receiver back into its cradle startling Jacobs into sitting up straighter. He'd hit another wall. His head throbbed with frustration.

"What's wrong?" asked his partner.

"I talked to the Cincinnati P. D. and they told me Grimes retired last month." Tyrone placed his elbows on the desk and rubbed his temples.

"He's old enough to retire?" said Jacobs.

"He was fifty-five when he was workin' this case, so I guess he is." Tyrone slammed his fist on his desk then flung himself back in his chair crossing his arms over his chest. "I tried to call his house and got the freakin' voice mail."

Jacobs started pecking away at his keyboard. "Any luck on the vet?"

"I've got my buddy lookin' for a vehicle registration for the guy. That's probably the only way we're going to find Golden."

Lieutenant Terhune came off the elevator heading in their direction. Tyrone couldn't read his mood. His boss would be a great poker player.

"While the two of you interviewed Mrs. Brennan, I got a call on Kirk Golden."

"That was fast," stated Jacobs. "We were just talking about him."

"Turns out Golden's working as a vet's assistant in Tipton."

"Sounds like our guy took a demotion," said Jacobs. "He must have done some fast talking to get this vet in Tipton to hire him."

"So where on Earth is Tipton?" said Tyrone.

"It's about fifteen to twenty miles north of Noblesville," said Lieutenant Terhune. "You take US 31 North to State Road 28 and head east. You can't miss it. Here's the address. Right now, it's quitting time. Go home and start fresh tomorrow."

"Sure, Lieutenant," said Jacobs. "Have a nice evening."

"Shit, I haven't even had time to look at my incoming mail." Tyrone grabbed the envelopes from the top of the stack glancing at each as he sorted through the correspondence. "How do these advertisers get hold of my work address?"

"They buy lists from other people. It's big business," said Jacobs, picking up a discarded flyer from Tyrone's desk. "Oh look, a discount coupon for a massage. Maybe you should get the wife one of those."

"Maybe. What the hell is this?" Tyrone found a typewritten envelope from a P. O. Box with a zip code from the south side of Indianapolis. "You got some gloves on you?"

"I keep some in my desk drawer," Jacobs said. He went back to his desk and pulled a couple out of the drawer and tossed them at Tyrone.

Tyrone opened the envelope, carefully pulling out the letter. Then he unfolded it by pulling it open at opposite corners. He read the typewritten note aloud.

"Dear Detective,

I hear you're working on the Matherson case again. It would be better for everyone involved if you would drop this case. You're only going to hurt people. Let sleeping dogs lie.

A Friend"

"Doesn't sound like much of a friend," said Jacobs.

"But somebody definitely wants us off this case. I'm goin' to bag this and take it to Forensics. The envelope might have some DNA on it if the sender licked it. Of course, the envelope's probably worthless for prints with so many people handling it. The letter might have some, but I doubt it. At least we'll have it to match against a printer."

"It's amazing that the way a printer prints is as accurate an ID as a fingerprint," said Jacobs.

"Now all we have to do is find the printer," said Tyrone.

Chapter 15

Reid Matherson approached the Backstreet Bar in Shelbyville. He didn't know anyone in the town so this little neighborhood bar would provide the privacy he needed for this meeting. He didn't want anyone he knew seeing him meet with this man.

He stepped inside and looked around at the dark, dank atmosphere. The décor looked like something out of a horror movie. Posters, once vibrant with color, were now yellowed and torn. Cracked and dusty mirrors merely reflected strange images back into the room. He hated to imagine the state of the dishes and glassware.

"Hey."

A man tapped Reid's shoulder nearly causing him to jump out of his skin.

"Still as skittish as ever, I see."

"What do you expect, sneaking up on a guy?" spouted Reid.

"I didn't sneak. Stop your whining and tell me why I had to drive to Shelbyville to meet you in this lovely establishment."

Reid gestured to a dark secluded booth. As soon as they sat down a waitress came by.

"What'll you have, gentlemen?"

"I'll have a beer. Whatever's on tap. What about you, Reid?"

"Scotch, neat," said Reid.

"I'll be right back."

"Like I told you on the phone, Sarge, they found Wendy's car." Reid shook nervously.

"So what's the problem?"

"Weren't you listening? They found Wendy's car in the reservoir."

"I heard you the first time. What happened to the bird sanctuary?"

"They moved it to the north side of the park. The dumb ass birds decided they liked it better, so they opened up the old bird sanctuary for fishing."

"Shit," Sarge said, frowning. "Who found it?"

"A couple of teenagers were out there fishing and one of them decided to dive in. He saw the car and they called the police." Reid started wringing his hands. "Now they've reopened the investigation."

"She wasn't inside it, so it's no big deal."

"No big deal!" Reid's voice was loud enough to cause customers to turn their heads in his direction.

"Quiet," Sarge hissed. "You got to stay calm, Reid."

"Easy for you to say, you're not their prime suspect."

"Look, they didn't figure it out before; they won't figure it out now."

"But they have the car." Reid felt more panic-stricken than before. "What if they find something?"

"Like what? The car's been submersed in lake water for ten years. Everyone knows the water has destroyed any evidence. If she's not in it, then it looks like she dumped it on her way out of town."

"I hope you're right," said Reid, unfocused and staring at the table. Then he looked up and stared into Sarge's eyes. "Detective Mayhew talked to Jared."

Sarge rubbed his cheek and bit his lip. "So what happened?"

"He's got Jared all worked up, that's what happened," said Reid as he saw the waitress coming out of the corner of his eye. Reid leaned back in his seat and Sarge took the hint to stop talking.

"A beer for you and a scotch, neat, for you." She smiled at Reid playfully. "It's $4.00 for the scotch and $3.00 for the beer."

Reid gave her a ten-dollar bill and told her to keep the change. When she was out of earshot, Reid continued. "Jared's been having nightmares for years. I'm afraid all of this will bring on something much worse."

"You're just going to have to keep these guys away from him."

"And how do you propose I do that?" Reid spewed in frustration. "Jared's an adult now. He wants to find out what happened to his mother."

Sarge sat back and looked away from Reid.

Reid knew him well enough to know he was thinking and would not say another word until Sarge spoke first.

Sarge leaned forward again. "I tell you what we're going to do. You're going home and relax while I figure something out. Just stick to your original story and keep working on Jared."

"But, what if…."

"No buts," he retorted. "I helped you before, I'll help you again."

"Okay," Reid relented.

Sarge raised his glass of beer, hinting at a toast. "To our success."

"To our success," Reid repeated, raising his glass with doubts streaming through his brain. Their glasses clinked. Reid downed his

Scotch in two gulps.

"Man, you are a nervous wreck, aren't you?"

Reid just looked at him, rose from his chair and headed for the door.

Chapter 16

Wednesday morning Tyrone and his partner went to the Bethel Insurance Company on North Meridian Street. He told the receptionist they needed to speak with Drew Blake. She called Drew then showed them to a conference room.

"Smaller than I pictured it," said Tyrone once the receptionist left them alone. The conference room was the size of a small bedroom. A round table with six captain's chairs much like you'd see in a kitchen graced the center of the room. A couple of inspirational framed posters hung on the wall.

"Hello, there." A stout man of only about five feet, seven inches in height, stood in the doorway. He wore glasses with thick black frames which did nothing but harden his looks. His curly bright orange hair reminded Tyrone of the comedian Carrot Top.

"I'm Detective Mayhew and this is Sergeant Jacobs," said Tyrone, extending his hand. "We're from the Missing Person Department."

"Drew Blake here," he said. "I had a feeling I'd see somebody from the police department when I heard they'd found Wendy Matherson's car."

Jacobs motioned to a chair. "May we sit?"

"Of course, would you gentleman like some coffee?"

"No, thanks." Tyrone saw the offer as a stall tactic. "We don't plan on stayin' very long."

"Mr. Blake, we understand Wendy Matherson worked here for about two years before her disappearance," said Jacobs.

"That's correct."

"We also understand you asked her out a couple of times, despite the fact she refused, citing her marriage as the reason," said Jacobs, pulling out his pad and a pen to take notes.

"The way she talked, I thought she planned to get a divorce." Drew shifted in his chair. "I liked her, that's all."

Tyrone glared at him. "According to witnesses, you didn't take no for an answer."

"Where'd you get such an idea?"

Tyrone could hear a slight change in Drew's voice, indicating his throat tightening from stress. "So, are you denyin' it?"

"I most certainly am." Drew sat up straighter and blushed a little.

"When a girl says no, she means no."

Jacobs leaned toward Drew. "Then why did you show up at the restaurant where Mrs. Matherson was dining with Portia Graves?"

"It was just a coincidence."

Tyrone noticed sweat beading up on Drew's upper lip. He exchanged a look with Jacobs then they both stared at Drew in silence for a moment.

"Mr. Blake, it doesn't really matter whether it was a coincidence or not. You approached the women and joined them without being asked," said Jacobs. "When you made further advances toward Mrs. Matherson and she rejected you, you threatened her."

"That's bull shit!" Drew said, slapping his hand on the table.

"We've already told you we have witnesses," said Jacobs. "Lying to us will only make things worse."

"How do you explain the nasty scratch you had on your neck a couple of days after Wendy Matherson disappeared?" asked Tyrone. In his opinion, this guy was a weasel. He would really enjoy taking him down.

"I went hiking that Sunday at Turtle Creek Park and ran into a low-hanging branch." He crossed his arms in a protective stance. "I was with my cousin. I'll gladly give you his contact information. Ask him, he'll tell you we were together all day."

Tyrone gave Drew his deepest look of contempt. "I find it amazing you remember so precisely. Believe me; we'll definitely want to talk to this cousin of yours."

"Wait here. I'll get you his card and home information." Drew stood, advancing toward the door.

"You're tellin' me you don't know your own cousin's home contact info," said Tyrone with all the intimidation he could muster.

"I don't have anything to write on," said Drew.

"Jacobs has a pad of paper and pen right here," said Tyrone. "What do you think he's been takin' notes on while we've been talkin'?"

"I wasn't thinking." Drew gave Jacobs his cousin's name, address and phone number.

"Thank you, Mr. Blake," said Jacobs. "We'll be in touch."

Drew stepped back from the table. He'd lost that cocky demeanor he'd displayed earlier. "I'm sure you gentlemen can find your way out," said Drew and he left the room without waiting for a response.

Tyrone glanced at his partner. "I guess we've been dismissed."

"So it would seem," said Jacobs.

They walked swiftly from the building. Once outside, Tyrone turned to Jacobs. "What you want to bet that asshole's in there right now calling his cousin and gettin' their story straight."

"I'm not taking that bet. Let's get back to the station. We've got to get ready to run to Tipton this afternoon."

As they approached the car, Tyrone noticed a piece of paper under the wiper.

"Damn solicitors," said Jacobs. "Always leaving crap on everybody's cars. Half of them wind up blowing away and...."

"Jacobs," Tyrone interrupted, grabbing his arm. "Wait a minute. Look around. You see any flyers on any other car in this lot? All these cars were already here when we went in the place."

Jacobs looked around and shook his head.

Tyrone got closer, noticing the flyer lay face down. He unlocked the door and slid into the driver's seat so he could read it from inside the car.

"It's a message for us." Irritated by its content, Tyrone read it aloud. "It says, *Leave well enough alone. Leave her family in peace.*"

"So while we're in there interviewing Drew Blake, someone's out here leaving us a love note."

Tyrone popped open the trunk and retrieved some gloves and an evidence bag. He carefully removed the note from under the windshield wiper then bagged and tagged it as evidence.

"Do you think we should have the car fingerprinted?"

"We'll have Mark Chatham do it at the station," answered Tyrone. "Glove up and let's take the car and this note to Forensics. We need to see if this note matches the note I received at the office."

"You don't think Blake came out here while we waited in the conference room, do you?"

Tyrone sealed the evidence bag and turned to his partner. "As much as I'd love to pin this on the slime ball, he didn't know we'd be here today. He didn't have time to type a note and put it out here."

Jacobs chuckled. "Yeah, I guess it couldn't be that simple."

"Besides, I don't see this guy requesting we give it up for the family's sake."

"Neither do I," said Jacobs. "We'd better get going. We can take my car to Tipton."

Chapter 17

After leaving Tyrone's car and the note with Forensics, they hopped into Jacobs' car and headed up 31 towards Tipton. The thick traffic seemed to disappear once they drove north of Carmel. The four-lane highway sported lots of farmland and very few traffic lights.

"I guess we're off to the land of cows and pigs," said Tyrone.

"Actually, it's mostly pigs. They've got a pretty famous pork festival in Tipton every September. I think it's the weekend after Labor Day. Maybe you should take the family up there some time."

"I'll think about it. Might do the kids good to see how the other half lives. How far did the lieutenant say Tipton was?" asked Tyrone.

"We should arrive in about twenty minutes," said Jacobs. "Look at it this way; it gets us out of the city for a while."

"Well, you'd better hope my car's ready when we return. If not, I'll need for you to chauffeur me home tonight and pick me up in the mornin'."

"Oh, joy."

"Now, now, you know you love my fabulous company," said Tyrone. "Otherwise, you'd be assigning somebody else to take these lovely trips with me."

Jacobs gave him a sideways glance and changed the subject. "I wonder how people can live out here in the middle of nowhere. Do you realize how far they drive just to go to a grocery store?"

"If it weren't for some of these people out here in the middle of nowhere, we wouldn't have any groceries for our very convenient grocery stores."

"True. How long is your mother-in-law staying with you?"

"Only a couple more days," said Tyrone. "She's not so bad. All I have to do is agree with everything she says."

Jacobs chuckled and looked to his right. "There's the sign for 28 already."

"Time flies when you're havin' fun...or so they say."

"Whoever *they* are," said Jacobs.

Jacobs made the turn onto State Road 28 and entered Tipton five minutes later. They found the Bradbury Veterinary Clinic after a few more minutes. It was a small building, probably a house at one time. They parked the car and entered.

"Hello." A middle-aged woman greeted them from the front desk. "May I help you?"

Jacobs introduced himself and Tyrone and asked if they could speak with Kirk Golden.

"Sure," she said brightly. "As soon as he and Dr. Bradbury are done with Miss Farlow's cat, I'll let him know you're here. You can have a seat right over there."

Tyrone grabbed a *Popular Mechanics* magazine from the rack and sat down in a hard wooden captain's chair. He assumed they preferred wooden chairs because of all the hair from people's pets. He flipped through a few pages more to give himself something to do while he waited rather than actually reading it. Then Tyrone heard a male speaking to someone.

"Baby Girl will be okay, Miss Farlow," he said. "Often cats of her age start losing teeth. As long as she's able to eat, she should be fine. If she loses any more or shows signs of pain, please call us."

"Thanks," said the young woman. She stepped up to the reception desk and paid her bill.

"Kirk Golden?" asked Jacobs, approaching the man. "We're from the Indianapolis Metropolitan Police and would like to ask for a few minutes of your time."

Golden glanced at Jacobs. "Certainly, I'm always willing to cooperate with the police. However, it's been quite a few years since I lived in Indianapolis. I'm not sure how I can help."

Golden led them to a cramped office just big enough to hold a desk, chair and two small guest chairs. "Have a seat gentleman. Now, what can I do for you?"

"I don't know if you've been watchin' the news lately," said Tyrone, "but we recovered Wendy Matherson's car a few days ago. You do remember Wendy Matherson, don't you?"

"Wendy Matherson?" He scratched his chin and paused for a few seconds. "Ah, yes. I treated her cat many years ago."

"Ten to be exact," said Tyrone.

"So what does finding her car have to do with me?"

"From what we gather, you and Mrs. Matherson had a very volatile relationship," said Jacobs. "She was ready to sue you and the cat clinic where you worked when her cat died after being treated by you."

"Yes, she was, but I got over it. I went to Michigan a few months after losing my job and stayed with my parents until I found this job."

Tyrone watched his body language for signs of discomfort. "But we understand you're now a veterinarian's assistant, not a vet."

"That's correct," he said, stiffening. "It's much easier to assist. If something goes wrong, the pet owner doesn't come after you."

Tyrone nodded. "You've had this job how long?" he asked.

"Eight years. It took a while to figure out what I wanted to do after what happened in Indianapolis."

"According to people who knew Mrs. Matherson, you harassed her for a while after the incident at the cat clinic," said Jacobs.

"We had words when she accused me of neglect," said Golden. "I'll admit I was extremely angry with her. I nearly lost my license because of her, although I don't need it now."

"Mrs. Matherson received a lot of harassing calls," said Jacobs. "Did you make any of those calls?"

"Look, if you're implying I was involved in Wendy Matherson's disappearance, I can tell you now I had nothing to do with it. I didn't even know she'd disappeared until a friend of mine from Indianapolis called to tell me what happened. I had already moved to Michigan when she went missing and I can prove it."

"That would be very helpful," said Tyrone. "I assume your parents can confirm this, correct?"

"Yes." Golden pulled a pen from his lab coat pocket and took a message pad from his desk drawer. He wrote down his parents' contact information and handed it to Tyrone.

"Here's my card," said Tyrone. "You can email me any time if you have others who can vouch for you or if you remember any other information regarding this case."

"I'll do that," said Golden.

"Thanks for your cooperation," said Jacobs, standing and extending his hand.

Golden stood and shook Jacobs' hand and then Tyrone's. "Thank you for coming by."

Once in the car, Jacobs turned to Tyrone. "So what do think of our illustrious ex-Dr. Golden?"

"I don't think he's our guy," said Tyrone. "Makin' crank calls and leavin' road kill at the clinic is cowardly. I don't think he has the guts to confront anyone face-to-face. We'll check his alibi, of course, but this seems like a dead end to me. "

Tyrone's cell phone rang. "Mayhew."

"It's Mark. We're finished with the car and note. No prints and the printer for the note is different."

"Are you kiddin' me," said Tyrone, soliciting a glance from Jacobs. "Thanks, Mark."

"I take it he came up with a big zero on the car," said Jacobs.

"Yep," answered Tyrone. "There's a bright side though."

Jacobs gave him the sideways stare.

"I don't need a chauffeur."

Chapter 18

The next morning as Tyrone concentrated on the Matherson file, Lieutenant Terhune approached him with a strange look on his face.

"Serena Walsh is here to see you, Mayhew. Remember her?"

"Yeah, she's the psychic lady who talked to Grimes. She said she had some kind of feelin' Miss Matherson was dead."

"Did you get to talk to her during the initial investigation?"

"No, sir. I'd gone to talk to Cindy Woods about her sister the day he talked to Miss Walsh. Grimes told me Miss Walsh had come by, but he said she was a nut case."

"So you guys didn't follow up on her claims?"

"Whose claims?" Jacobs asked as walked up beside them.

"A psychic who seems to have been brushed off the first time around." Lieutenant Terhune scowled at Tyrone.

"Like I said, I was off talkin' to the sister. Grimes indicated to me he'd taken care of it."

"Okay, okay. Jacobs you go in with Mayhew. I want two sets of ears in there. I don't put much stock in these psychics, but it's still a lead which should have followed up on the first time around. I put her in the small conference room. I didn't want her to feel like a criminal."

As Lieutenant Terhune left them to their task, Jacobs turned to Tyrone wide-eyed. "I've never met a real psychic before."

"Me neither." Tyrone wasn't sharing Jacobs' enthusiasm. He remembered some of his mama's stories about her ancestors who practiced Voodoo. She said it was evil because too many people used it to do harm. His mama showed him in the Bible where it said we aren't to deal with fortunetellers.

Tyrone opened the door and Serena Walsh rose from her chair. "Ah, you must be Detective Mayhew." She nodded but didn't offer him her hand.

"Yes, Miss Walsh, and this is Sergeant Jacobs."

Jacobs nodded his acknowledgement.

"Please have a seat, Miss Walsh." Tyrone realized she was nothing like he'd pictured. She wore jeans and a Cincinnati Reds tee shirt—no robes or bangles. Serena was pretty in an ordinary sense with light brown wavy hair highlighted with streaks of blonde. There was nothing mysterious about her—she looked normal.

Jacobs pulled out his notebook. "So, Miss Walsh, why have you come to see us today?"

"I saw on the news you've recovered Wendy Matherson's car from the reservoir."

"Yes, we did." Tyrone peered at her. "Is this why you wanted to talk to me?"

Serena nodded and when she spoke, Tyrone had a strange sensation of anticipation.

"Detective Mayhew, ten years ago I came here to report a dream I'd had along with some very strong feelings about the Matherson case."

"Detective Grimes told me you stopped by." Tyrone squirmed in discomfort, embarrassed at his own acceptance of Grimes' unwillingness to pursue her suggestions. "He said he checked out your claims and nothing came of it."

"So, he didn't tell you exactly what I said? Did he tell you I'd called several times after my initial visit? He never returned any of my calls."

"He said you thought Miss Matherson was dead," said Tyrone. He knew Grimes looked at psychic powers as hogwash. Tyrone also remembered there wasn't much in the file about Grimes' interview with Serena.

"Detective Mayhew, Sergeant Jacobs, I realize most people think that those of us who claim to have psychic abilities are crazy, or we're very clever frauds. I'm thirty-five years old and became aware from the age of five I was different. It scared my parents to the point of putting me into psychotherapy when I was ten. Fortunately, my counselor, a wonderful woman, taught me to accept myself for who I am and to embrace this rare gift."

"Sorry Miss Walsh, but Sergeant Jacobs and I need to deal in facts, not feelings."

"I get it, Detective," she said smiling at him. "When I talked to Detective Grimes, I told him about a dream. I had this dream the night Mrs. Matherson vanished."

"Do you still remember this dream?" Jacobs gazed at her.

"Like it was yesterday, Sergeant," she said. "I saw innocence. A child frightened beyond belief."

Jacobs leaned forward, abandoning his pen and notepad. "Did you see who it was?"

"All I saw was a small dark figure. I couldn't see his face, but his stature indicated a boy of nine or ten years of age."

Tyrone looked at Jacobs. They exchanged a knowing glance. Jared was only nine when his mother disappeared.

"Do you know what scared him?" asked Tyrone, still very uncomfortable with this process, but becoming more than curious.

"Something terrible happened. I could feel his terror. It had something to do with death."

"Shit." Tyrone spewed the word, regretting it immediately. "Sorry, Miss. I don't mean to be rude."

Serena shook her head and held up her hand. "No big deal, Detective. I understand your frustration. Especially since this is the first time you've heard the full story."

"Yeah," Tyrone admitted, shifting in his chair. "I guess Detective Grimes and I have different ideas about what's important."

"I can see that," said Serena. "I had no other dreams, but had feelings—uncomfortable, eerie feelings. One time I felt water rushing around and consuming me. Two days later, I felt dirt pelting my face. I knew she'd been buried somewhere dark and cold."

"Could you see where?" asked Jacobs.

"It's not that simple. This is why so many people are skeptical of a sensitive. We often see or feel things but only as clues or hints. It's very rare for one to see every detail. Most times it's the ones who claim to have all the details who you should suspect as frauds."

"Have you seen or felt anything lately?" Tyrone wasn't sure if he believed her. However, some of what she said made sense, like the frightened young boy and the rushing water. However, he couldn't figure out what the dirt and the burial meant.

"Detective Mayhew, I think Mrs. Matherson is buried in the woods not far from where the car was found. That came from logic, not feelings. However, I went to the reservoir yesterday and meditated until I got a sense of where she might be. I believe if you walk due south from the eastern shore where you found the car, you'll find her grave."

Tyrone looked at Jacobs reading his thoughts. A lead was a lead no matter who provided it. They'd have to check this out.

"I hope you realize I don't charge for my gift. I don't believe in making a profit from someone else's pain."

"I appreciate you tellin' me all of this. We'll check it out, Miss Walsh, I promise." Tyrone rose and so did Serena. They walked toward the door and he said, "Thank you for coming by."

Tyrone could see Jacobs reaching for the right words. He probably didn't want to offend her.

"Let us know if you see anything else helpful," said Jacobs, blushing slightly.

"I will," she said.

After Serena Walsh was out of sight, Tyrone turned to Jacobs. "Are you buyin' this?"

"Whether I buy it or not, we're still required to investigate her claim."

"Do you think she should come with us?"

"Nah," answered Jacobs. "If she's right, the recovery dogs will find the remains and Lieutenant Clark said he needed a water recovery dog anyway."

"Let's set it up then," said Tyrone. "I hate wasting the resources, but like she said, you don't need to be a psychic to see the logic in it."

Chapter 19

After speaking with Serena Walsh, Tyrone felt it more imperative than ever to speak with his old partner, Percy Grimes. He tried Grimes's home telephone number.

"If you're sellin' something, we're not interested." The voice of Percy Grimes had roughened with age.

"Hey, Grimes, you old dog, how's it goin' in Reds country?"

"Don't know about the Reds, but I'm doing fine. How the hell are you, Mayhew?"

"Great. Since you left, I have two more sons and a baby girl who was born almost two weeks ago."

"Congratulations. I hope that girl looks like her mom."

Tyrone could almost see Grimes sneering. He always did that when he used sarcasm or thought he'd said something funny. "Oh, she does," Tyrone assured him.

"Well, I doubt you called me to make idle chit chat about your productive prowess. What's up?"

"You're right. Do you remember the Matherson case?"

"Yeah, I got your voice mail. Sorry I didn't get back to you sooner. The wife and I just got back from Florida. Too hot down there this time of year, but the wife wanted to look at some rentals so we can become freakin' snowbirds."

"Percy, we found Matherson's car dumped in Eagle Creek Reservoir."

"No shit. What about Mrs. Matherson?"

"She wasn't in the car. Forensics is examinin' it as we speak, but with all the water damage I doubt they'll find much." Tyrone paused, feeling awkward about his next question. No matter, he had to ask it. "I had an interestin' visitor this morning."

"Really?"

"Do you remember talkin' to Serena Walsh?"

"The psychic broad?" Grimes snorted.

Tyrone could see that sneer again.

"What mumbo jumbo is she blabbering on about this time?"

"She told me about the dream she had ten years ago, the night Miss Matherson disappeared. I didn't find any notes in the file about your conversation with her. Why didn't you document it?"

"Come on, Tyrone," he laughed, showing Tyrone he was still as big a jerk as ever. "You don't believe this psychic crap, do you?"

"There are lots of cases where psychics have helped the police."

"Nonsense," said Grimes. "Lucky guesses in my book. Did she come up with anything new?"

"She thinks Mrs. Matherson is buried in the woods close to where we found the car. As soon as I finish our conversation, I'm going to call for a search and recovery team. They'll be scourin' the wooded areas near where we found the car."

"Sounds like the logical thing to do," said Grimes. "You didn't need a fraud like her to figure that one out."

"Actually, she said the same thing."

"So, how much money is the department shelling out for her services?"

"She doesn't want payment." Grimes' attitude was grating on Tyrone's nerves. He had to put out a real effort to remain professional and friendly. "She said it's a gift and she doesn't believe in being paid for it."

"Humph. How touching. She's a real citizen." The sarcasm in Grimes' voice was palpable.

"Look, Grimes, no matter how you feel about her, the stuff she told you about the water was correct." Tyrone decided not to say anything about the frightened boy in the dream. "What's your take on her car? Don't you have a gut feeling about what could have happened to Wendy Matherson?"

"The husband said she took off with her boyfriend. They dumped the car there to keep her husband guessing. She probably changed her name or something."

"So you're not even goin' to entertain the idea she could be dead?"

"I think you're wasting your time with the dogs, but as I recall, you can be pretty stubborn."

Tyrone held the phone away and grimaced at it. Grimes wrote the book on stubborn.

"Do you have any idea who this *boyfriend* was? Reid Matherson is quick to stick to his story, but he can't give me a name."

"Nah," said Grimes. "From what I remember, no one ever came up with a name for her lover. I guess she's pretty good at keeping secrets."

"Can you think of anything else you and Serena Walsh discussed during the initial investigation? Is there anything else I should know."

"Can't say I do. It's all in the file, so if that's all I've got things to do."

Grimes stunned Tyrone with his abruptness. He thought Grimes would be anxious to see this one solved. Apparently, retirement meant no more police work. "Okay, Grimes. Thanks. It was good talkin' to you."

"Same here," said Grimes before he hung up.

"Just as much an S.O.B. as I remembered," said Tyrone, turning to Jacobs. "He's probably offended I questioned his decisions."

"I take it from your end of the conversation Grimes just blew off Miss Walsh's opinions again."

"Yeah, and I can't help wonderin' what else he blew off."

"Well, right now, I'm blowing you off."

Tyrone noted the huge smile on his partner's face, something he hadn't seen in months. "*Really?*"

"Yeah, I'm meeting Erica for coffee. She wants to talk."

"I guess your charms must have worked the other night. I hope you're takin' her to a quality establishment. No more of that fast food stuff."

"That was her idea, so we wouldn't miss the movie."

"Okay, I'm just sayin'." Tyrone couldn't help teasing his partner. It had become second nature to him.

"I am a little nervous. We really didn't talk much about our relationship the other night. I hope she isn't meeting me in a public place to tell me she wants to break up."

Tyrone felt a pang of sympathy for the guy. He and Jada were about to celebrate their tenth wedding anniversary and he still couldn't figure her out. "Usually people sound sad if they're about to give you bad news. Did she give you any reason to think she wants to split up?"

"Well, no. Actually, she sounded really cheerful."

"There you go. Now get out of here before you're late. I'll finish this report on the Walsh interview and my conversation with Grimes. I'll see you in the mornin' and I want details."

Chapter 20

Although Tyrone's advice had calmed him for a while, the closer Ben got to the coffee shop the closer he came to losing his nerve. Except for the quick dinner and movie from a couple of days before, Ben and Erica had only spoken by phone. Since her leave of absence, most of the conversations they'd had began with him asking how she was doing, her telling him she was fine, and then discussing how her father was doing.

Their conversations usually ended with a goodbye when his greatest desire was to profess his love for her. However, he knew he had to take it slow. Going through such a horrible ordeal and having her father injured on top of it revealed a more vulnerable side of Erica. Although she's a very strong woman, we all have our breaking points.

Ben's stomach roiled. He wasn't sure he could keep a cup of coffee down. His chest tightened with anticipation. He had to hold onto what Tyrone said, because her tone of voice indicated this would be a good conversation. Ben's head started to ache. He was over thinking all of this.

Taking a deep breath, Ben yanked open the door of the coffee shop and the bells jingled above his head to announce his entrance.

Stepping in, he looked around. He had hoped she would be there first and he could join her without buying anything, but she wasn't there and now he felt obligated to purchase something. With his stomach still in knots, he decided to order some tea. Tea came in a cup, too, so Erica wouldn't notice his unmanly choice. He walked up to the counter and ordered, keeping watch on the door.

He sat at a table near the entrance, sipping his tea occasionally. She was late. Erica Barnes was never late. Surely, she wouldn't stand him up.

Wishing he had a saltine cracker or two to settle the churning, he sipped his tea once more. Hearing the doorbell tinkle, he saw her standing in the doorway scanning the room for him.

Ben stood up so quickly, he nearly knocked over his chair. Feeling his face flush with embarrassment, he gave her a smile and a wave.

"Hey, Ben," she called from the door making eye contact with him.

This was a good sign, he thought. She'd frown, or look away, or something if she had bad news for him. He walked around the table and was delighted when she hugged him, and then kissed him on the cheek. This was definitely progress.

He reached into his pocket for his wallet. "Do you want some coffee or tea?"

"I think I'll skip it," she said. "Let's sit down."

He pulled out her chair for her, and then hurried to take his seat. It would all be over in a minute. She would tell him she still loved him or kick him to the curb.

"Ben." She paused, looking down at her hands which she rested on the table. "I want to apologize."

"There's nothing to apologize for…."

"Let me finish. I've been upset and confused on more than one level since the Emerson case. None of it has been fair to you. I don't know why you've hung around."

"Because I love you," he blurted out before he could stop himself.

"I know you do." Erica's sorrowful eyes were brimmed with tears. "I love you, too. I just wasn't sure I was ready to make the kind of commitment you wanted. Living together is such a big step."

Ben prepared himself for the worse—I love you *but*. There shouldn't be any *buts* in I love you or any *it's not you, it's me's*. Love is love. If you love someone, you should work things out.

"During the investigation, I felt myself attracted to another man," she said, keeping her eyes focused downward. "However, in my therapy I've discovered this attraction helped me avoid what I was afraid of—the big step."

"So what's next?" He looked down, gripping his cup. Somehow, the heat of it soothed him.

"This, asking you to forgive me for being such an idiot."

He looked up and stared across at her beautiful face, her tears now spilling down her cheeks. His heart felt as though it would burst. Ben could feel his eyes stinging as he battled to keep from crying, too.

"I love you, Erica. Anybody would have been confused after the hell you went through. Of course, I forgive you. If I didn't then I'd be the idiot."

She laughed and wiped away her tears with the back of her hand. The tension in her face subsided giving way to her beautiful smile. Softness came back to her coffee brown eyes.

"I've missed your sense of humor, Ben."

"I've missed everything about you, Erica."

Chapter 21

Tyrone watched as the Indiana K9 Search and Recovery team assembled. Since the water search by the Fire Department had yielded nothing, they'd decided to use one dog, a Weimaraner named Apollo, to ride in a boat attempting a water recovery. It fascinated Tyrone to think these dogs could smell human remains in so many different depths and types of water.

Of course, he hoped Apollo wouldn't find remains there. Just because the dog can find where they are didn't mean the divers would be able to find them. After all these years in the water, the bones would be darkened and covered with silt. Many times, visibility is only good a few feet from the surface.

Three other dogs would head east into the wooded area Serena Walsh had indicated during her visit to IMPD. The two Pit Bull Terriers, Lex and Coal, had been very successful in human remains recovery. They'd been doing it for eight years now. Hazel, a newly trained two-year-old Rottweiler, was going on her first recovery assignment.

"Looks like everything's all set," Jacobs said, a telling smile on his face.

Tyrone looked him over. Jacobs had lost the sad, puppy dog look he'd had for the last couple of months. Things must have gone well last night with Erica.

Before Tyrone could ask about it, he saw Patrol Officer Anne Samuels escorting Jared and Reid Matherson along with two other young men, most likely Tanner and Ryan Matherson, towards him.

"Detective Mayhew. These gentlemen are the potential victim's family and insisted on being here. I told them it would have to be cleared with you."

"It's okay, Samuels. You and Bays doin' okay over there? We need to keep the press on the other side of the tape."

She grinned. "Oh, yeah, of course Miss Atkins is here with her crew. She's the biggest pest, as usual. It's always my pleasure to refuse her entrance."

"Tell them Lieutenant Terhune will be here soon to make a statement."

She nodded and went back to her post.

"Alright gentlemen, as a family man myself, I completely understand your need to be here," said Tyrone making eye contact with each of them in turn. "However, you may not accompany the search teams into the woods. Our team of detectives and forensics experts are set up over there near the picnic tables and you are welcome to hang out there. There's coffee, water, and probably some donuts left if you'd care for any."

"I don't want donuts, Detective," snapped Reid.

"Come on, Dad," said the shorter of the two eldest sons. Then he turned to Tyrone and extended his hand. "Detective Mayhew, I'm Ryan Matherson and this is my brother Tanner."

"It's nice to finally meet you. I'll want to talk to the two of you at some point, but not today. We'll need to concentrate on tryin' to determine if there's any more evidence in the area in regards to your mother's case."

Jared took a step forward. "You mean her body, don't you?"

Tyrone saw the pleading look in Jared's tortured face. Something was ensconced in Jared's mind—something well hidden by trauma and years of brainwashing. Tyrone had to find out how to extract those memories, but not today. Today he had to see if there truly was a body in the woods.

"We've no idea whether we'll find anything, Jared," said Tyrone. "We're searching here because the car was found in this area. We need to either confirm or rule out the possibility of a murder."

"Thanks for being honest with me," said Jared. "Everybody else wants to ignore it. I'm sick and tired of acting as if nothing happened." Jared swept his arm around indicating the rest of his family. "They want to forget. I want to remember." Jared briskly walked towards the picnic area.

"Jared's very upset by the reopening of this investigation," said Tanner. "My brother is extremely sensitive."

"I don't know, Tanner," said Tyrone. "He seems pretty tough and very determined to me. The only person who seems upset by all of this is your father."

Reid blushed and pursed his lips, but Tyrone didn't give him a chance at a comeback. Tyrone simply turned and followed Jared, ready for a cup of coffee.

* * *

"Shit!" exclaimed Tanner in a low voice once Tyrone was out of earshot. "What if Jared starts remembering?"

"Shut up, Tanner," said Ryan.

"Stop it," Reid said through gritted teeth. "Everything's under control. It's been ten years and he hasn't remembered a thing."

"What about all of those nightmares?" Ryan asked. "He might start realizing their significance."

"We have to stay calm," said Reid. "It'll be okay."

"I'm beginning to think Jared is right," said Ryan. "We never should have gone on like business as usual."

"Right now we'd better join him over there," said Tanner. "Detective Mayhew is eyeing us. Let's get some coffee."

Chapter 22

Erica yawned and stretched. She rolled over to check her alarm clock—9:00 a.m. Holy crap, she'd slept too late. Pop usually had his breakfast by 8:00 a.m. so he could take his medication. She jumped out of bed and threw on her robe.

The first thing that hit her as she opened her bedroom door was the aroma of brewed coffee. When she entered the kitchen, there sat her father reading the newspaper with a bowl coated with oatmeal leavings and a cup of coffee.

"Well, Kitten, seems you had a late night last night." He smiled, his eyes remaining on the newspaper.

"Yeah, I guess I did."

"You guess?" he said as he folded the paper and stared at her. "I heard you come in after midnight. Your good old dad's parental radar is still intact."

Erica blushed a little, but smiled at her father's obvious acceptance of her late night activities. She and Ben had grabbed a few groceries on the way to his place. They'd had a late night supper after making love for the first time in nearly two months. Her smile widened as she thought about that beautiful moment of finding their love again.

"So when you movin' out?" Her father's voice disrupted her thoughts and she snapped back to the present.

"What?" That threw her off. "What makes you think I'm moving out?"

"In case you hadn't noticed, I made my own breakfast *and* I took my medication without any trouble whatsoever. Don't you think it's about time to get out there again, livin' your own life?"

"But, what if…."

He held up his hand. "Kitten, you only get so many chances at love. I was damned lucky to find my one true love and be married to her for nearly thirty-eight years. You know you want to move in with Ben, so *do* it."

"What about my place?" She knew the minute she'd said it he'd have a retort.

"Why the hell would you want to go back there? All the wonderful memories?"

"The city is paying for the damage. I'd feel guilty...."

Again, Pop held up his hand. "The apartment complex is damn lucky the city is helpin' them out. Usually, a crime scene cleanup is the victim's responsibility. Of course, the apartment above yours is the complex's responsibility, but they'll recover. I bet they can write the repairs and loss of rent off on their taxes. Don't worry about those blood suckers."

"I see your point. How long's that coffee been in there?"

"An hour. Let's get crazy and make a new pot to celebrate your new found independence."

Erica laughed. Her father always knew how to bring humor into any situation.

"Kitten, that's the most beautiful sound I've heard in a long time."

She blushed. It felt good to laugh again. "Love you, Pop."

"Back at ya."

Chapter 23

Morning passed quickly. So far, the K9 recovery team had found nothing. Jacobs ordered lunch from the local deli and distributed it to the Mathersons and IMPD personnel. The two older Matherson brothers sat with their father out of earshot, but Jared asked if he could sit with Jacobs and Tyrone.

"This must be pretty tough for you," Jacobs commented.

"It's not easy when you find out everything you think is true turns into something totally different," said Jared.

Tyrone nodded. "So how do you get along with your brothers?" he asked.

"Ryan and I have always been close. He worries too much about me. Tanner's Dad's favorite. He was top of his class in high school and college. 'Course they're both smarter than I am."

"I don't know," said Tyrone. "Seems to me you're the one with the most common sense."

"Really?" Jared brightened for a moment, looking surprised.

Jacobs leaned in and lowered his voice. "Why do you suppose they all seem so nervous?"

"No idea. Dad's been acting extra jumpy ever since you found Mom's car. He's still insisting Mom left with some guy."

"Have you discussed the case with any of them?" asked Jacobs.

"Ryan and Tanner just arrived last night, so I haven't talked to them much. When I told Dad about your visit the other morning, he said she probably dumped the car in the reservoir to throw us off her trail."

"Interestin'," said Tyrone. Reid Matherson was still trying to control Jared's recollections. "Jared, do you remember what your mom wore the night she disappeared?"

"Let me think." Jared took a small bite of his sandwich and wrinkled his nose. He swallowed and took a sip of his soda before speaking. "It was summer. I don't need to remember exactly to know she was wearing blue jeans. She always wore jeans when she went out with her friends."

"Anything come to mind about a shirt or jewelry?" asked Jacobs.

"She had two piercings on each ear. In the top hole, she always wore some diamond stud earrings Dad had us give her for Christmas when I was six. She only took them out when she showered, and then put them right back in."

"Anything else?" asked Jacobs.

"She had a simple gold wedding band she wore all the time." Jared paused, squinting as though thinking hurt his eyes. "Oh, my gosh. How could I forget? She had a locket Grandma gave to her when Mom was a teenager. I don't remember seeing it after she disappeared. It had a picture of Grandma and Grandpa in it."

"You're doin' great," said Tyrone. "Is there anything else you remember?"

"What are you remembering, Bro?" asked Ryan, startling Tyrone.

"Just trying to give the detectives some idea of what Mom wore the night she didn't come home. I don't suppose you remember what kind of shirt she wore?"

"Seems to me it was a pale yellow. Jeans for sure," said Ryan, the latter of which confirmed Jared's recollection.

"Do you think she was wearing the locket?" asked Jared.

"The one Grandma gave her? Probably. She wore it most of the time. I hate to change the subject, but Dad's not feeling so hot. He wants to go home."

"I'm not going anywhere," said Jared defiantly. "I figured he'd pull something like this, that's why I drove my own car. I want to be here if they find her."

"Then I'm staying with you. They can take Dad's car and I'll ride with you," said Ryan smiling. "Let Daddy's boy take care of him." Ryan left to tell the others Jared and he were staying.

Tyrone could see by Reid's expression he wasn't pleased, but he and Tanner left without a fuss.

"What happens if they find her, Detective Mayhew?" asked Ryan upon his return.

"Our Crime Scene Investigators will very carefully excavate the site to try to keep any evidence intact. It's a little like doin' an archeological dig. Usually bodies aren't buried deep. People don't realize the ground is so packed and hard in the woods. Plus, they're usually in too big a hurry to do it right. They're afraid someone will see them."

"So how do the forensic guys do it without breaking the bones?" Jared asked.

"Once the dog identifies the site, CSI will use the GPR, or ground penetrating radar, and see if they can get an exact location of the remains," stated Jacobs. "Then they will use some long thin metal probes to try to determine how far to dig so they don't hit the bones with a shovel and cause damage. When they feel they are close, they will start using archeological tools to remove the dirt."

"Wow," said Ryan. "This could take a while."

"It's a long tedious process. Even after the skeletal remains are removed, they will continue to sift through the dirt with fine wire baskets to make sure no other bone fragments are left as well as jewelry, bits of cloth, or other evidence."

"How will they know it's her?" asked Jared.

"If the jewelry you said she was wearing is there, it would be a good indicator, but inconclusive," said Jacobs. "Dental records can be used to make the initial identification, but DNA will give us the final and most accurate means of identifying the remains."

One of the portable radio's beeped and a crackling male voice said, "Come in command center." Everyone went silent as Tyrone grabbed the radio from a nearby table.

"This is Mayhew. You find somethin'?"

"Hazel is indicating a spot in the fourth quadrant of the map. She refuses to move so I'm sure we've got something human here."

Tyrone checked the map. "The CSI team and I will be there in ten minutes."

"I want to go with you," said Jared.

"Not this time, son. I told you when you got here that no one except our personnel would be allowed to go out there."

"But I can identify her jewelry or her purse or something," he pleaded.

"We won't get in the way, Detective Mayhew," said Ryan.

"The two of you need to stay here," said Tyrone firmly. "Jacobs will be here with you. When we find something for you to identify, we'll put it into evidence bags and bring it back here to show you, but legally I can't allow you near the crime scene."

Jared began to cry. Ryan put his arm around his brother's shoulders and guided him to one of the picnic tables to sit down.

"I hated to tell him no," Tyrone said to Jacobs. "But if anything went awry, the lieutenant would put my ass in a sling."

"Don't worry. I'll stay with them and make sure they behave."

"Thanks, man." Tyrone walked away with a heavy heart. As much as he wanted to solve this case, he hated the idea of it turning out like this.

Chapter 24

When Tyrone arrived at the scene, he saw the Rottweiler standing next to her trainer. Tyrone watched as Hazel received her reward for a job well done. The control these dogs displayed amazed him. The dogs stop just short of the site, lie down, and stare at it. He'd always pictured frantic digging by the animal, but no. Every recovery dog was trained not to retrieve, but to show them where the remains of a human could be found.

Mark Chatham had arrived with the GPR cart. He would use the Ground Penetrating Radar to scan the area for skeletal remains. CSI used this information to determine where and at what depth they needed to dig. Evidence preservation was their top priority.

"Hey, Chatham."

Chatham smiled at him. He was dressed in an official CSI tee shirt and jeans. Not his normal attire, but this was going to be a hot sweaty job, so he dressed for the occasion. "This is the cold case you've been working on, right?"

"Yep. Wendy Matherson. The car was found in the reservoir close to where we set up."

"What made you think she might be buried out here?"

"Let's just say a little bird told me." Tyrone wasn't quite sure how Chatham would take the idea of a psychic coming up with the information.

"Okay." Chatham raised an eyebrow. "You're lucky it's been so dry this month, otherwise this thing might not pick up anything. It doesn't always give a clear image when it does pick up something. Whether it works will depend upon how deep the remains are buried. Skeletal remains are hard to detect with this thing, but I want to try to at least find the skull or other large bones so we have a starting point."

"Thank God the dogs don't have so many limitations. Let's stop talkin' and start scannin'."

Chapter 25

"Dad, what are we going to do?" Tanner ran his fingers through his hair as he paced in the living room of his father's house. "What if Jared remembers?"

"Tanner, we've got to stay calm or this whole thing will blow up in our faces," said Reid.

"I was sixteen. They'll try me as an adult."

"My friend has been informed of what's happening," replied Reid. "He'll take care of things."

"Oh, yeah!" Tanner's laugh bordered on hysteria. "Just like he handled it ten years ago? He said this wouldn't happen."

"Tanner, get a grip. The way you're acting now makes you your own worst enemy."

"I'm finally finishing school. I'm on the verge of a career and now this." Tanner continued to pace. "Why couldn't they leave it alone?"

"Seems to me you're only thinking of yourself. We need to concentrate on making sure Jared doesn't remember what really happened."

"And how are we supposed to do that, Dad? Jared doesn't listen to us. He's all hyped up. You heard him, he *wants* to remember."

Reid walked over to the liquor cabinet and pulled out a bottle of scotch. He poured a couple of fingers in a glass and downed it in one gulp. He turned to Tanner. "Want some?"

"Scotch isn't going to make this go away."

"No, but it might relax you."

"Or it might make me throw up." Tanner walked to the couch and plopped down hard. He leaned forward resting his elbows on his knees and rubbing his face in his hands. He could feel a migraine coming.

"Are you getting a headache?" Reid asked, and then downed another glass of scotch. "Maybe you should go to your room and lie down."

Tanner leapt to his feet. "Go lie down! I can't sleep."

"Tanner, you're making yourself sick. Take some of your medication and go lie down. It will knock you out in no time."

"Whatever you say, Dad." Tanner went to the kitchen to get a glass of water. His migraine medication was packed in a suitcase in his room. As he ascended the stairs, he heard the clink of his father pouring himself another scotch. He mumbled as he reached his room. "Maybe this is all a dream and when I wake I'll be in my apartment in Ohio. Then I can say I had a nightmare and none of this happened."

Of course, he knew this was all too real. Maybe he should confess what really happened. It certainly didn't do Jared any good to keep up this façade. If he didn't tell the police, then Ryan might crack. It would be better for him if he did it.

Of course, his father would be livid, but how could he continue to live the rest of his life like this. For now, he'd take the meds and sleep on it. Hopefully, the dogs wouldn't find anything, the case would go back to being cold, and they could resume their lives.

Chapter 26

"The sunset's beautiful," said Jared staring off to the west. "At least if she's buried out there, it's a gorgeous place." His eyes filled with tears.

"Hey, Bro, it might not be her." Ryan attempted to ease Jared's pain. His own guilt tore at his soul.

"Do you really believe it's not her?"

Before Ryan could answer, Sergeant Jacobs approached. "It's nearly dark and they've just started digging. This process will take all night. You two should go home and get some rest."

"I don't want to leave," Jared exclaimed. "I want to be here. I have to know if it's her."

Jacobs produced a half-hearted smile. "Until we take the remains to the morgue and start testing, we won't be able to positively identify them."

"Her clothes and jewelry, what about those?" Jared turned to his brother. "We can identify them, can't we Ryan?"

Ryan heard the desperation in his brother's voice, but he knew Sergeant Jacobs was right. "I'm sure Sergeant Jacobs and Detective Mayhew will contact us as soon as they find something."

"But...."

"No buts," said Ryan firmly. "If it's her, we'll need our strength to deal with it. Let's go home."

Ryan saw the hurt and disappointment in Jared's eyes just before he turned and stomped off toward the parking area. His own chest tightened with his brother's pain. Ryan looked at Jacobs.

"Thanks, Sergeant. You will call us when this is over, won't you?"

"Of course, however, until the pathologist checks your mother's dental records with the teeth of the remains we won't even know if it *could* be her. Clothing and other belongings are sometimes generic. For example, most people wear blue jeans. DNA is the best way for us to make a positive identification. Unfortunately, it could take weeks to get DNA results depending on the lab schedule."

Ryan nodded. Then he turned and walked swiftly to catch up to his brother.

* * *

Tyrone looked up to see Jacobs and a fresh group of CSIs approaching. The current team had set up a tent and portable tables where they could sort evidence. Chatham was right. It had been difficult to locate the bones with the GPR. He had spotted something large he'd hoped was the skull, but it turned out to be a hipbone.

They found the skeleton buried approximately four feet down. Whoever did this didn't want this person found.

Two members of the CSI team had a table full of human bones they were assembling. Others took scoops of dirt and used sifting pans to locate small pieces of evidence and smaller bones which may have separated from the skeleton due to rain and soil shifts. Tyrone wondered if they'd finally found Wendy Matherson.

"Mayhew," said Jacobs as he came nearer. "I finally talked Ryan and Jared into going home. Jared wasn't very happy about it, but he seems to listen to Ryan."

"That's good. Maybe you should take off, too. This is gonna be a long night."

"Me? You're the one with a wife and kids at home. I'll stay, you go."

"This is *my* case!" Tyrone was taken aback by his own volatile reaction. A sense of guilt and obligation washed over him. He'd waited ten years, how could he leave now?

"I get it," said Jacobs. "But you know as well as I do how long this could take. It'll still be your case in the morning. Please don't make me pull rank on you and make this an order."

Tyrone realized he was being unreasonable. He'd probably think more clearly with a good night's sleep.

"Okay, okay," Tyrone conceded. "But you call me if anything comes up."

"You know I will. Now go home."

"Yes, Sergeant." Tyrone could at least get one more moment of pleasure watching Jacobs roll his eyes and shake his head.

On his walk back toward the location of his vehicle, Tyrone caught up with Mark Chatham. "Goin' home, Mark?"

"Yeah, you?"

"The Sarge kicked me out," he said eliciting a smile from Chatham.

"Long day," said Chatham. "I was glad to see the evening shift.

I'm bushed."

"Does it look like a female?"

"From the size of the femur and the pelvic bone we found, yes. Whether it's Mrs. Matherson or not, only DNA can tell for sure."

"I wish we could put a rush on it," said Tyrone.

"Don't count on it, buddy. Of course, I heard the DNA lab hasn't been as busy, so you might actually get lucky and have it in a week, maybe two."

"I've waited ten years. What's another two weeks?"

Chapter 27

Tyrone wearily trudged up the walkway and slipped his key into the front door lock. It was late and he thought his three youngest children would probably already be in bed.

To his surprise, the moment he opened the door, Reggie threw his arms around him.

"Hey there little man. What's up?"

"Dad, do you think you'll be home on time tomorrow?" Reggie's eyes gleamed bright with anticipation.

"Don't know, why?" Tyrone knew immediately he'd forgotten something by the pained look on Reggie's face.

"Tyrone Mayhew." Jada walked up behind Reggie using her most critical voice. "Don't tell me your brain is so preoccupied you've forgotten what's going on tomorrow evening."

Tyrone thought for a moment then it hit him. "Oh, yeah, Reggie Jackson Mayhew's playin' in the big baseball tournament tomorrow night."

Reggie's big brown eyes lit up again and he gave his dad a big, toothy grin. "You was just pullin' my leg, huh, Dad?"

"'Course I was." Tyrone couldn't see how a little white lie could hurt if it spared his son's feelings.

"Time for bed now," said his mother still glowering at her husband. "You need to rest up for the big game."

"Okay, Mama."

She leaned over and Reggie gave her a big hug and kiss.

"Thanks, Dad." Reggie gave Tyrone another tight hug before running up the stairs to his room.

"I hate when a case gets me this distracted," said Tyrone.

"So do I," said Jada, walking toward the kitchen. "Come in here and talk to me while I heat something up for you."

He followed her with no hesitation.

She took a plate filled with meatloaf, mashed potatoes and green beans out of the refrigerator and put it in the microwave to reheat. Tyrone grabbed some sweet tea from the refrigerator then poured himself and Jada a glass.

"So, what happened today?" She set his dinner in front of him taking a seat across from him.

"One of the recovery dogs found some human remains in approximately the area the psychic told us to look."

"Wow. How long before you can determine if it's Mrs. Matherson?"

"At least a couple of weeks." He took a bite of meatloaf barely chewing before swallowing. "Superb meatloaf, Darlin'."

"Thanks, what about her family? Do they know?"

"They showed up. The older boys are in town now. Reid Matherson was extremely upset. The older boy, Tanner, took him home before the dog even found the remains."

"What about Jared? He seems more affected by this whole thing than anyone else?"

"He and the middle boy, Ryan, stuck around until dark. Jacobs finally convinced them to go home and wait."

"Good. Those boys don't need to be there."

"I couldn't let them near the crime scene anyway. I feel bad for Jared. The fact he can't remember tortures him day and night."

"What about hypnotherapy?"

"What?" Tyrone put down his fork intrigued by the suggestion.

"Hypnotherapy sometimes helps people relive and remember things their conscious mind refuses to recall."

"Jared would do anything to get those nightmares out of his head," said Tyrone. "But his dad will have a fit."

"Can't you meet with Jared privately? He *is* an adult after all. I hate to encourage him to do things behind his father's back, but it sounds like a necessary evil in this case."

"Do you know anyone at the clinic who could help us out?"

"When I was there, I worked with a woman named Daphne Swan," said Jada. "She used to hypnotize people to help them quit smoking or overeating. I could give the clinic a call in the morning and put her in touch with you."

"Have I told you lately how brilliant you are?"

Jada got up from the table and took her glass to the sink. "Finish your dinner then meet me upstairs. Just because I'm not cleared for sex yet doesn't mean I can't give my man a nice massage to relieve his stress."

Tyrone knew exactly what she meant. "Sounds like an offer I can't refuse."

"You'd be a fool if you did," she said, winking and swinging her hips seductively.

Instead of finishing his last few bites, he jumped up from his seat and chased her up the stairs. Jada giggled like a schoolgirl until he caught her just outside of their bedroom door.

"I love you more than anything, Jada Mayhew," he said, kissing the back of her neck while she swooned.

"Let's get in the bedroom before the kids hear all this racket," she whispered. "Take a shower and I'll get the lotion."

He followed her into the bedroom and locked the door.

Chapter 28

Tyrone sat down at his desk, remembering how wonderful and understanding his beautiful, vibrant wife had been the night before. He truly loved her more than life itself and would do anything for her and his children. Tyrone felt like the luckiest man in the world.

Chatham had left Tyrone a voicemail at 8:00 a.m. telling him the CSI team had found all the major bones by 3:00 a.m. and had transported them to the morgue. The other physical evidence was now in the forensics lab. His day team relieved the night shift still working to make sure they hadn't missed anything.

Tyrone wanted to call Dr. Patel regarding the remains, but he decided to call Jared Matherson first. He wanted to ask Jared to come down to the police station—alone. Even though not everyone can be hypnotized, Jared's susceptibility to his father's explanation of his mother's disappearance might mean Jared would respond well to hypnosis. Luckily, Tyrone had Jared's cell number so he wouldn't have to worry about any of the other family members answering and interfering.

"Hello," said Jared. "Detective Mayhew, is that you?"

"Yes, Jared. I wondered if you could find a way to get away from your family and come down here to talk to me this morning."

"Did you find anything for me to identify?"

"I'll check, but I have something else I need to talk to you about privately. It's actually an idea my wife came up with to help you recall repressed memories. It might help to stop those nightmares."

"Really?"

Tyrone could hear the excitement in Jared's voice. "The main thing is not to disclose to your dad or brothers what you're doing, at least not yet. With your dad's attitude I'm afraid he might try to interfere."

"I know exactly what you mean." Jared paused for a moment. "They all decided to go out to breakfast this morning since Dad took the day off again. I told them I didn't feel good. I could sneak out now if you're going to be there for a while."

"Perfect. I'll call our coroner's office to see if they have any information for us. I had a voice mail this morning from CSI Chatham telling me the remains are in the morgue. I'll see if they've had a chance to check the dental records this morning."

"Thank you, Detective Mayhew. I should be down there in forty-five minutes."

"Great, see you then."

Tyrone disconnected the call then immediately called Dr. Patel in the morgue.

"Dr. Patel, it's Tyrone Mayhew. Did you receive the skeletal remains found at Eagle Creek Reservoir yesterday?"

"Ah, yes," said Dr. Patel. "It was pretty quiet in here this morning, so I had my dental expert come in to compare the teeth of the remains to the dental records of Wendy Matherson. There were several teeth missing, but it looks like this could be her."

"How are you going to proceed from here?"

"I have called in a forensic anthropologist from Indiana University to assist me with this autopsy. She is more experienced with older bones than I am. She is also a facial reconstruction expert and can give us a picture of what this person looked like."

"Excellent." Tyrone felt encouraged for the first time in days. "Any idea from a preliminary exam what may have been the cause of death?"

"Besides the missing teeth, there are fractured vertebrae in the neck and lower spinal bones. There is a long hairline fracture in the bone above the right eye socket. The kneecap of the left leg is shattered, and there's an indentation and crack in the knee joint. The fibula of the right leg is cracked just under the knee."

"What do you suppose happened?"

"From the upper body injuries, my first guess would be a very nasty fall. However, the breaks in the leg aren't consistent with a fall. The kneecap would not have shattered in this way in a fall. I believe this happened by a blow to the knee with a heavy object. The indentation is also not consistent with a fall. A cylindrical object could have caused the shape of the indentation. It's as though the object was being held at a downward angle when it was used."

"Interesting." He paused momentarily mesmerized by this fact. "Could she have been beaten?"

"I thought of that as well," said Dr. Patel. "It's hard to say. Although it appears that her knee was definitely injured by a blow, the other apparent injuries do not. Usually when you see a separation of the skull from the spine, there is also damage to the skull in that area. In this case the only injury to the skull is the hairline fracture I mentioned earlier."

"And that wasn't enough damage to indicate she was struck in the head," said Tyrone.

"You are correct," said Dr. Patel. "If she'd been hit by the same object I believe struck her knee, she would have had a much more significant break in the skull."

"Well, I'll leave it to you and your colleague to figure out all the details," said Tyrone. "Thanks for the info."

"You're most welcome, Detective," she said, and disconnected.

Tyrone replaced the phone and looked up to see Jacobs escorting Serena Walsh into the area.

"Look who came to see us again," Jacobs said.

"Hello, Miss Walsh." Tyrone stood extending his hand. She shook it this time and held it for a moment.

"It was her, wasn't it?" She looked at him with an intensity that made him want to squirm. She looked tired and paler than she had two days ago.

"We don't know for sure, Miss Walsh," said Tyrone. "We have to do DNA tests to make a definite identification."

"I know it's her." Serena sounded distraught. "I've also come to tell you both I had a couple of visions yesterday. It wasn't clear to me who, but I am feeling the person who did this to her is very close to her—family."

Jacobs gave Tyrone a look of disappointment, then said, "But you don't know which family member, so I'm afraid you've given us too little to go on."

"You don't believe me do you, Sergeant?" Serena shifted her stance from leg-to-leg. "I did tell you where to look for her and I was right."

"It's okay, Miss Walsh. Sergeant Jacobs isn't implying you're not correct." Tyrone tried to diffuse the situation as he could see she was getting frustrated. Jacobs wasn't being very subtle after only a couple hours of sleep. "We'll check out what you've told us, but you have to realize without details we don't have any clue who to talk to. Family could mean anyone from her sons to third cousins. You must understand we can't even start investigating this as Miss Matherson's homicide until we have concrete evidence of the identification of the remains."

"Mayhew," shouted Detective Hill. "You've got more company. This fella was waiting downstairs for you. He said he had an appointment with you so I brought him up."

There stood Jared Matherson looking anxious. Tyrone saw Serena give Jared a curious wide-eyed look. She walked over to him. "You're Wendy Matherson's youngest son, aren't you?"

Jared nodded. "How do you know my mom?"

"I didn't know her in life, but I've had visions of her since her death," said Serena.

"You're the psychic everyone was talking about. You're the one who told them where to find her." Jared threw his arms around her. "Thank you. Thank you so much."

Serena quickly withdrew from Jared. She held his upper arms as though she might shake him. She looked straight into his eyes then spoke to him in a whisper. "Do whatever it takes to remember. You must remember." Then she let go of him and looked imploringly at Tyrone. "Help him," she said then walked away.

Everyone including Detective Hill stared at her as she left. Tyrone didn't recall telling her Jared couldn't remember anything from the night of his mother's disappearance.

"What a loon bucket," said Hill. "Glad she's your problem and not mine."

Jared started to open his mouth when Tyrone touched his shoulder. "Not worth your breath, kid. Let's go somewhere more private."

Tyrone started to walk towards a conference room, but stopped and turned to Jacobs. "Sarge, can you check with forensics to see if they found any jewelry or other personal items we can show Jared?"

"Sure."

"Want any coffee or water before we get started?" asked Tyrone.

"No," said Jared. "Coffee will just make me jittery and water will make me want to pee."

Nothing like being straight forward, thought Tyrone, as he closed the conference room door. "Jared, my wife is a nurse and she used to work at a clinic on the near west side. There's a woman there she worked with who hypnotizes people who want to kick bad habits."

"What's that got to do with me?"

"Hypnotherapists have been known to help people with repressed memories. I think these nightmares you've been having all these years indicate your subconscious is hidin' something from you. Something you saw. Between that and your father's persistence in telling you what he wanted you to remember, your conscious mind has accepted that you slept through everything."

Jared sat staring at his hands. He appeared to be processing what Tyrone had just told him.

"It sounds like you think my dad had something to do with my mother's death."

"Again, until we know for sure these remains are hers, we can't make the assumption she's dead."

"You heard the psychic lady." Jared started wringing his hands and shifted in his seat. "She's been having visions since my mom vanished. She knew where to find Mom's body. I've never believed my mom would just up and leave me like that. This is why I dream about death, because I knew deep down she was dead."

"Okay, okay. Calm down and let's get back on track," said Tyrone. "My point is we might be able to make these nightmares go away. You told me you'd do anything to remember."

"Yeah, I did." Jared gazed at the wall to his right, and then his eyes brightened. "The psychic told me I needed to remember. She knows something. Nobody is going to believe her, so that's why I need to remember. I'll do it."

"Great. I'll have my wife set up an appointment for you. Now as much as I hate to be tellin' a boy to deceive his father, we need to keep this between us. Don't even tell your brothers. I'm afraid they might give you a hard time and try to stop you from trying the therapy."

"Don't worry, Detective Mayhew, I'll keep my mouth shut. Even if they find out, I'm not going to let them stop me."

There was a knock at the door and Mark Chatham walked in with four small evidence bags. "These are some items of jewelry we found in the grave. I'll lay them on the table in front of you, but don't touch them."

The first bag had a pair of hoop earrings. Jared indicated he didn't recognize them. Tyrone thought they were just too common for anyone to know to whom they belonged. Next Mark set a bag containing a gold band.

"She had a wedding ring like it, but lots of people have plain gold wedding bands," said Jared, disappointment evident in his demeanor. He looked at the third bag containing two diamond stud earrings and shrugged. "She had hoop earrings like those and she wore diamond earrings all the time, but they could belong to anybody. I'd like to think they're hers, but I can't be positive."

"This piece is a little more unique," said Chatham. "There were photos in it, but they were damaged beyond recognition." He laid the bag containing an open locket in front of Jared.

Tears began to flow immediately from Jared's eyes. "Can you turn it over?"

Chatham complied.

"It's my mom's," said Jared, his voice cracking with pain.

"How can you tell?" asked Tyrone.

"See the etching of a double heart there?" They nodded and Jared went on. "It wasn't part of the original design. Grandma had the jeweler do it. This has to be her locket. No one else would have had one etched exactly like this one."

Tyrone looked at Chatham. He felt a sadness which was almost overwhelming. In his opinion, Jared was a great kid who'd been used to hide something horrendous. He nodded at Chatham to indicate he should take the evidence back to the lab.

"I'm sorry, son," said Tyrone. "I wasn't going to tell you this because it's not really conclusive, but her dental records matched the remains for the most part."

"What does that mean?"

"Some of her teeth were missing. They weren't found at the site so it looks like they were knocked out somewhere else."

"Great!" Jared said, crying again. "Somebody beat her up and killed her?"

Tyrone patted Jared's shoulders, trying to comfort him. He couldn't imagine what this young man must be going through and how these past ten years had been torture for him.

All he knew was the sooner he could get Jared an appointment with Daphne Swan, the better.

Chapter 29

When he pulled into the driveway, Jared noticed Tanner's car was back. He'd hoped he would get home before they did, but it wasn't meant to be. Now he had to prepare himself for the inquisition. He really didn't feel up to it, but he knew there was no avoiding it.

Jared pushed open the door.

"Where have you been?" asked his father, scowling at him.

"Wow, Dad, that must be some sort of record," Jared sniped.

"Don't be a smart ass," his father retorted. "We were worried sick about you."

"I went for a drive." Jared knew the answer was lame and his father wouldn't back down. He also knew the further he went into this hellhole, the more likely his brothers would ambush him as well.

"Hey, Bro," said Ryan cheerfully. "Thought you didn't feel good."

"I'm better." Jared lowered his gaze.

"You don't look so hot," said Ryan. "Have you been crying?"

Jared pushed past him into the living room. He didn't want to explain. Turning on the television, he plopped on the couch and sat back roughly. His father stormed into the room after him and grabbed the remote from his hand turning off the set.

"What the hell?" Jared yelled. "I want to watch TV."

"Not until you tell me where you've been."

"Come on, Dad," said Ryan. "Lighten up."

"I will not!"

"What's all the shouting about?" Tanner said as he entered the room.

"Dad's blowing a gasket because I went out for a little while," said Jared. Now that Daddy's favorite had arrived, things could only get worse.

"You're living in his house," stated Tanner. "You should abide by his rules."

"Very easy to say when you've lived hundreds of miles away for the past five years," Jared countered.

"Back off him, Tanner," said Ryan. Jared could usually depend upon Ryan to jump to his defense. "He's obviously upset about something." He turned to Jared. "Did you talk to the police today?"

Jared couldn't believe how Ryan zeroed in so quickly. Of course, Ryan had always been tuned into him, so it shouldn't have been a surprise.

"Yes, I went downtown to talk to Detective Mayhew. The CSI brought me some stuff to look at. They belonged to Mom."

The three men stood in place, staring at Jared. Tanner looked like he was about to have a panic attack. His breathing increased and he started pacing. His father sat heavily into the nearest chair looking stunned.

Ryan sat down on the coffee table placing his hand on Jared's knee. He was the only one who remained calm. "Are you sure? Did they find the locket?"

"Yes, it has the double heart etching on it. Her dental records also match the teeth she had left. Apparently, she took some sort of blow to the face which knocked some out because they couldn't find them all."

His father's face changed drastically. No longer stunned, he gave Jared a strange wild-eyed look. "I guess she didn't run away after all."

"No, Dad," Jared shouted as he jumped up from the couch and flung his arm, knocking a small statue off the coffee table to the hard wood floor where it shattered. "She didn't fucking run away! Nobody but you ever believed that!"

"Calm down, Jared," demanded Tanner.

"Fuck you! You're the same as he is! You never gave a shit about what happened to Mom. After that night, you never talked about her and if I tried to, you'd tell me to shut up!"

Jared saw Ryan coming towards him. "Don't, Ryan. You're always trying to take care of me, but I'm not a kid anymore."

Ryan stopped in his tracks.

"This family has been nothing but fucked up since Mom disappeared. Nobody but Ryan ever cared about my shitty nightmares. Remember what *you* told me, Dad. It's just your imagination, Jared. Think pleasant thoughts when you go to bed and the nightmares will go away. Well they didn't! I just stopped telling you about them."

"Son, I was just trying to do what was best for you," said his father looking defeated.

"*Really?* Taking all the feelings and hiding them away was good for me?"

"He tried to protect you," said Tanner.

"From what?" Jared turned on his older brother. "From remembering who *murdered* our mother? Well, I'm going to get to the bottom of this whole thing."

"What are you going to do?" His father rose from his chair.

"I saw the psychic at the police station. She knows what happened. She told me I needed to remember what happened that night."

"And you bought the word of a psychic!" Tanner laughed maniacally. "Are you out of your mind?"

"Probably am after what that son-of–a-bitch did to me." Jared pointed at his father.

In the next second, Tanner quit laughing, drew up his fist and clipped Jared in the jaw sending him to the floor.

"No, no!" Their father ran to his sons and pushed Tanner back. "We mustn't fight amongst ourselves."

"I'm not going to let him talk to you that way," said Tanner.

Ryan offered to help Jared up, but he slapped Ryan's hands away and scrambled up on his own.

"I'm going to my room now and I'm going to pack. Then I'm going to see if Aunt Cindy will let me stay with her. You remember her, Mom's sister, and the one you forbade us to see?"

"Jared, please don't," begged Ryan.

"I can't stay here anymore, Ryan. Aunt Cindy will understand. I'm sure she's heard about this by now. She needs someone with her who loved Mom, too."

"Son, you don't have to leave." His father breathed heavily as he let go of Tanner.

"Don't call me son," said Jared gritting his teeth. "Detective Mayhew has set me up with a hypnotist who's going to help me remember. I'm not going to suffer any more."

Jared turned and ran up the stairs, slamming the door as he entered his bedroom. As he started throwing some clothing into his duffle bag, he worried that he'd blown Detective Mayhew's trust by losing his temper and telling his family about the hypnosis. Of course, now that he was leaving, they wouldn't be able to pressure him anymore. He was sure Detective Mayhew would understand.

Chapter 30

Tanner paced and massaged his knuckles. "Shit! This is totally out of control and I've got an appointment to talk to the cops this afternoon."

"Just stay calm, Tanner, and stick to our story." His father rubbed his temples. Tanner wasn't the only one who got migraines.

"How am I supposed to stay calm with everything unraveling? What about your friend, Dad? What's he doing to help?"

Ryan's brow crinkled. "What are you talking about? Dad, you can't let this go any farther. You've got to tell the police what really happened."

"Shut up!" Tanner looked as though he would deck Ryan next. "I'm not going to jail."

"Stop bickering," commanded their father. He needed to think. Everything *was* out of control. He'd known the day would come when Jared would question what really happened. Perhaps Jared would even scour the country trying to find her. However, he never anticipated the discovery of the car or the body. "I'm going into my office to think. In the meantime, leave Jared alone."

"Whatever you say, Dad," said Tanner.

"We on the same page, Ryan?" asked Reid.

"Okay, Dad," said Ryan with a sigh. "But I'm telling you, this is only going to get worse the longer we wait."

Reid waved him off and walked toward his office. He wondered if he should chance making that call. With suspicion directed at him again, the police would watch his every move. They could obtain phone records, credit card records, and etcetera. He'd have to use the disposable cell he was given. Reid dialed the number and listened to it ring.

"This better be good."

"It's not, Sarge," said Reid. "Everything's gone haywire. That psychic bitch went to the police with another vision. They took dogs out to the woods and found her."

"Look, Reid," he said. "They've got no evidence. Seems to me her boyfriend got mad because she wouldn't leave you and the boys. Maybe she even took him out there to talk."

"And, he got pissed, killed her and buried her, then dumped the car in the reservoir," Reid said, finishing the thought.

"Exactly," he said. "So no worries, right?"

"Except it seems Detective Mayhew had a little talk with Jared this morning and now Jared's going to see some shrink."

"Big deal. What can a shrink do? Tell him his nightmares are because of his problems with his daddy's control issues or because his mommy deserted him."

"He said Mayhew recommended a hypnotist."

"Really?"

Reid waited through the silence, hoping his friend would come up with a viable solution.

"So pretend you're in favor of it and ask him about his progress. No need to worry about it now."

"There's more," said Reid. "While Jared was at the police station the psychic showed up again."

"Why can't that nosy bitch mind her own business? What did she say to him?"

"He should *try to remember*. This is why he's even more determined than ever. He's also going to be out of my reach."

"Why?"

"He's angry with all of us," said Reid. "He doesn't want to be here and is going to ask Wendy's sister if he can stay with her."

"That could be a problem." There was another long pause.

Reid waited patiently. He was used to these long periods of thinking time.

"Okay, leave it to me. I'll take care of things."

"What are you going to do?" asked Reid.

"Better for you if you don't know. Trust me."

The cell phone went dead. Reid stared at it a long time wondering whether he'd been wise to ask for help. No telling what might happen now.

Chapter 31

Jacobs shuffled through his files. "Mayhew, which one of the Matherson kids is coming in this afternoon?"

"Daddy's boy, Tanner. He's the most likely to have seen or heard something that night. How many sixteen-year-olds do you know who go to bed early on a Saturday night?"

Jacobs shook his head. "You make a good point. Are we going to gang up on him, or do you want to take this one on your own?"

"Actually, I thought you should take this one. Tanner and his daddy don't trust me. He's more likely to open up to you than to me. I can watch on the computer and if I think we need to 'good cop-bad cop' him, I'll make an entrance."

Jacobs crossed his arms in front of him and sat back in his chair. Tyrone could see the wheels turning as Jacobs thought it through. "Well, Tyrone, I guess you do come up with a good idea every now and then."

"Thanks."

Jacobs sat forward and finally found the file he needed. He grabbed a notebook. Before he could leave his desk, his phone rang. When he hung up, he looked at Tyrone. "Tanner's here. He'll be in number three so watch and learn."

Tyrone snickered as he pulled up the video feed from interrogation room number three on his computer. Jacobs' cocky attitude could only mean one thing—he and his ladylove had truly reconciled. Tyrone had been so busy yesterday with the search he'd completely forgotten to get the juicy details about Ben and Erica's *coffee date*. All he knew was Jacobs said things were heading in the right direction.

Focusing now on Tanner, he could see the young man fidgeting. He crossed his arms and uncrossed them, then crossed his legs, uncrossed them, got up and walked around then sat back down when he heard Jacobs entering. Tyrone was sure this boy knew something. If he was asleep in his bed on the night in question, there'd be no reason to be so nervous.

"Mr. Matherson," Jacobs began, "have you spoken with Jared this morning?"

"Yes, he told us he came here earlier. He said you found some of my mother's things."

"I have a photo of the evidence." Jacobs pulled some photos out of his folder. "Could you take a look at these and tell me if you recognize any of them?"

Tanner took his time before speaking. A glossy layer of sweat formed on his upper lip. "Some of this stuff could belong to anybody, but this locket belonged to my mother. My grandmother had it engraved with the hearts."

"Jared said the same thing. Speaking of Jared, he seems to have a lot of trouble with nightmares. Do you know anything about them?"

"I know he used to complain about bad dreams when he was a kid. Something about dying. Can I have some water?"

"Sure, I'll be right back."

"Good deal," said Tyrone aloud. Most people became more nervous when they had to wait. Jacobs would get the water and take his sweet time about it. Again, Tanner stood up and paced. He wiped his lip with the back of his right hand then ran his left hand through his hair. This guy's blood pressure must be sky high.

Jacobs returned with a bottle of water. "Here you go, Mr. Matherson. May I call you Tanner?"

Tanner nodded, sat down, and then took a long swig from the bottle. He breathed deeply, seeming to relax a bit.

"Where were we?" Jacobs glanced at his notes. "Oh, yes. We were talking about Jared's bad dreams."

Tanner took another drink and swallowed hard. "Sergeant, until I came home, I didn't realize Jared was still having these nightmares. As a matter of fact, the last time I remember him talking about them was after his eleventh birthday party, just before I moved to Ohio to go to college. He woke up screaming in the middle of the night. Dad took care of it and I don't recall anyone talking about it the next morning."

"Any idea what might be causing Jared to have these dreams?"

"Not a clue."

Jacobs put his hands together as though he were praying. He rested them on his lips and stared into Tanner's eyes. Tyrone was impressed. That look would scare him.

Tanner started to rock. "I swear I don't know anything about the dreams. Jared and I weren't close. If you want to ask someone about them, ask Ryan. He shared a room with Jared and they were really close. As far as I know, they still are." Tanner looked around the room avoiding Jacobs' stare.

Jacobs finally brought down his hands to the desk. "Enough about Jared. What do you remember about the night your mother vanished?"

"Nothing. I was sleeping."

"What time did you go to bed that night?"

Tyrone studied Tanner's physical reactions. He noticed Tanner wiping his hands on his jeans, obviously more sweating. Then Tanner looked away from Jacobs again before answering.

"That was ten years ago. How the hell am I supposed to remember the exact time?" Tanner's discomfort seemed to increase. He shifted in his chair. "It seems like I went to bed early that night, probably around 10:00."

"Kind of early for a teenager on a Saturday night."

"If I recall correctly, I wasn't feeling well that day. I decided to hit the sack early."

Jacobs wrote something in his notebook. "So, you went to bed at approximately 10:00 p.m. that night, went to sleep and didn't wake until morning."

"That's right."

"Can anyone besides your father corroborate your story?"

Tanner stood, his face blushing with anger. "What are you implying?"

"I'm not implying anything, Tanner. Now sit down." Jacobs' stern tone did the trick. Tanner deflated as quickly as he'd inflated. "Now, I'll ask again and reword the question. Did anyone outside of your household know of your illness? A friend you talked to about plans you had to cancel? Did you have a job you had to blow off that day? You know, that sort of thing."

"Not that I can recall."

"I see." Jacobs made a few more notes.

Tyrone knew this stall tactic would create paranoia in Tanner.

"Did you overhear any phone conversations your mother might have had that seemed hostile?"

Tanner shook his head.

"To your knowledge, did she have any enemies? Were there any neighbors who were angry with her?"

"No, my mother was great. I miss her just as much as Jared does."

To Tyrone's surprise, he saw tears welling up in Tanner's eyes. Man, Jacobs was good.

"I'm sure you do," said Jacobs. "It's horrible to lose a parent at such a young age. I'm sure it was terrible to think she would abandon you, and now you have to accept a new truth. There was no boyfriend, she didn't leave willingly and we only need to run the DNA to say without a doubt that the remains we found belong to your mother."

Tanner stood again. "I've told you all I know. I need to go home and check on my father. This whole thing has been quite a shock for him."

"Sure, I get it," said Jacobs. "I only have a couple more questions and you can go."

"Okay."

"At sixteen, you would have been pretty savvy to what goes on around you," said Jacobs. "Did you ever see your mother with anyone who might have been a bit too friendly?"

"What do you mean, too friendly?" asked Tanner.

"You know, someone who might have touched her in an intimate way or said something to her that wasn't really appropriate since she was a married woman."

"Oh, you mean did I see anyone who could have been her boyfriend?"

"Precisely."

"No, Sergeant Jacobs. As far as I knew, my mother was a faithful wife. I didn't know about the affair until Dad told us she'd run off with someone."

"Doesn't it strike you as a little weird that he'd say that, but didn't know who her lover was?"

"No," said Tanner, shaking his head. "I trust my father to tell me the truth. I really don't know anything else, so may I go. My father had quite an argument with Jared today and he was very distraught when Jared moved out. I really need to go check to make sure Dad is okay."

"Sure. We'll let you know if there's anything else we need." Jacobs rose and opened the door. "And, Tanner, please make sure you call us if you remember anything else which might be helpful."

Tyrone turned off his view of the interrogation room. He rubbed his chin, thinking about Tanner's state of mind. The boy was very protective of his father and trusted him implicitly.

Jacobs strolled up to his desk. "So, what did you think?"

"He's definitely hidin' something. When you look at the recording, you'll see he was even more nervous when you aren't in the room. If his dad did this, I believe he'd do anything to protect him."

"I don't see a lot about the neighbors in the file. Did you and Grimes question them?"

Tyrone thought for a moment. "There were a few we talked to, but Grimes seemed to think it was a waste of time. I'm beginnin' to think he wanted to believe Reid's story so he could close the case."

"Didn't get closed, though, did it?" Jacobs tossed the file in his top desk tray. Then he sat there looking off into space and smiling.

"Wait a minute," said Tyrone. "I know that look. Seems to me you had more than coffee the other night."

Jacobs blushed.

"Ooo, yeah. My Jada is going to be thrilled to hear you two are back on track."

"I think Erica's going to move into my place. She said her father was getting sick of her hovering. She's not too keen on going back to her old apartment."

"Well, then, looks like we've got some celebratin' to do. How about I get my sister to watch the kids day after tomorrow and we all go out. Jada hasn't been out on the town since the baby was born."

"Sounds good to me. I'll check with Erica and let you know first thing tomorrow. I'm really happy, Tyrone."

"I can see that, my brother. Now don't screw it up again."

Chapter 32

Serena ran into the mist of the woods. She stopped momentarily to listen, so frightened that the only thing she could hear was her thudding heart. The crack of a branch to her left sent her fleeing again. The fog thickened, her terror increased and then he was there— right in front of her. She looked at the figure in Army fatigues and night vision goggles. He reached for her and then....

The creak of her bedroom door and the thump of her tabby cat, Alice, leaping on her bed woke her. She sat straight up, heart pounding in her ears. Dazed from such a rude awakening, she grabbed Alice.

"How did you get the door open?" Normally she didn't allow the cat in her room at night. A night prowler, Alice woke Serena several times if she allowed Alice in the room.

She started to get up to put Alice out when she saw a man standing at the foot of her bed, his gun silhouetted in the moonlight. He wore dark clothing and his night vision goggles masked his face. She held her breath unable to release it and sat still as a rabbit hoping not to be seen.

"Don't scream or I'll shoot you and your feline friend."

In shock, the only thing Serena could think to do was let go of Alice who leapt from the bed and disappeared. Her voice trembled as she spoke. "Who are you and what do you want?"

"It's come to my attention you're nosing into things which are none of your business."

Nonplussed she said, "I don't know what you're talking about."

"Let me make it perfectly clear." He approached her, pointing the gun at her face. "You've been telling stories which are confusing a young man whom I care deeply for and it must stop."

The young man had to be Jared Matherson. His mother's death had been the only incident weighing on her mind lately. In addition, this man's voice sounded vaguely familiar, but she couldn't place it. Serena shook uncontrollably when he put the gun to her temple.

"Lay down," he commanded.

She obeyed. One wrong move and she was sure he'd kill her.

"If you tell me what I've done wrong, I can make it right. I'll stop. I promise. Just don't hurt me." Her nerves turned into tears. Serena couldn't understand why Jared remembering would matter, unless…unless this was his mother's killer.

A new wave of terror hit her. If this man killed Wendy Matherson, he'd not think twice about killing her.

He climbed onto the bed, the goggles giving him the appearance of some alien creature. Continuing to point the gun at her, she felt there was nothing to do but despair. Did he intend to rape her first? How could she fight her assailant with a gun in her face?

Straddling her across her hips, he pulled a pair of handcuffs from his left pocket. He clamped one end to her right wrist. "Put your arms up over your head," he said, motioning toward the headboard with his gun.

At first, she simply stared at him and lay motionless.

"I said, put your hands over your head," he said gruffly, and then back-handed her across the cheek.

She did what he told this time, despite her dizziness. Beads of sweat started to form on her face as he wove the handcuffs around the wooden bar of the headboard and clamped the cuff on her other wrist.

He moved further up her body squeezing her ribs between his legs. "If you move, I'll blow your brains out."

Terror seized her as Serena realized she was imprisoned. There was no escape unless *he* set her free, but it was evident that this man from her nightmare had no intention of letting her go. Tears began to flow down her cheeks despite her efforts to stop them.

He placed the gun on the bed and moved up her body with both knees cutting into her ribcage. He looked at her tilting his head from side-to-side as though peering at something curious.

"You know what I don't get," he finally said. "I don't understand why you didn't foresee this."

"I did," she said, choking down tear-inspired mucus.

He tightened his legs, pushing in on her sides.

"Please, I can't breathe very well."

"Really?" He sounded delighted. He slowly sat down on her chest pushing the air from her lungs. "Actually, I had hoped you couldn't breathe at all."

Survival instinct finally kicked in as Serena gasped and tried desperately to move sideways to buck him off. She drew up her legs to try to gain some leverage, but he was too heavy. Serena realized he'd never planned to shoot her, but he *was* going to make her death as terrifying and painful as possible. Desperate and weakening, Serena pulled her arms forward meeting with resistance, tearing her tender skin until warm blood trickled down her arms.

Then the monster grabbed her chin and forced her mouth closed and pinched her nose. The pressure was so intense she thought she'd explode. There was no way to breathe, no way to stop him.

The more she struggled, the weaker she became until she could barely move. With little oxygen reaching her brain, her head began to feel dizzy; flashes of light seemed to pop in front of her eyes. She wished she could tell her mother she loved her just one more time. Then Serena Walsh stopped struggling and everything went black.

Chapter 33

He checked her pulse through his latex gloves. Gone. He pulled a plastic bag and a tiny key from his pocket. Removing the handcuffs, he slipped them into the bag. Retrieving his gun, he went to the back door where he found his satchel of tools making sure everything he'd used to enter the home was there, including the plastic bag with the handcuffs. He ejected the clip from the gun, and then placed it and the clip inside the satchel. When he was sure he had everything, he slipped out the back door not bothering to close it.

He continued to wear the night vision goggles so he could find his way back to his car without using a flashlight. Stealthily he walked, checking for lights in the neighbors' houses. It was past 2:00 in the morning, but one never knew when there would be someone up for a midnight snack.

The car sat behind a line of pine trees giving him shelter from curious eyes. Before he'd arrived, he'd turned off the dome light in the car and pulled the bulb in the trunk to avoid unwanted attention when he opened them. Quietly, he placed the tool satchel in the trunk removing the handcuffs and retrieved a garbage bag. Slipping out of his fatigues, he put them in the garbage bag along with the handcuffs.

A few nights from now he'd put them in some dumpster at an apartment complex far away from here. No one would be the wiser. He tossed the night vision goggles in the trunk bringing the lid down slowly and pressing it closed to make minimal noise in this all too quiet place.

He didn't slam the car door either, but simply brought it to the point of closing then pulled it hard hearing it latch. The only noise he couldn't avoid was that of starting the engine. Fortunately, this line of trees was next to an alleyway he could follow to the next street. He definitely didn't want to go out the way he came in and go past her house.

Breathing deeply for the first time since he left Serena Walsh's house, he hoped he had solved at least part of their problem. Now, how was he going to convince Detective Mayhew to leave them alone and look elsewhere for the killer?

Chapter 34

As Jared drove along Meridian Street, he recalled the relief he felt when his Aunt Cindy had taken him in the day before. He feared she'd say no when he asked if he could stay with her. They hadn't seen one another since his father forbade it ten years ago. Contrary to Jared's fears, Cindy welcomed him into her home as though they'd never been apart.

She encouraged him to tell her everything. They grieved together over the ever-closer reality the remains found were his mother's. He'd finally found someone who he could talk to about his mother—someone who wouldn't steer him away from the subject. Someone who cared his mother was gone.

Detective Mayhew had called late yesterday to give him the time of his appointment with the hypnotherapist, Daphne Swan. Jared confessed to the detective how he'd blown their deal about telling his family. At first Detective Mayhew sounded disappointed; however, his attitude seemed to change when Jared told him he'd moved in with his Aunt Cindy.

He pulled up to the clinic feeling the heaviness of anticipation in his chest. Conflicts swirled through his mind and soul, creating a battle between his desire to know the truth and his fear of what he may learn. He closed his eyes and took a deep breath. When he opened his eyes, the need to know won out.

A very pleasant older woman with more gray than mousy brown in her short curly hair sat at the reception desk. Her round face and sweet smile made him yearn for his grandmother who passed away two years before his mom disappeared. He remembered the depression his mother suffered when his grandmother died. She once told him she wore her locket every day to keep her mother close to her heart.

"What can I do for you, young man?"

"My name's Jared Matherson. I have an appointment to see Doctor Swan."

"So, you're new here."

"Yes."

She pulled open a drawer and retrieved a clipboard with some forms attached. "Fill these out and return them to me when they're complete. I'll let Daphne know you're here."

Jared took a seat in the reception area to fill in the forms. He pulled out his insurance card and smiled at the fact his father would get the bills. Once complete, he returned the forms to the receptionist and sat back down.

He nervously leafed through a few magazines. He read the captions under the pictures, because he couldn't concentrate long enough to read any of the articles. After about fifteen minutes of waiting, a nurse came to the doorway and called him in. His pulse began to quicken with anticipation.

The nurse opened the door to the therapist's office and closed it upon her departure. There stood a tall, thin woman with long auburn hair and blue eyes. Jared guessed she was probably in her thirties. She wore blue jeans, an emerald silk shirt, and black flat shoes. Her casual appearance made him feel more relaxed. He'd expected to see a staunch woman dressed in a suit and heels.

She extended her hand to him and he accepted it, shaking it lightly. "Hello, I'm Daphne Swan, Jared. It's a pleasure to meet you."

Jared simply nodded, not sure why he couldn't find his voice.

"I've spoken with Detective Mayhew about your case. It's my understanding you have a repressed memory you would like to work on."

"Yes, Doctor Swan," he said.

"Please call me Daphne," she said. "I appreciate your polite respect; however, you and I will be working on your inner most thoughts. One of the secrets to a successful hypnotic state is trust."

"That makes sense."

"We won't try the hypnosis today."

Jared couldn't stop the disappointment from showing on his face.

"Please don't be discouraged, Jared. We need to get to know one another a little better. We need to build a level of trust. Since this is something I'm doing upon the request of the police, I've blocked out time every day this week, if that's okay with you."

Jared's eyes widened with renewed hope. "Sure. You name the time and I'll be here."

"I also want to assure you, anything you tell me during these sessions is held in strictest confidence. Detective Mayhew may have requested I help you, but patient privacy laws prevent me from sharing the information with him without your consent. Do you understand?"

"Yes." He nodded.

"Great, now let's get started."

By the time his hour ended, Jared had given her every detail of what he could remember from the months before his mom disappeared and for the years after. Jared included his father's insistence he'd been asleep the night his mother vanished. Then last, and most important in his opinion, he gave her the details of the horrendous nightmares he'd been having.

"So these nightmares have been going on for the past ten years?" she asked, although it seemed more like a statement.

"What do you think they mean?" he asked.

"It's hard to tell right now, Jared," said Daphne. "Our minds tend to try to push bad memories aside to protect us. A traumatic experience can cause memory loss or suppression. You may have seen or heard something that you don't want to believe. Your mother's disappearance must have been very hard on you."

"It was weird," said Jared.

"In what way?" Daphne asked.

"Sometimes I remember little bits and pieces, but nothing concrete," said Jared. "I think I see her face. She looks scared, and then she's gone. Sometimes I hear shouting, you know, my dad and brothers. But they tell me I'm imagining it."

"We'll work on sorting out those images and finding out whether they are real memories or not. For now, our time is up. Can you be here tomorrow at the same time?"

"I told you before, you give me a time and I'll be here." He jumped out of his chair, emotionally drained but hopeful. It felt good to talk with an objective person.

On the drive back to his aunt's house, Jared had a multitude of things racing through his mind. Then something on the radio caught his attention.

"This just in. Police are at the home of Serena Walsh, the psychic who we understand was instrumental in leading police to a body found in the woods at Eagle Creek Reservoir two days ago. It is believed an intruder broke into her home on North Pine Street last evening to rob her and murdered her in her bed."

"What the hell?" Jared turned up the volume.

"Police aren't speculating on the cause of death at this time. Ms. Walsh was found this morning after a neighbor discovered Ms. Walsh's cat wandering around the yard. The neighbor stated that Ms. Walsh never let her cat outside, so she became suspicious. She went to the back of the house finding a window and door open. She

immediately went home and called 911."

Jared turned off the radio. His heart pounded so loudly it made his ears throb. Breathing heavily, he started to cry. Immediately he began to speculate whether this had something to do with what she knew about his mom's death.

"Oh, God," he said aloud. "Did somebody do this to shut her up? The only people who knew she'd talked to me were the police." Then he wiped his eyes and it hit him. "Shit, shit, shit!" He pounded the steering wheel with his left hand. "I told Dad!"

Chapter 35

Homicide Detective Chennelle Kendall stood outside of Serena Walsh's house. She took notes as she questioned first responder, Patrol Officer Anne Samuels.

"So, it appears the intruder popped out the screen, and then neatly cut the glass of the window in back. He or she gained entrance by unlocking the window and climbing through," repeated Detective Kendall. "Then the intruder decided to take an easier way out by going out the back door."

"That's correct," said Officer Samuels.

"Who called it in?"

"The elderly lady next door. Her name is Edna Givens. She's pretty shaken up."

"Did she actually go in and find the body?"

"No. When she saw the screen on the ground and the open door, she went home and called the 911 operator."

"Great, thanks. Oh, Samuels."

"Yeah."

"I heard you're studying for the detective exam. Good luck. I'd love to have you on our team."

"Thanks, Detective Kendall."

"Call me Chennelle," she said, then walked toward the back of the house. There she found Detective Brent Freeman examining the window where they suspected the intruder entered. He wore a white dress shirt and blue tie, but had his sleeves rolled up on this exceptionally hot, late-June morning. His wavy brown hair gleamed in the bright sunlight.

Freeman turned and stared at her. "This has got to be where the intruder went in. Looks like our bad guy used a professional tool to cut the hole in the top pane. It's just large enough to slip a man-sized hand in and unlatch the lock. There's the piece of glass lying next to the screen."

"A professional burglary gone wrong?" Kendall crinkled her brow.

"I would have thought so, but as far as I can tell, there wasn't anything taken. Her purse is still in the house with money in her wallet. Her cell phone, computer, e-book, television, and stereo are all still here."

"Is Spalding finished with the preliminary exam of the body?"

"Don't know. Let's go find out." Freeman led the way into the house.

As Kendall and Freeman entered Serena Walsh's bedroom, she saw Nate Spalding leaning over, showing off the bald spot on the pate of his head in the midst of his thinning black hair. He carefully lifted one of Serena's eyelids with a gloved finger. Gently he lowered her eyelid and stood up to his full six-foot frame.

Kendall leaned in to get a closer look. "Do you see anything which might tell us what happened?"

"She's got petechiae of the eyes," said Spalding.

"And?" She waited for an answer, but Spalding looked puzzled. She lost her patience. "Was she strangled, smothered with a pillow, what?"

"The petechiae is a sign someone *helped* her stop breathing; however, I can't tell how by looking at her. There aren't any marks on her neck indicating strangulation. In addition, no apparent bone fractures in the neck. A pillow could have been used. If it was, we'll find pillow case fibers in her mouth and nose when Dr. Patel does the autopsy. CSI should bag the pillows and test them for her saliva and epithelial from our killer."

"I guess we'll have to wait for the doc to check this one out," said Freeman.

"Take a look at her wrists. See the marks and the cuts on them?" Spalding pointed to the areas. "Now look at the headboard. I believe from the wounds and the damage to this post, she may have been handcuffed during the assault."

"Can you tell if she was sexually assaulted?"

"From the outward signs, I would say no. The way her pajama top is hiked up and from the bruising on her torso, it appears someone sat on her. I see no signs of semen present on the outside of the clothing. I checked her thighs. There are no wounds or bruising indicating a forced sexual assault. However, she does have bruising on the upper *front* of her thighs. Again, like someone sat on her." He frowned. "At any rate, Dr. Patel will have to do the rape kit to make a conclusive determination."

"Thanks," said Freeman. "Let's go check the rest of the house, Kendall."

As Kendall checked the living room, she happened to glance out the window and spotted Detective Mayhew and Sergeant Jacobs advancing. "What are they doing here?"

"Who?" Freeman asked.

Kendall didn't answer, but walked out the front door. Freeman followed.

"What are you doing here?" she asked.

"Don't know if you heard, but we worked with your victim recently," said Mayhew. "She's the one who pointed us in the right direction to look for what I'm ninety-nine percent positive are the remains of Wendy Matherson."

Freeman stepped up. "Got any idea why somebody wanted Serena Walsh dead?"

Mayhew and Jacobs looked at one another. Mayhew opened his mouth to explain, but screeching tires drew his attention to the street. A young man ran up to the tape but was held back by patrol officers.

"Detective Mayhew," he screamed. "Detective Mayhew, I need to talk to you!"

"Who the hell is that, Mayhew?" asked Kendall.

"That's Jared Matherson. He must have heard about the murder."

"Let's go talk to him. He seems pretty freaked out," said Jacobs. "We don't want him getting arrested."

"I'll go with them and meet you inside in a few minutes," Kendall said to Freeman and he headed back to the house.

"I told you, I need to speak with Detective Mayhew," said a frantic Jared.

"You don't have any business here, kid," said the patrol officer sternly. "I said, beat it."

"It's okay, Lloyd," said Kendall. "We'll talk to him over there." She pointed towards the garage.

The officer let Jared pass under the crime scene tape. The three detectives followed him to the other side of the garage. With the media nearby, Kendall didn't want the press overhearing their conversation.

"Calm down, Jared," said Jacobs. "Take a few deep breaths and tell us what's so urgent."

Jared looked at Jacobs as though he'd just been slapped, stopping abruptly and staring at him. "I'm here because I heard someone killed the psychic."

Kendall could see the look of panic on his face.

"She talks to me one day and the next day she's dead!"

Mayhew moved in front of Jared. "So you're thinkin' that's got somethin' to do with this?"

Jared shook his head and turned around a couple of times. Then he stopped to face Mayhew again. "I was driving home from the clinic when I heard it on the news." He paused momentarily. "When I heard what happened, of course, I figured it had something to do with me. My dad and brothers know about her telling me to remember. I told them yesterday during my tirade."

"If you think they had something to do with this, we can check it out," said Kendall. "We'll question them."

"But in the meantime, you need to go back to your aunt's house and chill out," said Jacobs.

"How?" Jared shouted.

"Come on, Jared," said Mayhew. "Sergeant Jacobs is trying to help you."

"We're gathering evidence and will check out any and all leads, including the possibility this may be related to your mother's case," said Kendall. She wanted to send him on his way so she could get back to work. "Detective Mayhew and I will escort you back to your car."

She motioned for Jacobs to join Freeman in the house. He nodded and walked away.

Mayhew put both hands on Jared's shoulders. "I know you feel a lot of responsibility 'cause you can't remember what happened the night your mama vanished. However, none of this is your fault."

"But...."

"Listen," said Mayhew in a commanding voice. "You can't control what other people do. What happened here may or may not have anything to do with your mama's case. Understand? We've got to wait until they figure out what happened here."

"And we will," said Kendall.

Jared nodded. His arms gave way under Tyrone's strong hands. "Okay," he said. "But it seems strange this would happen right now."

"Let's go." Mayhew guided Jared back towards his car, Kendall following. "So how'd it go this mornin'? Did you like Daphne?"

"Yeah, she's great. We didn't do the hypnotism today though. She wanted to get to know me first. I go back same time tomorrow."

"It'll come, son," said Mayhew. "Don't forget you can call me any time you need to talk."

Jared smiled at him then nodded to Kendall. He got into his car and slowly left the scene.

"You'll have to fill me in," said Kendall.

"Long story. I just hope that boy can find peace someday."

Chapter 36

Tyrone took off his suit jacket and loosened his tie. The sun beat down hot from its noontime position, but he was far from hungry. He viewed Serena Walsh's death as a frustrating setback. He walked around her house once more watching CSI technicians do their work. His mind wandered to the Matherson case and how this case might link to it.

"Mayhew." Freeman beckoned him to come into the house.

Tyrone walked swiftly, hoping someone had found a clue. He entered the kitchen to find Jacobs, Kendall and Freeman congregated. "Did you find anything?"

Freeman turned. "I'll tell you what we *didn't* find—signs of a robbery. Her wallet's still in her purse along with her cell phone and checkbook. No gaps in the wallet where credit cards might have been, but we'll check to see if she had others besides what's in there."

"We found fifty dollars cash in the wallet and another two-hundred in a box in the freezer," said Kendall. "It looks like the jewelry box wasn't touched, not that she had much more than costume stuff."

"When we opened her dresser drawers, we found everything meticulously folded," said Freeman. "Was she ever in the service?"

"Not to my knowledge," said Tyrone. "Did you find anything personal to indicate a jealous boyfriend or ex?"

"Nope," said Freeman. "The CSI techs will take her laptop in for someone in computer forensics to go through. We'll let you know if we find anything. How was the Matherson kid when he left?"

"Calmer, but still upset." Tyrone remembered the anxious look of fear on the boy's face. "He thinks she was killed because he'd talked to her. He's seein' a hypnotherapist to work on what happened the night his mama went missing."

Freeman shook his head. "Damn, that must be rough."

"Yeah," Jacobs said, making them all aware of his presence.

Tyrone thought he'd been unusually quiet.

Jacobs looked at Freeman. "Have you seen Erica lately?"

"No, but I talked to her yesterday," said Freeman. "Stevenson wants her to take at least a ninety-day leave. You should call her," Freeman said with a smirk. "She asks me about you too, you know."

"As a matter of fact, we went to the movies a few days ago. Then

I had coffee with her the other day." Jacobs smiled. "We're going to make another go of it."

"That's great," said Freeman.

"Okay, Romeo," laughed Tyrone. "We'd better get back to the station since our friends from homicide have everything under control here." Tyrone looked at Freeman. "Let us know if anything comes up."

"Will do."

Chapter 37

Jared pulled into the driveway a little too quickly, barely missing his Aunt's vehicle. His head pounded with thoughts he'd rather not be having. He couldn't get rid of the idea that his dad or one of his brothers might have had something to do with Serena's murder? Immediately, he eliminated Ryan as a suspect. Despite Ryan's tough military background, he was a gentle soul. Jared refused to believe Ryan capable of cold-blooded murder.

Then there's Tanner. He always did his father's bidding. Did he do it to protect their father? Of course, his dad had been acting very strangely since the police reopened the investigation. He might be capable of almost anything.

Jared shook his head hoping to clear it. It didn't work so he decided to do the next best thing—talk to Aunt Cindy.

He knew where to find her as soon as he walked in the door. The fabulous aroma of chocolate chip cookies wafted from the kitchen. He hadn't had homemade cookies in ages. When he found her, she'd just removed the last one from a cookie sheet.

"Jared, I'm so glad you're home." She beamed at him.

Home. What a wonderful thing to hear. Despite his troubled thoughts, he smiled at her, but it wasn't good enough to fool her.

"Jared, honey, is something wrong?" Her smile turned to concern.

"I need to talk to someone," he said, tears spilling from his eyes.

"Sit down, sweetheart. Can I get you some water or something?"

"No thanks." He swallowed hard. He could hardly swallow his own saliva with his stomach tied up in knots. Consuming anything else would be impossible. "Have you listened to the news today?"

"No. What's happened?"

"You remember I told you I met the psychic who helped the police find mom?"

"Yes."

"She's been murdered," he said, sobbing. "And it's my fault!"

Cindy's mouth dropped open and she looked away. She didn't say anything for a few moments. Then she turned to him. "I want you to get that idea right out of your head, young man. Even if this has something to do with Wendy's murder, it's definitely not *your* fault. The murderer probably feared this woman knew something about what happened to my sister. Whoever killed both of them is at fault."

Jared pulled himself upright. Cindy handed him a napkin so he could wipe his tears. He needed to stop thinking about this and allowing it to stifle him. Solving his mother's murder hinged on his memories.

"I know you're right," he told her. "But it's weird, isn't it? I talked to her yesterday and now she's dead."

"That would make it seem like it's connected," said Cindy. "Of course, we don't know anything about her social life. She might have had an ex-husband or an angry boyfriend. She may even have been helping the police with some other case and that got her killed."

"I hadn't thought about that," he said.

"Now, can I talk you into some freshly made cookies and some milk or coffee?" she asked.

"Milk would be great."

Cindy grabbed a dessert plate from the cabinet and placed four cookies on it. She then poured a large glass of milk for him. "Here you go, sweetheart. Now, how did things go with the therapist?"

"It was a get-to-know you session," said Jared. "Tomorrow morning I'm going back and she's going to start the hypnosis. I'm going to remember for you as well as for myself. I'll make you proud of me."

"Too late, I already am."

Chapter 38

"So I heard you and Natalie are going on a Caribbean cruise in October," said Kendall from the passenger's seat of Freeman's car. "Things progressing nicely then?"

Although her superior, Freeman still blushed when confronted with things of a personal nature. Women tended to get the better of him, the plight of someone who grew up with three sisters, a mother, and an absent father.

"You would be correct on both counts," he replied, a smile slowly forming. Ben and Erica weren't the only ones whose relationship had been tested. Natalie nearly died two months ago when some gang bangers tried to make a point. "I think it will do us both some good after all she's been through."

"Hopefully we can put this case to rest so you won't worry about it," said Kendall.

"Easy to say, hard to do," he said. "Even if we finish this one, there'll be another to take its place."

"Of course, I could handle this one on my own. I've a gut feeling this murder *is* linked to the Matherson case. It's too coincidental for my taste."

"I think you're right," he confirmed. "Serena Walsh talks to Mayhew and Jacobs about their case and a few days later she's in the morgue. I don't believe in coincidence. You're good, Kendall. I'm sure I could leave this in your capable hands, should it go into October."

Kendall spotted the house number they sought. "There's the Matherson house. Three cars in the driveway, maybe we lucked out and they're all home."

Freeman slowed the car and they headed towards the front door. Kendall rang the doorbell. Freeman could hear footsteps approaching. A tall lanky young man opened the door. Freeman and Kendall showed their badges to him before anyone uttered a word. He opened the door and led them to the living room.

"Dad," he said. There were two other men in the room. They both stood and the older of the two approached. "These are cops."

"I thought Detective Mayhew and Sergeant Jacobs were handling my wife's case," he said with the crinkled brow of confusion.

"They are," said Freeman. "We aren't from the Missing Person Department, Mr. Matherson. This is Detective Kendall and I'm Detective Freeman. We're from Homicide."

Reid Matherson grabbed the back of the nearest chair. He held his chest as though in pain. Both of his sons ran to his side. "Are you alright, Dad?" asked the shorter, more muscular man.

"Yes." He brushed off their hands as they tried to help him. "I'm fine. What murder are you speaking of if not my wife's, Detective? Nothing's happened to Jared, has it?"

"No." Kendall took out her notepad and pen. "We didn't come about Jared. As far as we know he's perfectly fine."

"My name is Ryan," offered the shorter man. "This is my brother, Tanner. If it's not Mom or Jared, then who was killed?"

"Serena Walsh," said Freeman.

"She's the psychic who's been helping the police, isn't she?" said Ryan. "She was murdered?"

"Yes, in her home last night," said Kendall.

Freeman could see shock and confusion on Ryan's face. A quick appraisal of his father's and brother's faces made Freeman uneasy. Tanner looked panicked and his father remorseful. He couldn't help but wonder what was going on.

"Can the three of you tell me where you were between 11:00 p.m. and 2:00 a.m. last night?" asked Freeman.

"In bed of course," said Reid.

"What about the two of you?" Freeman directed to the sons.

"I don't know about Tanner, but I was asleep," said Ryan. "Matter of fact, I woke up at about 3:00 this morning hearing the front door open. What time did you come in, Tanner?"

Tanner wiped a few beads of sweat from his upper lip.

Freeman could see Tanner getting more nervous by the minute. "Answer the question, Tanner is it? Where were you last night?"

Tanner gulped. "I went out to a bar with friends. Ryan's correct. I got back at about 3:00 a.m."

"Can anyone corroborate your whereabouts during the entire time period?" Kendall poised her pen over the notepad.

"I think so," he said, voice cracking under the strain. "I was with Parnell Higgins most of the night."

"What do you mean by 'most of the night'?" Kendall peered at him.

"Well, I met him there...."

"Where?" she asked.

"I met him at Ned's on 82nd Street at around 10:00 last night. I was there until about 2:00 a.m. and then left to go home."

"It takes you an hour to get home from Ned's?" Freeman said, becoming more suspicious.

"No, not usually," said Tanner.

Before Freeman could go on, Reid Matherson moved between the detectives and his son. "Are you implying Tanner had something to do with this fortuneteller's death? If you are, then I'm stopping this interrogation right now. Next time you want to talk to any of us, do it through our attorney."

Freeman stopped the interview. He'd need to request a search warrant before he could look for evidence implicating someone in this household had gone to Serena's house and killed her. He hoped he hadn't screwed up coming here first. Now they had time to dispose of evidence.

"Thank you for your time gentlemen," said Kendall as she and Freeman walked out the door.

"Wish I was a fly on the wall," said Freeman when they reached the car. "I'd love to know what's being said right now."

"Me, too," said Kendall. "Me, too.

Chapter 39

Ben couldn't stop thinking about Erica. From his conversation with Freeman, he felt more confident that Erica really meant it when she said she wanted to try again. He loved her so much, but feared he might push her farther away if he put on too much pressure. Things were looking up now that she was considering the idea of moving in with him.

Jacobs took out his cell and pushed the number one button, the speed dial he set for her. After two rings, she answered.

"Hello."

Her voice was sweet music to his ears. "Hey, there."

"How are you?" Erica's cheerful tone implied her delight at his call.

"I'm good," he said. "Sorry I haven't made plans with you since our coffee date. I've been a little busy with this cold case."

"The Matherson case, I've been following it on the news," she said. "Sounds like you two found her body."

"It looks like it. Do you think we could get together soon? Maybe lunch or dinner?"

"Is tonight too soon?"

His heart leapt in his chest. He wanted to shout *yes, yes*, but kept his cool. Instead he laughed. "No, it's fine. Do you want to go out?"

"Pop's been asking about you. Why don't you join us for dinner tonight? I'm fixing pot roast, potatoes and carrots. It's way too much for the two of us to eat."

"Sounds great. I'm waiting for Mayhew to come out of Terhune's office. I can come over after he gives me the update."

"It's in the crock pot so come on over whenever you're done. I may have to feed Pop before you get here though. You know how older folks can be."

"I heard that." Ben heard her father say in the background. "'Bout time you got that boy over here."

"See you later," she said.

"You bet."

He hung up a minute before Mayhew came stomping over to his desk.

"It's been a crappy freakin' day. I can't believe somebody killed

Serena Walsh. She must have been gettin' too close to givin' us this asshole's identity."

"We've already got Mrs. Matherson's body," said Ben.

Mayhew sat down hard in his chair. "Apparently this guy thought she'd see him in one of her dreams and expose him."

"You could be right," said Ben.

"What makes it worse is I disappointed my son—again. I told Reggie last night I'd be there for his game today and now he's goin' to think he can't count on me. And, of course, Jada was fit to be tied when I called her to tell her earlier."

"Speaking of our ladies, I called Erica."

"'Bout time. It's been four days since you had that *coffee*." Mayhew raised an eyebrow. "Good lookin' woman like that won't wait around forever."

"Erica invited me over tonight for dinner with her and her dad."

"That's progress." Tyrone got up, turned to leave and almost ran head on into Lieutenant Terhune.

"Hate to bust up your plans for the evening fellas, but I need you to follow up on a tip we just got. Caller says he knows something about Wendy Matherson's disappearance."

"Are you serious, Lieutenant?" asked Ben.

"Very," said Terhune handing a note to him. "Here's the info on where to meet him. You call your significant others and tell them you're going to be late for dinner."

"Damn it!" said Mayhew as the lieutenant disappeared behind his office door. "I've already missed Reggie's game, but I told Jada I'd at least make it home for supper. The kids will be in bed by the time I get home."

"So much for spending time with Erica." Ben's heart beat heavy with disappointment.

"Barnes is a cop. She'll understand, but Jada doesn't always understand why I have to work past my assigned hours. Especially now with four kids to take care of."

"Let's get out of here," said Jacobs. "If we hurry, maybe we can save some portion of our evening."

Chapter 40

"Are you kidding me, Tyrone?" Jada exclaimed. "You didn't make it to the game. This baby's been fussing all day. I already fed the kids and Reggie's helping Malcolm with his bath. If it wasn't for Darryl helping with his sister, I'd be totally insane now that Mom's gone home."

She breathed deeply as she listened to her husband explain his position. Mixed emotions swirled through her brain. Should she be the dutiful, understanding wife or strangle him *and* his lieutenant.

"Okay, Tyrone," she conceded. "I get it. Just get home as soon as you can. I'll heat up something for you when you get home."

Jada put the portable phone back in its cradle. She heard Malcolm's laughter and Reggie telling him to stop splashing. She knew she'd have a mess to clean up afterwards, but at least Reggie was stepping up and taking on some of the responsibility. He was only six but seemed so grown up.

Before her mother left, she'd told Darryl he was the man while his father was away. Taking her words to heart, he'd mowed the grass that afternoon then took turns with Jada trying to comfort a very fussy Adanne. As bad as her day had been, she found solace in her two eldest sons. How grateful she was for them and for a husband who taught his boys to respect women. These thoughts soothed her, and her anger with Tyrone subsided. She could never imagine life without him.

Feeling guilty about her treatment of him, she went to the kitchen. Once she'd loaded the dishwasher, she'd work on a special dessert for Tyrone.

As she set to the task, the only sound she heard was Malcolm's giggles as he ran to his room. After all the effort Darryl put into getting Adanne to go to sleep, Malcolm had better not wake her.

A noise like a car backfiring many times over shattered the silence. Breaking glass and the thudding of something hitting the walls instinctively sent Jada to the floor. She lay on the kitchen floor in shock until she heard Malcolm screaming and she realized someone was shooting at her house. The gunfire stopped and tires screeched. Jada leapt to her feet running to the stairway in search of her children.

"Darryl! Where are you? Malcolm! Reggie!"

"Mama! Mama!" Malcolm cried.

She heard someone running in the hall. "Me and Adanne are okay, Mama," said Darryl. Of course, Adanne was crying at full capacity again. She and Darryl with Adanne in his arms reached Malcolm's room at the same time.

"Mama!" Malcolm screamed then cried hysterically when he spotted her. She saw her youngest son standing by the bed, blood spatter smeared all over his little face and bare chest where he'd tried to wipe it off.

She ran to him, her heart pounding. "Are you hurt, baby?"

Malcolm shook his head and pointed to the floor unable to speak through his hysterical tears. She heard Reggie's moans before she saw him.

Tears filled her eyes and panic almost stopped her heart as she looked at her son, blood oozing from his upper left chest. "Oh, my God! No, not my baby! Darryl, call 911! Tell them your brother's been shot and we need paramedics."

"Is he going to be okay, Mama?" asked Darryl.

"Go make that call. Hurry."

With Adanne in his arms, Darryl grabbed Malcolm's hand, but he screamed and sat down on the floor.

"Malcolm will be okay, call 911," she yelled.

Darryl ran out of the room to find the phone.

Jada could not believe what just happened. Not in this neighborhood. Not to her family. She grabbed Malcolm's pillow and pulled off the case. She used it to apply pressure to the wound. Reggie winced in pain.

"It hurts, Mama. It hurts."

"I know it hurts, baby," she said trying to keep her voice steady, "but I've got to stop the bleeding. The paramedics will be here any minute. You're going to be all right."

"Promise," he said weakly.

"I promise, Reggie. You know Mama never lies to you."

"Yes, Mama," he whispered, and then closed his eyes.

"Reggie, Reggie, honey," she said, shaking him gently. "Try to stay awake, baby."

"But it hurts, Mama."

She gently ran her free hand along the side of his face. She could hear Malcolm still crying hysterically behind her, but she couldn't take the pressure from Reggie's wound. Then she heard the sirens.

"They're coming, Mama," said Darryl with Adanne screaming at full capacity.

"Go down and let them in," she instructed. "I've got to keep pressure on this wound."

In seconds, there were two EMTs and a police officer in the room. Everything was loud and confusing. Malcolm was screaming for her and she wasn't sure where Darryl was.

"Mrs. Mayhew," said a familiar voice. "Mrs. Mayhew you can let go now. The paramedics need to get to him so we can get him to the hospital."

Jada felt a slight tug of her arm and tried to resist, but one of the EMTs pulled her hand away from the wound and before she knew it she was on her feet. As she turned, she saw the friendly face of Officer Donovan Bays. She'd met him at one of the police's balls or something.

"Let's go over here and give them some room, Mrs. Mayhew," he said.

Jada looked down and saw there was blood all over her hands and clothing. Her son's blood. She started to shake. She could no longer contain her grief over what had just happened. Jada couldn't take her eyes off of her hands, healing hands that now felt helpless."

"We've got him stabilized," said one of the paramedics. "Let's get him out of here."

Jada turned toward them. "I want to go with you."

"Okay, as long as you stay out of the way," he said.

"Officer Bays," said Jada, turning back to see him holding a calmer Malcolm by the hand. "Can you keep an eye on my other children until someone comes to get them?"

"Of course," he said. "There are already four patrols out here, so there's plenty of help."

"Darryl will know who to call," she said.

"Don't worry, Mrs. Mayhew," said Bays. "We always take care of our own."

Chapter 41

"Where is this asshole?" said Tyrone in frustration. "He told Terhune he'd be here at 7:30 and it's after 8:00 already."

"I don't know, maybe he chickened out," said Jacobs as his cell phone began to ring. "Jacobs."

Tyrone watched as Jacobs's face paled. Jacobs turned and walked a few feet away. He barely heard him say they'd leave right away.

"Get in the car," commanded Jacobs without explanation. "I'm driving."

A horrendous knot clenched Tyrone's stomach. Jacobs rarely used his authority as shift supervisor to demand Tyrone do anything. He wouldn't insist on driving Tyrone's car if there wasn't something terribly wrong. Jacobs started the car and turned on the lights and siren.

"What the hell's goin' on?" Tyrone asked, dreading the answer.

"I'll get us to Methodist as fast as I can, but you have to stay calm."

"What's wrong, Ben?" Tyrone insisted. "What's happened?" He knew someone he loved must be hurt for Jacobs to act this way. "Is it Jada? Is it one of my kids?"

"It's Reggie, Tyrone. Someone drove past your house about twenty minutes ago and shot up the place. Reggie took a bullet in the shoulder. Terhune says the paramedics were optimistic."

"What the *hell* does that mean?" he shouted. "Does anybody know what's goin' on?"

"Terhune said Reggie's in surgery. Officer Bays is watching the other three kids until your sister gets there to pick them up. None of them were hit, but Malcolm saw Reggie get shot. He's pretty shook up."

"Oh, my poor babies," Tyrone wailed as the tears could no longer be held. "I should have been there, Ben. I should have been there to protect my family."

"You can cut that shit right now, Tyrone. This was a blitz attack. Whoever did this is a sneaky bastard who had the element of surprise on his side."

"Jada was so upset with me when I got called out," said Tyrone. "I don't know if she'll ever forgive me for this."

"She loves you. She knew you had a dangerous job when she married you."

"Yeah, but she sure wasn't countin' on something like this."

Tyrone turned and stared out the window, guilt tugging at every fiber in his body and tears of pain running down his cheeks. Silence reigned until they reached the Methodist Hospital's emergency entrance.

"I'll drop you off and find a parking space," said Jacobs.

"Thanks." Tyrone jumped out of the car, slamming the door. He ran into the emergency area and told them whom he was. They directed him to the surgical unit waiting area. There he found Jada weeping into her hands with Erica at her side. Erica gave him a weak smile, and then gently rubbed Jada's back softly telling her of Tyrone's arrival.

Jada stood up and looked at her husband, face screwed up in pain. She ran to him and started beating on his chest. "Where were you? Where were you when somebody shot our baby?"

Tyrone grabbed her wrists to keep her from striking him any further. He shut his eyes to stop the tears, but it didn't help. "Please, Jada. Please. I'm so sorry, baby. I should have been there."

She jerked away from him and flung herself into Erica's arms, weeping on her shoulder.

"Come on now, Jada," Erica said softly, patting Jada's back. "Listen to me. You and Tyrone need to stick together through this, just as you always do. If you don't, this son-of-a-bitch wins."

Tyrone wiped his eyes with the heels of his hands. He had no idea what to do. He couldn't blame her for her anger. Nothing she could say could hurt him more than the way he felt at that moment. Nevertheless, he still wanted to hold his wife, to comfort her and to be comforted.

"I need to know my Reggie is going to be alright," Jada told Erica once she'd calmed down. "Why would someone do this to us? We moved to that neighborhood because these things just don't happen out there."

No one realized Jacobs had come in until he spoke. "Jada, this sort of thing happens everywhere. I think that call Terhune got was a fake because the guy never showed up. Someone wants us off of the Matherson case—bad."

"Then you need to get someone else assigned to it, Tyrone Mayhew," Jada shouted, pointing her finger and advancing on him.

"It's not that easy," said Tyrone wiping his hands on his shirt. "This is my job. I'll find a place where you and the kids will be safe until we finish this."

"This case has been going on for ten years," she retorted. "Am I supposed to wait it out for another ten?"

"That's not what he means," said Erica. "They have Mrs. Matherson's remains and the car, which proves a crime was committed. Now this bastard's nervous. He's trying to scare Tyrone off the case."

Tyrone took a step toward his wife. "Jada, if I leave the case now then other criminals will think it's okay to use these kinds of scare tactics against other cops and their families. I'll get him honey. I swear it. Nobody comes after my family," he said, fierceness in his voice and on his face that could melt steel. "Nobody."

Their interaction was so intense that no one saw the surgeon enter the waiting room. "Mr. and Mrs. Mayhew."

"Doctor," said Jada, rushing over to him. "Is Reggie okay?"

"Yes. He's a very healthy young man so I expect him to heal very quickly," said the surgeon. "It was very fortunate that the bullet went through him at such an odd angle. I brought a diagram so I could explain it. The bullet entered the left side of the chest just under the clavicle, angled upward. Then it hit the top of the scapula. That caused the bullet to ricochet slightly and exit just missing the joint."

The doctor paused and folded his diagram. "We had to remove a few scapula bone chips and do some muscle repair. There's a crack in the scapula that will heal nicely as long as he takes it easy. Your son was very lucky. If the bullet had gone the other direction, it could have nicked the lung or gone into his neck."

Jada shook then grabbed Tyrone's arm as if trying to steady herself. Tyrone put his arm around her shoulders, gulping back more tears.

"We recovered some fragments of wood and wall board from the wound and have sealed and tagged it for the police. A friend of yours, Detective Freeman, has already contacted us and is aware of this evidence."

"See, Jada," said Tyrone. "Brent's already on the case."

"Reggie will be in recovery for at least an hour," said the doctor. "I'm afraid it's a very small area, so only one of you can sit with him."

"Then his mother should go," said Tyrone. "She needs to see that he's okay. When he wakes up, hers needs to be the first face he sees.

I've got to go check on the rest of our children and let them know Reggie's okay."

Jada smiled at him and mouthed, *thank you honey*, before she followed the doctor out of the room. Relieved, Tyrone knew she would eventually forgive him. When he turned, he looked Jacobs in the eye.

"I'm goin' to call my sister to see if she's picked up the kids yet," said Tyrone, then he turned to Erica. "Can you take Ben back to the station to get his car?"

"No problem," said Erica.

Tyrone placed his hand on Jacobs' shoulder. "I need to spend the next few days with my family, but I want you to promise me you'll keep working this case."

"Partner," said Jacobs, "that's a promise I'll have no trouble keeping."

Chapter 42

Morning came too fast. Tyrone decided it must be later than he thought when he heard footsteps in the hallway. He peered over at his bed partner. It wasn't Jada. She'd stayed at the hospital all night with Reggie. There lay his sweet little Malcolm who must have been exhausted not to have woken already.

Tyrone stared at Malcolm's angelic face. He shuddered at the idea of his baby boy splattered with his brother's blood. Only three and already witnessed something no child should ever see.

Tyrone slipped out of bed making sure he didn't disturb his son. He opened and closed the door gently making a minimal amount of noise. The wonderful smells floating into the hallway told him his sister was busy making breakfast.

Approaching the kitchen, Tyrone heard the deep baritone of his brother-in-law conversing with Ophelia.

There sat Judge Norman Jackson feasting on bacon and eggs, while Ophelia fussed over Adanne who occupied her infant seat in the middle of the kitchen table. She responded joyfully to her Aunt and Uncle, smiling and kicking her feet.

"Well, look who it is." Norman tickled Adanne's foot and she jerked, crinkling her nose. "Your daddy finally decided to grace us with his presence."

"Good mornin', Norman." Tyrone walked around the table and gave Ophelia a kiss on the top of the head. "How are two of my favorite girls this mornin'?"

Adanne flailed her arms about and gave her father one of those snort-like sounds babies often produce. Tyrone smiled at her and took both of her feet in his large hands, caressing them gently.

"Coffee?" asked Ophelia.

"Yes, please," said Tyrone. "Thanks for coming to get the kids last night."

"No thanks necessary," said Norman. "We love those children like they're our own."

"You know Malcolm's going to need a lot of T. L. C.," said Ophelia. "Officer Bays said the CSI had to swab him and photograph him before they'd let Darryl bathe him. Poor little guy. Thank goodness he had on his underwear. It embarrassed him having all those strangers poking him and taking photos."

"I should have been there." Tyrone's feelings of guilt gnawed at his gut again.

"Detective Freeman said someone called and lured you and Jacobs away," said Norman.

"He didn't show up, so we're sure it was him," said Tyrone.

"I called the hospital this morning, Ty." Ophelia set his coffee in front of him. "Reggie had a good night. His temperature and all his vital signs are good. He's going to be okay."

That was a relief, but then Tyrone's heart thumped with panic. "What if this guy doesn't stop? What if he tries it again?"

"You've got to stop thinking like that," she said. "If you're going to help your sons survive this horrible experience, you've got to stop blamin' yourself. Worry about what you can do, not what you should've done."

"Okay, I get it. You're right." It made sense that if he continued to make himself crazy over this he'd fail his family. He took a long gulp of coffee, wondering what he should do next. Then it came to him.

"Sis, Norman, what about your cabin in Brown County? When Reggie gets out of the hospital, can Jada and the kids go there?"

Norman and Ophelia looked at one another, then at Tyrone. Ophelia nodded, and then Norman said, "I don't see why not. How likely is it the person who did this would know anything about the cabin?"

Tyrone smiled at them. Then he heard the tapping of small bare feet on the hardwood floor. He turned to see Malcolm in the kitchen doorway rubbing his eyes.

"Daddy, did Reggie die?"

"No, no, son." Tyrone rose from his chair and hoisted his youngest son into his arms. "He was hurt pretty bad and the doctor had to do some surgery to fix him, but he's doing much better now."

"Is Mama with him?"

"Yes, she is. She'll call us later and let us know when I can bring you and Darryl to see Reggie."

Malcolm looked at him with such sweet innocence. "Can't Adanne come, too?"

"I don't think so," said Ophelia. "She's just a baby and if she gets fussy she'll disturb the other patients. Only children who understand how to behave get to visit at the hospital. Would you like some chocolate milk, sweetheart?"

"Yes, Auntie." Malcolm's eyes widened as though all thoughts of death and hospitals now pushed aside.

Funny how the little things excite them at this age, thought Tyrone. He placed his son on a chair.

"You've become quite a grown up young man," said Norman. Malcolm smiled at him then looked at his dad with a huge toothy grin.

"Thank you, Auntie," said Malcolm as Ophelia set the glass in front of him.

"You're welcome," said Ophelia. "How about I fix you some chocolate chip pancakes?"

"Those are my favorite," said Tyrone.

"Mine too, Daddy," beamed Malcolm.

"Then chocolate chip pancakes it is," she said. "Norman you go roust up Darryl. By the time these boys are fed and dressed, it will be time to go visit Reggie."

"Thanks, Sis." Tyrone turned away gulping back his tears. He didn't want to upset Malcolm.

"You helped take care of me when Daddy died," she said. "Now it's my turn to help take care of you."

Chapter 43

After a wonderful breakfast with Natalie, Brent headed into the city to meet with Dr. Patel. Natalie had promised Brent she would stop by the hospital to check on Reggie and lend her support to Tyrone and Jada. After all, Tyrone was one of her heroes.

As Brent entered the morgue area, he heard Ben Jacobs call out his name. "Hey, Freeman. Wait up."

"You here for the autopsy results on your skeleton?"

"Yes, and I hope to find out if they've completed the autopsy on Serena Walsh as well," said Jacobs. "I don't know about you, but I think they're linked."

"Kendall and I were thinking along those same lines," said Brent. "Have you talked to Tyrone today?"

"Briefly. Kids bounce back so quickly. He said he talked to Reggie on the phone this morning, and he sounds better than Jada does."

"I can't imagine having something like that happen to one of my kids," said Brent. "Natalie's going up to see them this morning before she heads to the office."

"She might get to see all the boys today. From what Mayhew told me, he's bringing Malcolm and Darryl with him. I'm sure they want to see Reggie for themselves. Poor Malcolm asked his dad if Reggie was dead."

"That must have been rough for Tyrone to hear."

Jacobs nodded, and then asked, "Are you the primary on the Walsh case?"

Brent shook his head. "I'm going to let Kendall handle it on her own as soon as she and I go over this report. Then I'm going to concentrate on finding the son-of-a-bitch who did this to Mayhew's family. As far as the higher ups are concerned, this was an attempted murder of a police officer."

"Lieutenant Terhune is working on the number the guy used to send us on the wild goose chase. I bet it's a disposable cell."

Brent nodded, and then yanked open the door leading to Dr. Patel's office.

One of the most meticulous forensic pathologists he'd ever met, Dr. Patel produced quick and accurate results.

"Hey, Doc." Brent was the only person she allowed to call her Doc. "I found Jacobs here in the hallway. Seems he and I have way too much in common at the moment."

"Well, then, I'm glad you're both here so I don't have to repeat myself." She walked to her desk with the two men following. They took seats in the chairs across from her.

"Sergeant Jacobs, here is the report on the skeletal remains, which I received three days ago—the remains of Wendy Matherson."

Jacobs looked up at her with a wide-eyed expression.

"Yes, the DNA is in. These remains are definitely those of Mrs. Matherson. As you know, I had a colleague from Indiana University come by who specializes in anthropological forensics. She concurred these skeletal remains were most likely buried within six months after Mrs. Matherson's disappearance."

Jacobs leafed through the report. "Did you both agree on the cause of death?"

"Most definitely. As I told you before, some of the bone injuries indicate she may have taken a long fall. I understand there's a stairway in her home, so this may have been where the fall occurred. The fractures and separation of the vertebrae located at the base of the skull would have caused immediate brain hemorrhaging and certain death. Even if a neurosurgeon had been standing right there, she would not have survived. This definitely could have been the cause of death."

"Could have?" Jacobs said.

"In cases like this where all we have is bone, it is difficult to determine without a doubt what injuries caused her death. However, this gives us a pretty good theory with which to work. We found no indication of gunshot wounds. A shot to the chest would have left marks on her rib bones or sternum. We found nothing of the sort. Same for the skull, no bullet holes were found."

Jacobs turned a few more pages. "No indication of bullet wounds. What about stab wounds?"

Dr. Patel shook her head. "Stab wound injuries are usually found in the chest area—ribs or sternum—where the killer can do maximum damage. These types of wounds are also typical to the hands and arms as the victim instinctively tries to ward off the attack. We found no nicks of this sort in her bones to indicate someone stabbed her. In any case, this woman did not die from natural causes."

"What about her legs? You said those breaks were strange."

"My colleague agreed these were caused by a cylindrical object," said Dr. Patel. "Something the size and shape of a large pipe or a baseball bat."

"With three young boys, I'll bet there were a few baseball bats around," commented Brent.

"I'll check the old reports," said Jacobs. "I don't know any boy who hasn't at least tried his hand at baseball."

"The one thing we cannot tell you with absolutely no doubt is that she was murdered," said Dr. Patel. "Although the way her knee and leg were damaged could be a contributing factor to her fall, we don't know if the fall was accidental or not."

"So, unless someone in the house confirms that's what happened, we're stuck," said Jacobs.

"Now, onto the Walsh autopsy," said Dr. Patel handing a file to Brent. "I am in agreement with D. I. Spalding's initial assessment regarding the bruising and cuts around the wrists. This indicates she tried to free herself from something metal. Rope or cloth would have left other types of marks and fibers."

Brent thought he knew the answer to his next question, but had to ask. "Do you know what was used?"

"You see the markings here." She pulled out a photo and pointed to a pattern on the skin of Serena's right wrist. "I would venture to say this mark was left by handcuffs."

"Was she sexually assaulted?" asked Brent.

"No, and apparently there wasn't much of a struggle at the beginning. She had no bruising on her back, arms, and etcetera, only on the front of her upper thighs and torso. The petechiae of her eyes, the marks on her nose and chin, and her collapsed lungs tell us she was burked."

"Burked?" Jacobs' mouth dropped. "What's that?"

"Burking is a common expression for asphyxiation caused by compression of the torso. Our examination indicates the killer sat on the victim's chest, which in turn put so much pressure on her lungs she couldn't take in air. He also pinched her nose and pushed her chin up so she couldn't open her mouth. This was a lengthy and frightening death. I'm sure she sustained the cuts on her wrists and bruising on her thighs by instinctually trying to escape."

"What a bastard," Brent exclaimed. "Couldn't just do one shot to the head, he had to torture the girl."

"That's why I feel it's connected to the Matherson case," said Jacobs. "She told us she never used her abilities to make money, so she'd have no pissed off clients for us to question. It's obviously not robbery with all the valuable items left behind. Coming to us when we found Mrs. Matherson's car is the only thing she's done recently out of the ordinary."

"Is there anything else we should know, Doc?" asked Brent.

"No, that's all I have for now," she said. "You'll have my full written report tomorrow morning."

Brent set down his file and looked at Jacobs. "Do you want to accompany me this morning while I interview the Matherson clan?"

"You bet I do," said Jacobs. "I doubt Jared had anything to do with this because he's really anxious to find out what happened. However, the other three haven't exactly been very cooperative. Let's see what excuses they give us today."

Chapter 44

"Oh, no, this is awful," said Cindy, setting her cup of coffee on the table. She always watched the local morning news in the kitchen after her husband left for work and the children left for school. This gave her a chance to catch up on the latest events while cleaning up the breakfast dishes.

"What's awful?" asked Jared as he entered the kitchen.

She grabbed the remote and turned off the TV. "Sit down, sweetie. Let me grab you a cup of coffee and we can talk."

"Okay." He frowned at her. "Is there anything new about Serena Walsh's murder?"

"It's something different. Whether it has anything to do with what's been happening lately is anyone's guess."

She poured a cup of coffee and joined him at the kitchen table. "I just heard on the news there was a drive by shooting last night. It happened at Detective Mayhew's house."

"*What?*" he shouted, nearly choking on a sip of coffee. "Is he okay? Did anyone get hurt?"

"Yes, someone got hurt. His six-year old son was shot." She could see Jared's face go pale. "They said the boy is listed in stable condition at Methodist Hospital, which is really good. Please don't be upset."

Jared put his head in his hands squinting as though he had a monstrous headache. "This is my fault, Aunt Cindy, all my fault."

Cindy grasped his hands, pulling them away from his face. "Now you listen to me, Jared Lee Matherson. The person who murdered Ms. Walsh, who shot that little boy, and who probably killed your mother is at fault. Not you. Do you hear me?"

"Yes." Jared pulled his hands away and rubbed his chest. "I understand, but why? Why would they do this?"

"Who can explain the cruelty in the world, Jared? Nobody. If we ask this lunatic why, he may give us an excuse, but will it make sense to us? Probably not."

"Thanks." He took her hand, held it to his face and closed his eyes.

The pain in her nephew's face ripped at her heart. "You're welcome. Now, what can I make you for breakfast? You have an appointment with Dr. Swan this morning, right?"

Jared opened his eyes and released her hand. "Yes, but I'm not sure I can eat anything. My stomach hurts."

"Then I'll make you some toast and tea." She gave him a loving glance and he responded with a smile. She knew he'd missed this sort of nurturing for a very long time. Jared probably couldn't remember the last time he had this sort of attention. He finally agreed to eat, most likely to appease her.

"Thanks, Aunt Cindy. I suppose eating something is much better for me."

"You're darned right it is."

"You know, I think I remember Mom saying that sometimes. You look a lot like her you know."

"I'll take that as a very high compliment." Cindy walked around to the back of his chair and hugged him from behind. "Thank you. Now, you'd better get your shower. You don't want to be late."

* * *

By the time Jared reached the clinic, he'd had too much time to think again. Panic caused his heart to beat faster and his stomach to tighten. All he could think about was that poor little boy. Kids shouldn't be caught up in such horrible circumstances. His heart sank and he felt confused by his own sudden twinge of fear. He prayed the boy wouldn't start having nightmares, too.

Jared stopped at the reception desk to sign in, and then his anxiety kicked in. He demanded to see Daphne immediately. "I know I'm early, but I've got to see her now!"

"Please, Mr. Matherson. Take a seat and I'll tell her you're here."

"You don't understand. This is very important."

"Jared, what's wrong?" Daphne walked toward him quickening her pace. "I could hear you in my office."

"I'm sorry," he said, his cheeks hot with embarrassment. "I really, really need to start now. I have to remember. People are getting hurt because of what I can't recall."

"Okay, okay, you're my first appointment so let's go on back."

He slumped as he followed her back. If he kept this up, people would think he was crazy.

She sat in her winged back leather chair and motioned for him to sit on the couch. "You will want to get into a comfortable position. You may sit on the couch and lean back, or lay down—whatever helps you relax. I can see you're very agitated right now, but I cannot emphasize enough the need to become relaxed. If you don't, if you try too hard, the hypnosis won't work."

"I understand. I think I'll lie down."

"Alright, Jared. Would it bother you if I record our sessions?"

He shook his head.

"Good. Sometimes it helps later on if we can listen to them together. Now lie down and get comfortable."

He squirmed a few times and finally settled in. She told him to close his eyes and take several deep breaths—inhale through his nose then exhale out of his mouth. With each cleansing breathe he could feel his muscles relax more and more.

"Jared, I want you to try to clear your mind. Push all of your current problems to the side for a while. Keep your eyes closed and keep breathing deeply."

It was difficult for him to push aside his thoughts. Serena Walsh's face came to mind, telling him to remember. Her death haunted him, but he pushed the thoughts aside for now. Jared concentrated as best he could on Daphne's voice. The more he concentrated, the more relaxed he became. He could hear traffic sounds, her voice and his own breathing, and kept his mind on what Daphne told him to do.

"Now, I want you to visualize a pleasant place. Somewhere you find peaceful. Do you see it?"

Still allowing his breathing to relax him, he tried to visualize a peaceful place. Then he saw it—a beach, beautiful and sunny. He could almost feel the warmth of the sun and the ocean breeze. The clear turquoise sea lay in front of him, waves gently caressing the clean white sand leaving small, curious creatures behind as it receded. As he watched, he heard Daphne's soft voice.

"I want you to look around. We need to find the doorway which leads to your memories."

He moved his focus away from the foamy waves and turned to see a beach house. "There's a house," he mumbled.

"Good. Do you believe the doorway is there?"

Jared stared at it for a moment before he answered. "Yes, I believe it's in there."

"How are you feeling about it? Do you want to enter?"

Jared's heart raced. "I'm a little scared, but I'm more scared not to go in."

"Take your time. Keep breathing. Inhale…exhale. When you are ready, walk slowly toward the house. Let me know when you are inside."

He looked at the bright white house with its screened-in porch. Bright red hibiscus lined the walkway. He approached the doorway cautiously. Reaching out, he touched the golden doorknob and felt a rush of dread. He knew something awful must be inside, but he had to see.

"I'm going in," he said. As he entered, he saw a long hallway with three doors on each side. Now he must decide which one was the right one. "There are lots of doors in here."

"Do you have a sense of which door you'd like to try? If not, just walk down the corridor and it will come to you."

Walking down the hallway, he noticed they all looked the same. However, the second door on his right seemed to beckon to him. "I've found it."

"When you're ready, open the door slowly and step inside," she instructed.

Jared reached out. The door opened without his touch.

He heard Daphne speaking. "When you're ready, tell me what you see."

"It's dark. Really dark."

"Do you know how old you are?"

Thinking for a moment, he finally said, "I think I'm nine."

"How do you feel?"

"I'm scared. I hear strange noises." His heart raced. Terror gripped him as he tried to see through the darkness. "There's a bat, there's a bat!"

"Is it flying?"

"NO," he screamed. He knew she didn't understand. He continued to scream. "NO, NO, NO!"

"Jared, go out of the room and shut the door. Now!"

He did as she instructed, but breathed rapidly in panic.

"Jared, you're safe now. No one can hurt you. I want you to come back to my office now."

On the verge of hyperventilating, he breathed so rapidly his chest hurt. He tried to concentrate on Daphne's soothing voice. He wanted to believe her. He wanted to be safe.

"Jared, I will count to three. On three, you will open your eyes and be back in the room with me. One...two...three."

Jared's eyes popped open. Still trying to catch his breath from the fright, he sat up much too quickly. He felt dizzy thinking maybe he should lie back down. Daphne's look of concern made him realize he must look awful.

"Look at me. Slow your breathing," she said.

He looked into her bright blue eyes and she breathed with him. Soon his rhythm matched hers and the dizziness went away.

"That's better," she said. "As soon as you're ready, let's talk about what you saw."

"I'm ready now, but I don't think I remembered enough."

"But you did remember something very significant or you wouldn't have panicked. Do you remember the bat? Did it hurt you?"

"You don't understand. It was a baseball bat, not an animal. One minute I couldn't see anything through the darkness; the next, this wooden bat just hung in the darkness illuminated by a soft bright light."

"You've done very well today."

"But I didn't remember enough," he repeated.

"Jared, I know how anxious you are, but this takes time. It could take months before we are able to tap into the cause of your nightmares."

"But we don't have that kind of time," he said in frustration. "Somebody killed the psychic who told the police where to find Mom and someone shot at Detective Mayhew's house. They hurt his son."

"I heard. However, that is not your responsibility. Are you afraid the person who's doing this will come after you?"

Jared gasped and looked away, shocked at the implication. He hadn't thought about someone coming after him. "No. I was worried about the other people involved."

Daphne smiled at him. "I know how much you and Detective Mayhew want to find those memories. That is why I cleared my calendar so we can meet daily. You will continue to be my first appointment of the day until we solve this puzzle. Okay?"

"Thank you. Will you report this to Detective Mayhew?"

"No. I consider this therapist-client privilege. If you want him to know about your sessions, you will need to be the one to tell him."

Thanking her, he left the office. He didn't want to intrude on Detective Mayhew at the hospital. However, he could call Sergeant Jacobs instead. Yeah, that made more sense. He'd call him as soon as he got home.

Chapter 45

Ben met Detective Freeman in the parking lot so they could head over to the Matherson house. He was afraid the Mathersons would just give one another an alibi. However, he and Freeman might get some feel for their truthfulness by their reactions. Sometimes body language told more about a person than the words they spoke.

"I'll drive, if that's okay with you," said Freeman.

"That works for me. They don't know your vehicle, so they won't see the car and make a run for it."

"You're hilarious, Jacobs."

"Actually, I'm thankful that you suggested I ride along since I'm already familiar with the Mathersons. I'm also sure the shooting at Mayhew's house is connected. I can't wait to get my hands on the guy who called us out on that no show."

"Yeah, I hear you," said Freeman. "You, Kendall and I need to keep a close eye on these three cases and share everything. Wendy Matherson, died mysteriously ten years ago, Serena Walsh knows too much so she's murdered, and now the attempt on Tyrone."

"If Grimes hadn't screwed things up during the initial investigation and had listened to Miss Walsh, we might have solved this one a long time ago," said Ben, regret tugging at his brain. He'd been skeptical, but everything Serena Walsh had told him was true. She didn't tell fortunes for a living. All she wanted to do was help people, and look what it got her.

Freeman glanced his way. "You've got to let it go. We can't change the past, but we can sure keep the pressure on until we find this bastard."

They arrived at the Matherson house within twenty minutes. Ben didn't see Reid's car, so he assumed Reid had gone back to work. It was just as well since it might make the boys more vulnerable without him around.

Freeman rang the doorbell and took a step back.

"What do you want now?" Tanner sighed as he held the front door open.

"We need to talk to you and Ryan," said Ben. "I assume Jared is still staying with his aunt?"

"Yes, Jared is at Aunt Cindy's." Tanner showed his displeasure at having his morning interrupted by rolling his eyes and yanking the door open wider. "Come on in."

Ben didn't miss the sudden reddening of Tanner's face either. Could he be the one who killed Serena Walsh and shot up Mayhew's house? At sixteen, was Tanner capable of murdering his own mother?

Ryan entered the foyer. "What's going on? Oh, hello, Sergeant Jacobs."

Ben had found Ryan the more pleasant of the two older brothers. If he was hiding something, he was quite good at it—much better than his older brother and father. Ben introduced Freeman to Ryan.

"Why don't we go into the kitchen?" said Ryan. "I've got a fresh pot of coffee. It's more comfortable to sit at the kitchen table."

"Dad said we weren't to talk to them again without an attorney," said Tanner poking his brother's shoulder.

Ryan slapped his hand away. "Shut up! I don't care what Dad said. I want to know what's going on. If you don't, then go call Daddy's lawyer."

Tanner didn't make the call, but followed them as they all walked single file into the kitchen. After accepting cups of coffee, Ben pulled out his notebook and wrote down his observation of Tanner's continued nervous reactions and Ryan's calm composed manner.

Ryan sat across from Ben fixing him with an intense gaze. "Is the final report in? Are those bones my mom's?"

"Yes," answered Ben. "The DNA matches. She apparently died from injuries to her neck. How she sustained those injuries is still in question. However, that's not the only reason Detective Freeman and I came here today."

Tanner leaned forward, wide-eyed. "What else could it be? Did something else happen besides the Walsh lady getting herself killed?"

Tanner's last remark didn't slip past Ben. How exactly Tanner could think Serena Walsh *got herself killed* peaked Ben's curiosity. He'd make note of this statement in case he wanted to pursue it later.

Freeman frowned. "Don't you boys watch the news?"

Tanner and Ryan looked at one another, obviously perplexed by the question. Maybe they really didn't know.

Ben looked down at his notebook. "Where were you two at about 7:30 last night?"

"Upstairs sending emails to my friends back in Oklahoma," said Ryan. "You want to tell us what's going on? What does our whereabouts last night have to do with my mother's death?"

Ben decided to get Tanner's response before they started divulging why they were truly there. "And you Tanner, where were you?"

"I went across the street to visit with the Millers from about 6:00 p.m. to 9:00 p.m. Their son was one of my best friends growing up. They'd invited me to dinner and showed me a bunch of photos of Bud, his wife and new son."

"Where was your father during this time period?" asked Freeman.

"As far as I know, he was here," answered Tanner. Ryan nodded his agreement.

Freeman glanced at Ben, then back to Tanner. "How was your father's demeanor yesterday? Did he act nervous or upset?"

"No." Tanner bristled as though he'd been offended. "He was fine. He seemed perfectly normal to me."

Ben caught Ryan rolling his eyes at his brother. Ryan apparently wasn't buying that his father was *perfectly normal*.

"He was in the living room watching TV when I left," said Tanner.

"What about you, Ryan?" Freeman asked. "Do you know whether or not your father was here the whole evening?"

Ryan sat thoughtfully for a few moments. Ben noticed Tanner looking at Ryan pleadingly.

"I can't say for sure," said Ryan. "I was sending emails and chatting on the internet for two or three hours. His car was in the driveway and my room is at the back of the house. I wore my earphones with my music up pretty loud. If he left, I wouldn't necessarily have heard him."

Ben scribbled some notes and then looked at Ryan. "You didn't come down for a drink or snack?"

"Not from about 7:00 to 9:00 p.m.," said Ryan. "I came down just before Tanner came home. Dad was sitting in the living room watching some educational channel. I got a soda and went back to my room just as Tanner came through the door."

"I think it's about time the two of you tell us what really brought you here, Detectives," Tanner's face reddened with apparent anger. "What happened last night?"

"Does anyone in this house own a gun which uses 9mm ammo?" asked Freeman.

"I do," said Ryan.

Ben set his pen down on the table. "Where is it?"

"It's up in my room," said Ryan. "It's a 90-Two Beretta."

Wary, Ben momentarily entertained the idea that maybe Ryan's cool demeanor misrepresented him. "Can we see it?"

"Sure." Ryan rose to go upstairs.

"I'll go with you," said Freeman.

Ben and Tanner sat at the table in uncomfortable silence. He wondered if Tanner had actually been at the neighbors. He felt Tanner the more likely suspect. Even now, Tanner fidgeted in his seat, crossing and uncrossing his legs, and his upper lip had broken out in a light sweat. What was going on in that head of his?

The silence broke when someone ran down the stairs. "It's gone," Ryan shouted. "My gun is gone."

Freeman came in just two steps behind him. "Ryan here said his gun was unloaded in a lock box he placed at the back of the top shelf of his closet. The lock box is gone. We pulled crap out of the closet to see if it had fallen on the floor, not there."

"I searched under my bed, in my desk." Ryan's calm manner had dissolved into panic. "I can't find it."

Ben rose from his chair intent on calming Ryan. "Focus, Ryan. When did you see it last?"

"I haven't gone to the range since I arrived from Oklahoma," said Ryan, stroking his jaw. "I put it up there when I got here and hadn't thought to check on it. What's happened?"

"Sit down, please," said Ben. "At approximately 7:50 p.m. last night, someone drove past Detective Mayhew's house and blasted it with bullets. One of those bullets hit his six-year-old son. Luckily, the injury wasn't life threatening, but the boy did have to go through surgery and is now in stable condition."

Surprise lit up Ryan's and Tanner's eyes. Shaking his head, Ryan said, "Oh my God! The psychic? Detective Mayhew's family? What the *hell* is going on?" His last question he directed to his brother.

"How the hell am I supposed to know?" Tanner said defensively. "This is all news to me."

"Unfreakin' believable!" Ryan started to pace. "And you think this has something to do with my mother's case or you wouldn't be here, right Sergeant?"

"That's correct," answered Freeman.

"Detective Freeman and I will leave now. We'll check out your alibis," said Ben. "If that weapon shows up, you need to call me immediately."

"Sergeant Jacobs," said Ryan. "Does Jared know?"

"He knows about Serena Walsh. He heard it on the radio yesterday," said Ben. "I have no idea whether or not he's heard about the shooting at the Mayhew's."

"We'll be in touch," said Freeman ending the interview, then he and Ben left the house. The Matherson brothers stood at the door as still as statues watching them go.

"You think they know anything?" asked Freeman as he drove down their street.

"I don't think they're involved in what happened," said Ben. "However, I believe they have a good idea who *is* involved. We need to see a judge quick. We need a search warrant for the house, grounds and all three of their cars. If any of them are involved, we don't want to give them a chance to get rid of the evidence."

"I'm pretty sure we can get Mayhew's brother-in-law to help us," said Freeman.

"After what happened to Reggie, I'll bet Judge Jackson won't hesitate."

"I'll put a couple of patrols out here to make sure these guys don't go anywhere without eyes on them," said Freeman. "If one of them did it, we'll catch him."

Chapter 46

"Hey, Daddy," said Malcolm from the back seat. "You sure Reggie's okay?"

"Yes, I'm very sure," answered Tyrone. "He was hurt pretty bad, but real lucky it wasn't worse. You'll see when we get there."

"No wrestlin' around though, Bro," said Darryl. "When we're at the hospital you gotta be quiet. Right, Dad?"

Tyrone smiled at Darryl in the rearview mirror. How could a nine-year-old be so grown up already? "Your brother's right, Malcolm. Some of the other kids are pretty sick. We've got to respect their needs."

"Okay, Daddy," said Malcolm. "Is that why Adanne didn't come?"

"She's too little to know what's goin' on. If she gets one of her belly aches, she won't understand why she can't cry," said Darryl. "Aunt Ophelia will take good care of her."

"Besides, she don't know Reggie that good yet," declared Malcolm.

Tyrone cringed at Malcolm's misuse of grammar, but then smiled. Jada would have been all over that one. He remembered how she'd tried to get him to stop dropping the 'g' off of words ending in 'ing'. He finally told her it was a Hoosier thing which was part of his genetic makeup. Eventually, she gave up on him. However, she wasn't going to allow her Hoosier born children to continue the tradition.

"Here we are boys," said Tyrone, pulling into a parking space. Tyrone got out and opened the door to retrieve Malcolm. Darryl had already unfastened him so Malcolm scrambled out of his seat and into his father's arms. Tyrone set him down and grabbed his hand. "You stay close to me and your brother, Malcolm."

Malcolm nodded. He took his brother's hand as soon as he got out of the car. When they entered the lobby, Jada was waiting for them.

"Mama, Mama!" exclaimed Malcolm, running to her. She bent down just in time to snap him up in her arms. Tyrone could see tears glistening in her eyes. He knew his wife was worried sick about Malcolm's reaction to the shooting.

"How's my little man?" she asked, hugging him close.

"I missed you last night, Mama."

"I missed you, too," she said. "Did Daddy read you a story before bed?"

"Nah, I was too sleepy to wait up for Daddy, so Auntie read one. She's pretty good, but you're gooder."

To Tyrone's surprise, Jada held her tongue on that grammatical error.

She held her free arm out to their eldest son. "Come here boy. You know you aren't ever going to be old enough you can't give your mama a hug." He gladly moved into the crook of her arm.

"Mmm, mmm, it sure feels good to have my man hugs. How's your sister doing?"

"She's just eating and sleeping," said Darryl. "You ain't missing much."

"Aren't missing much," she corrected, and Tyrone smiled at her.

"You all just missed seeing Natalie."

"Did she bring Reggie a present?" asked Malcolm.

"Not today," she answered. "But she stayed with Reggie so Mama could get some breakfast. Sometimes when people do nice things for us, those are the best kinds of presents."

Malcolm looked confused, so Jada continued. "We'll talk about it later; right now, we should go up and see Reggie. He's been asking for you."

Tyrone beamed with pride as he watched his family interact. Unfortunately, his cell phone rang, rudely interrupting his reverie. "I gotta take this, baby. It could be an update."

"You go ahead," she said. "The boys and I will manage. Right, boys?"

"Right, Mama," they said in unison.

Tyrone pulled his cell from his pocket and walked outside to make sure he had good reception. The call waiting said *unknown number*. "Hello, this is Detective Mayhew speaking."

A strange electronic voice came over the line. "Detective Mayhew, I thought you would stop this ridiculous investigation after you got my note."

Rage suddenly ripped at Tyrone's gut. He walked away from the doors so people entering the hospital wouldn't hear his end of the conversation. "Are you the one who shot my boy, you stinkin' coward?"

"Temper, temper, Detective."

"Temper! You think *this* is temper? Somebody messes with my family best not think he can get away with it. You better hope somebody besides me finds your sorry ass, because I'm gonna rip your fuckin' head off!"

"I didn't mean for the kid to get hurt, just be glad he's still alive."

"You didn't mean…what the hell you think is gonna happen when you shoot a gun into a house full of people? You think sayin' sorry's gonna help you?" Tyrone tried to stay in control, but he could feel his blood pressure rising and he broke into a sweat.

"I wanted you to realize what could happen if this investigation continues. If it doesn't stop, neither will I."

"I couldn't stop this investigation even if I wanted to. We already know the bones we found are Wendy Matherson's. Killing Serena Walsh and shootin' up my house weren't necessary."

"She should have stayed away from Jared."

"Jared was already determined to do what he could to remember what happened to his mother," said Tyrone, breathing hard and trying to focus although every fiber of his being wanted to reach into the phone and choke this guy. "He's not going to stop, even if we do."

"That's too bad," said the electronic voice. "Watch your back, Detective."

The call disconnected. Tyrone kicked the air and cursed the caller with every vulgar word that came to mind.

"What's going on, Tyrone," said a familiar voice. Tyrone turned to see Lieutenant Terhune headed in his direction.

"That fucking son-of-a-bitch just called me! Can you believe the fucking balls on this guy? How the hell did he get my cell number?"

"Come on, man. Calm down…."

"How the hell am I supposed to calm down? He shot my son, Lieutenant! He shot my Reggie! He as much as told me this wasn't the end of it."

"Was there a caller ID number?"

"No," said Tyrone. Shaking violently, he pushed the phone into Terhune's hand. "Take it to the lab or somethin'. Find out who called."

"We can check your call record, but these types usually use disposable cells," said the lieutenant. "Did you recognize the voice?"

"Hell, no. The bastard's usin' some sort of electronic device to warp his voice." Tyrone paced, rubbing his chin and cheeks as though to wash some stench off. He looked Terhune square in the eye. "What am I gonna tell Jada? How am I supposed to tell my wife she and my precious children are still in danger?"

"Do you know of any place we can put them in hiding for a while?" asked Terhune.

"I guess, but what if we don't catch him right away? What if it takes another ten years? I can't live without my family that long."

"Look, Tyrone, this guy's starting to get desperate and desperate criminals make mistakes. That's how we'll catch him. He probably didn't think we'd ever find the car, or Wendy Matherson's grave. He thought he'd committed the perfect crime. Now it's all starting to unravel on him."

"My brother-in-law and sister have a cabin in Brown County. I already asked if Jada and the kids could go there while Reggie recovers," said Tyrone. "Do you think we could get police protection for them?"

"We'd have to check with locals first," said Terhune. "If they don't have the manpower then maybe we can get the state police involved."

"Nothing's wrong with Reggie I hope," said Erica as she approached.

"Nah," said Tyrone wiping his brow. His anger still seeping from his pores.

"So what's going on? You look awful," she said to Tyrone.

The lieutenant quickly gave her the rundown of the latest phone call. When he finished, she turned to Tyrone and rubbed his big muscular arms.

"You're going to get through this. Look at me," she said smiling. "I'll go with them and play off-duty cop/security guard."

"Nuh uh," he said pulling back from her. "You've been through enough lately. Besides, if I put you in harm's way Jacobs would tear me apart."

"Well, Ben Jacobs doesn't run my life," she said. "Even if I was married to the guy, I make my own decisions. I love Jada and the kids. Please don't say no. I really want to help."

"That's not a bad idea," said Terhune. "She can't go as a police officer, because it's out of our jurisdiction. However, she's trained to handle these situations and still has some off time."

"We'll keep the local P. D. in the loop," said Erica.

"Okay, I give," said Tyrone. "Thank you for volunteering." He took Erica in his arms and hugged her.

"You, too, Lieutenant." He extended his hand and Terhune shook it vigorously. "I don't know how I'd get through this without all of you. Right now we'd better get up there before Jada thinks I left her alone with those rowdy boys."

Chapter 47

"I can't believe that," shouted Ben into his cell phone. "This guy actually called Mayhew on his cell phone and threatened him?"

"I walked up to him just as the call ended," said Lieutenant Terhune.

"Did he recognize the voice?"

"He said the guy used a device to disguise his voice," said the lieutenant. "Of course, as much as those devices distort the human voice, it could have been a woman."

"Tyrone didn't need this on top of everything else." Ben ran his fingers through his hair in frustration. "So what is he going to do? We can't stop investigating. You don't just throw two murders and a drive-by shooting into a drawer and forget about them."

Freeman parked the car along the street across from the Matherson house. He killed the engine and removed his seatbelt.

"I'll tell you precisely what we're doing next," said Terhune.

Ben's eyes widened when Terhune got to the part involving Erica.

"Oh, hell no," Ben spewed. "She's been through enough. She doesn't need to be playing security guard."

"You can discuss that later," said Terhune. "You at the Matherson house yet?"

"Yes, sir," said Ben. "I'll update you later."

Ben hung up the phone and unbuckled his seat belt, and then looked at Freeman.

"I take it Erica is getting involved," said Freeman.

Ben nodded. "She wants to go into hiding with Jada and the kids to play bodyguard."

"I've known Erica Barnes a lot longer than you have. Telling her she *can't* do something will only make her more determined to do it, and she'll be pissed at you for trying to stop her."

"I know, but...."

"There are no buts about it, Ben. If she's hell bent on going with Jada and the kids to the cabin, no amount of pressure will keep her here."

Ben slumped in defeat. "I guess if I want to keep this relationship going in a positive direction, I'd better accept it."

"You're a wise man, Jacobs." Freeman clapped Ben's shoulder

then turned to look out his window. "Here are the troops."

Just as they exited Freeman's car, Detective Kendall approached.

"I've got both warrants," she said. "Judge Jackson was more than willing to call in some favors and find another judge to sign them. He was concerned that signing them himself might give a defense attorney ammunition to throw out the evidence in court since he's related to some of the victims."

"Good idea." Ben pointed at the warrants. "Do you mind if I serve those?"

"Be my guest," said Freeman.

Kendall handed the warrants to Ben. They all walked toward the house and Ben signaled for the rest of the team to follow.

Reid Matherson answered the door, mouth dropping when he saw the army of police officers standing on his doorstep. "What the hell is this?"

"Mr. Matherson," said Jacobs. "We are here to search your property...."

"The hell you are," interrupted Reid. "Not without a search warrant and my lawyer present."

"Sir, I don't have to wait for your lawyer to serve these two search warrants," said Ben glaring at Reid. "The first warrant gives us permission to search your property, including all vehicles, for a 90-Two Berretta owned by Ryan Matherson. We have cause to believe that handgun was used in a drive by shooting at Detective Mayhew's house."

Reid started to speak but Jacobs held up his hand.

"The second warrant allows us to have our CSI team check your stairway for blood evidence and for us to search for the weapon used in the death of your wife, Wendy Matherson."

That put the brakes on Reid's ability to speak. He snatched the warrants from Ben's hand and looked at them as though in shock. *Busted*, thought Ben.

Ryan and Tanner appeared. "What is it, Dad?" asked Tanner. Reid simply shoved the papers into Tanner's hands and walked into the house.

"You guys couldn't even give us time to tell Dad you came by this morning," said Tanner, anger blushing in his cheeks.

"They came by today and you didn't call me," Reid shouted.

"No, Dad," said Ryan, rolling his eyes. "They wanted to ask us a few questions about our whereabouts last night when somebody shot

Detective Mayhew's son."

The veins in Reid's face were so pronounced; Ben thought the man was going to have a stroke.

"I told you boys not to talk to them without a lawyer present," shouted Reid.

Ryan's face became fierce and flush. He advanced on his father and poked him in the chest, sending Reid backward. "That's just it, *Father*. We're not *boys* any longer. We're men. Maybe Tanner likes being treated like a twelve-year-old, but I don't."

Ben spotted Tanner's angry face and decided he'd better intervene before things came to blows. "We need for the three of you to step outside with these officers while we do our search."

Ben instructed the two patrol officers to stay with them and make sure they didn't go back into the house or the garage. He saw Reid pull out a cell phone on his way out the door. He was probably calling that lawyer he's always screaming about.

"Parelli," said Freeman, "go upstairs and start with the master bedroom." She nodded and went up the stairs. "Chatham, I need you to work on the stairway. Pull up the fucking carpet if you have to. I'm positive Wendy Matherson died here."

"Let's check the cars, Jacobs," said Kendall. "I'd bet the gun's in one of them. Want to take bets on whose?"

"Sounds good," said Freeman. "I'll handle the house."

Ben peered out the open doorway. He could see all three men looking tense. Tanner was wringing his hands and looking around nervously. Reid was still on the phone. He was shouting something Ben couldn't hear. On the other hand, Ryan had slumped to the ground next to a large maple tree with his elbows on his knees holding his head in his hands as if he had a horrendous headache.

"Coming, Jacobs?" said Kendall.

As they walked into the kitchen, Kendall walked straight over to the door that connected to the garage. "I thought they'd have one of these by the door."

Ben watched as Kendall pulled three sets of keys off of the key board on the wall. "I think we should search Dad's car first, don't you?"

"He's the one I'd bet on. He can't account for his whereabouts last night," said Ben. "Let's do it."

When they reached Reid's vehicle, it was unlocked. Ben opened the driver's door and pressed the trunk release button. The trunk would be the first place an amateur like Reid might try to hide something. Kendall searched the trunk while Ben started on the inside of the car.

"Jacobs! I found the lock box," she shouted.

He got out of the car, but when he reached her, all he saw was an open box and no gun. "Let's finish searching the car," he said. "It may be in here somewhere."

"If he didn't take it somewhere and dump it," Kendall remarked.

"Maybe, but why not ditch the lock box, too? It doesn't make sense."

They pulled out the carpeting in the trunk, searching the spare tire area. They checked behind the speakers. Then they started on the inside of the vehicle, searching under the seats and glove box. Nothing. Ben decided they'd have to ask CSI to tow it in and tear it apart.

After searching the other two vehicles and finding nothing, Ben fumed as he grabbed the lock box and opened the garage door to step outside. He walked quickly over to Ryan with Kendall on his heels. "Ryan, is this the lockbox your gun was in?"

Ryan rose, but Jacobs wouldn't allow him to touch it now that it was evidence. Ryan pointed to a metal bar with etching.

"That's it," he said. "Those are my initials."

Before he knew it, Reid and Tanner were at Ben's side.

Ben's eyes narrowed as he turned to Reid. "Where's the gun, Mr. Matherson?"

"I have no idea what you're talking about," Reid answered.

"We found this lockbox in the trunk of your car," said Kendall. "Can you explain how it got there?"

"No idea," said Reid, crossing his arms in a defiant, stubborn stance.

"Fine," said Jacobs about to lose it. "I guess we'll take our little chat downtown." Jacobs turned to one of the patrol officers. "Take him downtown on suspicion of attempted murder of a police officer. We'll meet you there and decide what the other charges will be."

"You might want to add suspicion of the murder of his wife to that," said Freeman, who had apparently come outside unnoticed. "Chatham found human blood under the carpet on the stairway. We can rush this and have the results in a couple of days to see if the DNA matches Wendy Matherson's."

"My, my, Mr. Matherson," said Kendall. "You've been a very naughty boy. Telling us where Ryan's gun is would go a long way with the prosecutor."

"Bullshit!" cried Reid. "Tanner, call my lawyer and have him meet me at the police station." He looked at Jacobs. "I've got no more to say without my attorney present."

"Get him out of here," said Freeman to the patrol officer. "They're searching for a weapon now. It may be hard to find since her sons probably haven't played baseball for years."

"Should we go in and question Matherson?" asked Kendall.

Freeman nodded. "I'll meet the two of you there as soon as I check on the team. I'll see you back at the ranch."

Chapter 48

"Major Stevenson," said Ben as he and Kendall walked into the Homicide Department, "did you see Reid Matherson come in?"

"I saw him all right," answered Stevenson with a frown. "He's been crying foul ever since he arrived. His attorney must have an office downtown because he arrived before Matherson got here."

"Damn it," spouted Jacobs. "We can still hold him for a couple of days on what we have, can't we?"

Major Stevenson rubbed his chin. "If CSI finds a significant amount of blood in the house, we can arrest him on suspicion of murdering his wife. The sooner they get the DNA results to us the stronger our case, but it's still not solid. Finding the murder weapon would certainly boost our case. What about the Mayhew case?"

"I'm afraid the evidence we have so far on the shooting is pretty flimsy," said Kendall. "The missing gun could be the weapon, but unless we get our hands on it we can't match the bullets found at the scene."

"Let's hope Chatham and his team find it in the house or in one of the cars before they're finished," said the major.

Ben paced and ran his fingers through his hair, thinking hard about their next step. What was he going to tell Tyrone when he saw him? They were so close to putting Reid away, but not close enough. They could only hold him for seventy-two hours, but what good would it do if they couldn't find more evidence and he refused to answer any questions.

"I've talked to Terhune. We think Kendall and Freeman should deal with this one," said Major Stevenson. "Kendall, concentrate on trying to get him to tell us what he did with the gun."

"It's obvious he doesn't trust cops," said Kendall. "Maybe he took it to have it cleaned or something, but I'm sure he'll be too stubborn to tell us."

"*Bullshit!* The bastard tried to kill my partner and nearly killed Reggie," Ben exclaimed, anger pushing his temper to the limit.

"We know it looks that way, and we know how you feel," said Kendall raising an eyebrow. "That's why it's better for us to take care of it. Mayhew is Freeman's case. Walsh is mine. If this guy thought the two of them would expose what happened to his wife, we'll find out. All of us will get a piece of the pie before this is over."

"I didn't mean it like that," Ben said, realizing how it must have sounded. "I know you're right. I'm too connected to Reggie to be objective."

"I have a meeting so I need to go," said Stevenson. "Don't worry, Jacobs. We'll get this son-of-a-bitch."

Ben nodded and watched Major Stevenson walk down the hallway. "Thanks for keeping me straight, Kendall."

He heard footsteps behind him.

"Look who I found wondering the hallways," said Freeman, pointing to Erica.

Erica flashed them a smile and asked, "What's going on?"

"What are you doing here?" asked Ben, testiness in his tone.

"Nice welcome," she said. "I just finished talking to the department shrink. He wanted an update on how I'm doing. I'll probably be off a few more weeks. I love being with Dad, but I'm getting bored."

"That's my girl," said Freeman.

"Watch it," Ben said.

"Hey, she was mine first," laughed Freeman.

"Kendall, these two are such children," said Erica. "What were you two talking about when I walked up?"

Kendall gave her a quick overview of what they'd found at the Matherson house.

"Stevenson wants Freeman and me to handle the Matherson interrogation," said Kendall. "We need to concentrate on finding the gun used on Mayhew's house."

"I don't suppose his attorney's late?" asked Freeman.

Kendall raised an eyebrow and crossed her arms in front of her.

"I didn't think we'd be that lucky," said Freeman. Then he excused himself and signaled for Kendall to follow him to the interrogation room to see if Reid Matherson was ready to talk.

"Holy crap, Ben," said Erica. "This gets more complicated by the minute, doesn't it?"

"That's what frustrates me. More people are getting hurt and it all seems to have something to do with Wendy Matherson."

"It sucks when you know in your gut who did it, but there isn't enough evidence to get an arrest and conviction," she said. "Nowadays so many people watch shows that display every type of forensics known to man and they expect it to be done. They don't realize that not every jurisdiction has a lab. If they do, they can't afford the equipment to do every test."

"They also don't seem to understand tests take time," said Ben. "They think we can get DNA results in twenty minutes when it takes days."

"Do you have time to get some dinner?" she asked, smiling sweetly.

"I need to type up a report on what happened today, but it is after 5:00," he said, his serious frown softening to a smile. "Come with me and I'll ask the lieutenant if I can take a couple of hours if I promise to come back and finish my report. I could really use the break."

"Sounds great."

Chapter 49

"I'm reaching for the bat, but something is keeping me from it. Like a force field," said Jared. He was lying on the couch in Daphne's office trying desperately to grab the baseball bat he was seeing in his hypnotic state. "It looks like it's right there, but I can't touch it."

"Jared," said Daphne, "I think that's as far as you can go today. You should come back now."

"No, I want to keep going." His frustration made him squirm. "I have to remember."

"I know," she whispered. "But you sound stuck. You've done very well today. I'm going to bring you back now so we can talk about it. I'm going to count backward from three and when I reach one you'll be back in the room with me."

Jared thought he could resist and stay where he was, but as she reached two, he was back in the hallway. Then his eyes fluttered open at the sound of the word one.

"Why didn't you let me stay there, Daphne? I needed to find out what the bat is all about."

"I understand your frustration, but these things take time. Your mind has buried this memory for ten years. Besides, we only have about ten more minutes and there is something I need to tell you."

"What is it? No one else has died, have they?"

She gave him an empathetic smile. "No, no, nothing like that. This concerns your father."

Jared's forehead crinkled in confusion. "What about my father?"

"Detective Jacobs called me this morning to let me know your father has been taken into custody and is in the Marion County Jail."

Jared sat straight up at this comment. "Do they think he killed my mother?"

"They're holding him on suspicion of killing your mother and of the shooting at Detective Mayhew's house. They can hold him on suspicion for at least 72 hours."

"So he hasn't been arrested?"

"Not yet. From the way Detective Jacobs talked, they may not have enough evidence to prosecute him. Your father won't tell the police what happened to Ryan's gun." Daphne paused looking down at her hands.

Jared's heart began to race. "What is it? Is there something else you need to tell me?"

"Jared, they're also looking for a baseball bat. It could be the bat you're seeing in your dreams and during hypnosis. Do you remember whether or not those things were given away or if they are still in the house somewhere?"

"Ryan was the athlete. I tried baseball for a while when I was little, but I don't remember playing after Mom left...I mean died." Boy, did it feel weird to say she was dead after all of these years.

"Are you alright, Jared?"

"Yeah, I'm good. Do you think I should go see him?"

"I can't advise you on that. You know whether or not to go. Just make sure you go for the right reasons."

"What do you mean?"

Daphne smiled at him. "Don't go expecting him to confess everything to you, or to try to help you remember. For some reason, keeping you in the dark has been very important to your father. He's not likely to help you remember the truth now."

"I see what you mean." Jared sat forward and rubbed his face. Was his dad truly capable of shooting up a man's home and hurting a six-year-old without remorse? Did his father actually kill his mother?

"Time's up for today," said Daphne. "Will I see you again in the morning?"

"Definitely. I'm not going to miss any appointments. I want to know what really happened."

Jared left Daphne's office barely noticing the reception area. The next thing he knew, he was standing next to his car and wasn't sure how he'd arrived. He really didn't want to see his dad, especially after the way things ended the last time they were together. Of course, curiosity tempted him to ignore his reservations.

He stopped for a light at the corner of Illinois and East Ohio Streets. What should he do? Continue on Illinois for home, or should he make that right-hand turn down East Ohio and head for the jail? The sudden blasting of several car horns woke him from his dilemma and he opted to make the turn.

In minutes, he was at the jail. Jared had no idea what the procedure was for this visitation. He sat in his car for a few minutes wondering if this had been a mistake. Was Daphne wrong? Could he finally get his dad to tell him the cause of his nightmares? No way he'd find out sitting here.

He entered the jail and went through the first security point. Then he stopped at the information desk where he found a very stern looking female Sheriff's Department officer.

"May I help you," she said, not even cracking a smile.

"I wondered if I could see my father, Reid Matherson."

"Sorry, Mr. Matherson was taken over to Homicide fifteen minutes ago for interrogation."

"Oh," said Jared. "Thanks."

Jared went back outside; he looked up at the clear blue sky. He'd go over to the police station and ask Detective Jacobs for permission to see his father. Deciding to leave his car in the jail parking lot, Jared set out to walk the short distance to the City-County Building.

When he arrived, he remembered his Indiana History teacher telling them that the City-County Building was the first skyscraper built in Indianapolis. Then he looked at the door berating himself for thinking of historical trivia at a time like this.

"No time like the present," he said aloud. "I don't know if this will work, but maybe being in jail will make Dad more vulnerable somehow. I've got to try—for Mom."

Chapter 50

Tyrone had received the news of Matherson's detainment late the night before. Erica had come by to visit Reggie at the hospital. She told him she and Ben had just had dinner and that he had to go back to the office to finish the reports on the search of Matherson's home and vehicles.

It upset Tyrone to think that he and Jacobs were prohibited from talking to the suspect. However, he understood the shooting at his home brought him into the victim category and a defense attorney would be screaming police brutality should he get Reid to confess.

The decision for him to go to the office to check things out had Jada's stamp of approval. He'd stopped by to see Reggie earlier. Jada told him it would do him good to run in to the office for a while and find out what was going on. Of course, *she* wanted the guy who shot up their house put away as much as, if not more, than he did.

"Reggie doing better?" asked Jacobs.

"You need to stop sneakin' up on me, jackass."

"Still as grumpy as ever, I see." Jacobs smiled at him as he sat down at his desk. "Erica said she filled you in. The guy brought in a lawyer and is holding fast to his story. He won't say anything about what happened to Ryan's gun."

Tyrone pounded his fist on his desk. "If we don't find somethin' else, this guy's gonna walk. How can this be happening? We're so close, but not close enough."

"They're not finished tearing the house apart. We made Tanner and Ryan go stay with friends until we're finished with the crime scene. We haven't found the bat, but I'm going back there shortly."

"I'm coming with you. I hope it's still there. If he has half a brain, he'll have disposed of it."

Jacobs' phone rang. "Jacobs." He brightened as he looked at Tyrone. "Sure, send him up."

"Send who up?"

"Jared is here. He wants to see his father," said Jacobs. "I think we'll let him do just that."

"You thinkin' what I'm thinkin'," said Tyrone feeling hopeful.

"Reid's at the breaking point. If anybody can get him to talk, it's Jared. He's the one your anonymous pen pal wanted to protect. Reid's been feeding him crap all these years to keep him from remembering what really happened."

"Detective Mayhew," Jared exclaimed. "I wasn't expecting to see you. How's your son?"

"Reggie is doin' real well. He should get out of the hospital in a day or two. How are you?"

"I'm fine." His tone wasn't very convincing.

"How is the therapy going?" asked Jacobs. "Have you remembered anything new?"

"I'm stuck at a place where I see this baseball bat," said Jared, his face scrunching as though something pained him. "I know it's significant or it wouldn't keep showing up."

"We think a baseball bat may have been used in your mother's murder. Do you have any idea where that type of thing might be stored in your house?"

Jared's face screwed up in thought. "Daphne asked me that same question this morning. I stopped playing baseball after Mom..., but wait. Did anybody look in our attic? We have a finished attic where we store old stuff, Christmas decorations, you know. All the things you don't use all the time, maybe some memorabilia."

"Excellent," said Tyrone. "Jared, if we let you talk to your dad, do you think you can get him to tell you anything about what happened with your mom?"

"He hasn't told me anything for ten years so I doubt it. I'll see what I can do though. I want to help."

"Let's go down to Homicide," said Jacobs. "I'm sure Freeman and Kendall will be happy for any help they can get."

When the three of them arrived in the Homicide Department, they found Kendall and Freeman conversing at Freeman's desk. Freeman looked up and motioned for them to come over.

"Matherson's in Interrogation Three," said Freeman. "He won't talk to us until his attorney arrives so we're waiting out here for him."

"Jared wanted to know if he can talk to his father," said Jacobs. "Is it okay if I take him back?"

"Sure. You can wait in the observation room. Jared, you just signal the sergeant when you want to come out," said Freeman. "Tyrone, you can stay here and watch with us on the computer. Grab Erica's chair and bring it over."

Tyrone wheeled the chair from behind the desk across from Freeman's. Kendall had already brought her chair. They heard the knock on the door and watched as Jared entered the room.

At first, Jared looked shocked at seeing his father in his new orange jumpsuit; however, he recovered quickly. He stood with his hands in his pockets and shuffled his feet.

"Hello, Dad."

"Jared," said Reid with a wide-eyed expression of surprise. He started to stand, but Jared shook his head and Reid stayed put staring down at his clasped hands.

Jared sat down in the chair across from his father. Taking his hands from his pockets, he laced his fingers on the desk and focused on them, apparently unable to look his father in the eye. "Well, I thought that one day this might happen, I mean you and I across a table in the police station. But, I actually thought it would be the other way around with me in the orange get up."

"Jared, this isn't a joke."

Slowly lifting his face so he was eye-to-eye with his father, Jared leaned forward a bit. "I'm not joking. As fucked up as I've been this past ten years since Mom was *murdered*, I thought I'd end up in jail someday."

"Your mother wasn't murdered."

"I'm thinking the runaway story has been exposed as a lie now, Dad. Give it a rest and tell me the truth for once."

Reid's pained expression almost made Tyrone feel sorry for him. Surely, he wasn't talking about his wife running away any longer. On the other hand, had he been telling that story so long he actually believed it.

"I know she didn't run away, but I didn't kill her," said Reid. "You've got to believe me."

"I don't have to *do* anything. You're the one who's in trouble here, so tell me what really happened to Mom."

"I can't."

"You can't?" said Jared, his face wrinkled and red with anger. "You can't or you won't? You obviously don't give a shit about me or you'd tell the police what really happened. My life has been hell since she died. I want the nightmares to stop!"

"Please, Jared, you have to let it go. Stop trying to remember. It will be worse if you remember." Now Reid was crying.

Jared jumped up out of his seat and backed away from his father. "Really? You're going to sit there and cry! What do you have to cry about? Do you know how tortured I've been all these years? Even when I tried to forget, the nightmares still came. You kept me away from Aunt Cindy and Uncle Kevin because you knew they'd listen and they'd help me remember. You and Tanner made me feel like an idiot because I couldn't control my dreams."

"Please, Jared, you don't understand," pleaded Reid. "I love you, I wanted to protect you."

"Bull…shit! You were protecting yourself." He turned away from his father for a moment, and then looked at him strangely. "Was it Tanner? Are you protecting Tanner?"

"No!"

Jared advanced toward the table slamming his hands on the tabletop. "Tell me the truth right now or I swear you'll never see me again!"

Reid simply shook his head, tears still streaming down his cheeks.

"I remember the baseball bat, Dad. It's only a matter of time before I remember everything. Your silence won't stop me." He turned to the two-way glass and said, "Let me out of here, Sergeant Jacobs."

Tyrone and his companions saw the door open and watched in silence for a few moments as Reid's head hit the table and he sobbed. Something about this whole thing didn't make sense. Reid's reactions were off. He adamantly claimed he and Tanner didn't kill Wendy, yet he still said he needed to protect Jared.

Jacobs entered the room alone a few minutes later. "He took off. Jared said he'd talk to you later."

Tyrone pushed Erica's chair back to its place behind her desk. "Looks like we've got an attic to search."

Chapter 51

Tyrone and Ben headed for the Matherson home to search for the baseball bat he believed had caused Wendy Matherson to fall down the stairs to her death.

Before Jared gave Tyrone the clue about the attic, the crime scene had been released and the elder Matherson brothers had moved back in. When Tyrone and Jacobs arrived at the Matherson house, they found Ryan the only one home.

"Dad's lawyer called and said you'd be coming back. We just cleaned up the mess from the last time the cops were in here," said Ryan. For the first time, Tyrone thought he sensed some tension on Ryan's part.

"You'll need to wait outside with the patrol officer when he arrives," said Tyrone.

Ryan rolled his eyes and stomped out of the house.

"I can't allow you back into the house until we're finished."

Without a word, Ryan waived him off and started walking down the sidewalk. Soon he was out of sight.

After the patrol officer arrived to guard the front door, Tyrone went in to the house to join Jacobs in the search.

"Jacobs, where you at?" shouted Tyrone.

"In the attic," Jacobs shouted.

Tyrone entered the master bedroom to find Jacobs peering down at him from an entrance to the attic, a drop ladder waiting for him. "Get up here. Let's see if we can find that bat."

Tyrone climbed the ladder into the dusty attic. Someone had added some plywood flooring and walls to add storage space. Several labeled boxes occupied the area. Tyrone read the labels finding some marked *CHRISTMAS*, some marked *BOOKS*, and then finally found the box labeled *SPORTS STUFF*.

"Let's start with this one. It's long enough to hold a bat," said Tyrone as he handed a pair of gloves to Jacobs. He tore off the tape and they started to sort through sports gear. There was a football helmet, kneepads, soccer ball, three baseballs, two baseball mitts, and finally two wooden bats. "Let's bag 'em and tag 'em."

They went through several other boxes to make sure they had all the bats in the house. Tyrone didn't think they'd get another warrant if they screwed up this search, so they looked in the boys' bedrooms as well.

Once finished, Tyrone found Ryan waiting in the front yard. Ryan stared at what Jacobs was holding and didn't look happy.

"Where'd you get those?" Ryan asked. "I thought Dad gave all that sports stuff away a long time ago."

"In the attic," answered Jacobs. "Looks like your dad won't be coming home for a while."

"So what happens next?" asked Ryan.

"We'll take them to our lab and find out if there's any blood on either of them," said Tyrone. "If there is, then we'll hope there's an adequate sample for DNA testing. It doesn't take much blood these days to get a good sample."

"I see," said Ryan, turning away.

"Do you have anything you want to tell me?" asked Tyrone.

Ryan sighed, not meeting Tyrone's eyes. "No, Detective. I don't."

"Okay," said Tyrone, shaking his head. "Jacobs, let's get these down to the lab."

Chapter 52

Tyrone wanted to show this new evidence to Matherson to see what sort of reaction he might get. He had called ahead to ask Freeman if Reid was still in the interrogation room. Freeman told him yes. Kendall had been asking questions about Jared's visit with Reid when his lawyer arrived and stopped the interview to confer with his client.

When he arrived at the station, Tyrone went straight to Interrogation Room Three. "Hey there, Mr. Matherson. Recognize these?"

"What's the meaning of this?" bellowed the attorney.

Reid Matherson's eyes bulged as he looked at the baseball bats. Tyrone bet he'd put them in the attic intending to get rid of them. He'd probably forgotten they were in there.

"What's wrong, Mr. Matherson? Did we find something you didn't want us to have?" asked Tyrone.

"Don't answer that," said his attorney.

Reid looked at Tyrone, his face turning pale as a ghost. His lips moved, but nothing came out.

"We'll take these to the lab for testing," said Tyrone pointing at the bats. "I suspect the Forensics Lab will find your wife's blood on at least one of them. I'm sure it'll strengthen our case."

"That doesn't prove anything," said Reid's attorney. "It's all circumstantial."

Tyrone squinted at the attorney, doing everything he could to keep his temper in check. "Circumstantial or not, your client knows what happened to his wife. Somebody moved her body and drove her car into the reservoir. Somebody cleaned up the blood from the staircase and walls. It's not likely that a jury is going to believe someone outside of that household did this."

"That's enough," said Reid. "Leave me alone. My wife wasn't murdered. She simply fell down the stairs."

"Reid, stop talking," advised his attorney. "*Now.*"

Reid turned away and Tyrone waited. When it was evident Reid was following his attorney's advice, Tyrone took the evidence bag and headed for the forensics lab.

* * *

As Tyrone approached the lab, he found Valerie Cambridge behind the window where she logged materials brought to the Forensics Department. Tyrone gave her the case number and requested the techs check the bats for blood and epithelial evidence, and then check for blood type and DNA.

"Must be a cold case," said Valerie. "I haven't seen a number this low in a while."

"Yeah, this case is ten years old. We just found the body a few days ago."

"Family must be relieved," she said.

"Not really." Tyrone frowned. He knew he'd opened himself up for more questions.

"Sounds like one of them did it then."

Tyrone grinned at her sharp perception of the situation. "Thanks, Valerie. Tell the vampire we'd like a rush on this."

She laughed. "I'll tell him, but I can't guarantee he'll heed your request."

"Just do the best you can," he said. Tyrone walked out the door muttering to himself, "That's all anyone can do."

Chapter 53

The next morning, Tyrone got the okay from the doctor for Reggie to leave the hospital. To his dismay, Reggie would not be going home or to Ophelia's house. His family along with Erica Barnes had headed for the cabin in Brown County.

The blood evidence from the bats would take a few days at best to process and Reid Matherson was out on bail. The only thing they could even come close to charging him with was the murder of his wife. Since Ryan's Beretta was still missing, there was no solid evidence that Reid participated in the drive-by shooting of Tyrone's house. That didn't mean Tyrone had changed his mind about Reid's involvement, and with him out of jail, Tyrone needed to move his family out of the city.

It had been hard for Tyrone to sit down with his wife and tell her she and the children needed to go into hiding. He explained that despite the fact Reid Matherson was under suspicion for the shooting, he hadn't been officially arrested. Reid's alibi for the night Serena Walsh died was solid, but Tyrone still suspected Reid didn't act alone.

Jada had reacted more calmly than he'd expected. He knew she had no desire to go back to their house at this point. The bullet holes were still there and would be a constant reminder of how close she and her children had come to dying.

His family had left early with a state police escort. Despite his repeated objections, Erica Barnes accompanied them to Brown County. She'd bullied him into it after getting Jada to take her side on the issue. Nevertheless, he couldn't help but feel relieved. Barnes was a great cop, so having her with his family gave him an added sense of security.

His family safely away, Tyrone needed to turn his thoughts to his case. Lieutenant Terhune had been correct. The son-of-a-bitch who'd called and threatened Tyrone had used a disposable cell phone. The caller had apparently turned it off and thrown it away, because they were unable to locate it. In his office at the time of the call, Matherson had allowed police to search it. That search, and a search of the surrounding area, revealed nothing.

This entanglement of cases got more frustrating by the minute. Tyrone went over the recent interviews Jacobs, Freeman and Kendall had conducted with the Mathersons. He studied the coroner's reports on the Walsh case as well as the one on Mrs. Matherson's remains. Ballistics had been examining the 9 mm bullets they'd found in his home, but without Ryan's Beretta the testing was incomplete.

As he studied the Matherson file, he realized the search warrant they'd exercised ten years ago on the Matherson house did not include CSI involvement. He remembered Detective Grimes had said there wasn't any need because Wendy Matherson had never come home that evening.

Tyrone looked at Jacobs. "So nobody checked for physical evidence at the house."

"What'd you say?"

"Here in this report. I don't know why I never noticed this before. We never had a CSI team go to the house and look for evidence to make sure a violent crime wasn't committed there."

"I noticed the same thing. That's why Kendall and I got a second warrant to cover a search for blood evidence," said Jacobs. "Dr. Patel said the injuries were consistent with a fall like tumbling down a stairway. Since we had to look for the gun, we thought we'd look for the blood, too."

"When will the DNA results be in?"

"Mark Chatham found several samples and put a rush on it hoping the results would come in today," said Jacobs. "Did you check your email this morning?"

Tyrone shook his head, and then checked his email.

"According to Chatham, there was human blood on one of the bats," said Tyrone. "Blood type matches Wendy Matherson's, but it could also match her kids. They can't get the DNA results to us for at least two more days."

"Why don't you just put this one on a chain and wear him around your neck," said Hill sneering. Tyrone turned to see Jared Matherson standing beside Detective Hill. Then Hill rolled his eyes and walked away.

"Jared, it's good to see you," said Tyrone. "Have a seat."

Jared sat in Tyrone's side chair. His unkempt appearance and the bags under his eyes indicated a lack of sleep and possible depression.

"Are you okay?" asked Tyrone with concern.

"I've been seeing that hypnotherapist you recommended. I've seen her every morning this week."

"How's it going?"

"Good. I keep remembering bits and pieces. Nothing concrete except the baseball bat," said Jared, wringing his hands. He was staring at the floor, obviously having a hard time saying what he'd come to say.

"You know you don't need to hold back from me or Sergeant Jacobs, don't you?" said Tyrone.

"Yes. I guess that's why I'm feeling so bad. It's my fault. You know—the shooting. If I could just remember, Ms. Walsh would still be alive and your son wouldn't have been hurt."

"Don't know where you came up with that one," said Tyrone gently. He didn't believe for a moment Jared was at fault. "In my line of work, we see all kinds of rotten people. You aren't one of them."

"How's your son?" asked Jared.

"He's doin' well. The wound wasn't life threatening. He has to wear a sling for a while so he doesn't tear the incision, but he's gonna to be just fine."

"That's good to hear." Jared's face brightened a little.

Apparently, this young man had been carrying this weight on his shoulders. Tyrone hoped this would relieve the burden and put him back on track.

"Did you find the bats in our house yesterday?"

"Yes, we did," said Jacobs. "There's human blood on them, but we have to wait until the DNA testing is completed to know if it's *her* blood."

"I always wondered if Dad had done something to Mom," said Jared. "Then shooting at your house and being stupid enough to leave the gun case in the car. If you're going to ditch a gun, I'd think you'd ditch the case, too."

"It does seem strange, doesn't it?" said Tyrone, crinkling his brow. "Thing is, the evidence in the shooting at my house is pretty flimsy and circumstantial right now. Anyone could have put the empty gun box in his trunk. The keys are hangin' in the kitchen where anyone can get to them. Then there's the Serena Walsh case. His alibi for that night is solid so we're sure he didn't murder her."

Jared sat there staring into space as though in a trance. Tyrone glanced toward Jacobs who shrugged.

"You remember something?" asked Tyrone.

"The day after Mom disappeared, we spent the night with Grandma Matherson," he said. "When we came back, there was new carpeting in the living room and on the stairs."

"We believe the blood we found in the wood under the carpeting on the stairs is your mother's," said Jacobs. "Proving it was from the injuries she sustained in the fall that killed her may be hard, since there wasn't a lot found."

"So you really need for me to remember in order to have a strong case," said Jared.

"Did you have anything you want to tell me about your memories?" asked Tyrone.

"Noises, being scared, darkness, flashes of my dad's angry face," said Jared. He squinted and rubbed his eyes. "But nothing to pull them together, to actually see what happened."

"I think maybe you've been workin' too hard on this," said Tyrone. "Maybe you should take a break and...."

Jared's eyes flared almost maniacally. "No! I can't give up now. I've got to remember before somebody else gets hurt."

"Okay, okay," said Tyrone. He stood and touched Jared's shoulder. "It's gonna happen. But, I'm worried about you. You obviously haven't been getting enough sleep. Are the nightmares worse?"

Jared shook his head. "Not really. They've actually been better. I see most of this in the hypnosis."

"That's good," said Jacobs.

Jared squinted again as though he had a migraine. "So, you really think she died in our house?"

"Yes, we do," said Tyrone. The pain in Jared's face caused Tyrone to cringe. "Headache?"

Jared nodded. "Yeah. I should probably go home."

Tyrone walked Jared to the elevator. "Jared, we knew going into this it could take a while. These memories must be real, not something you *think* you remember."

"I see Daphne again tomorrow morning. Maybe I'll remember who used the bat." The elevator door opened. Jared nodded with a weak smile on his face as he entered the elevator.

Jacobs stood when Tyrone returned to his desk. "Do you think his brain will ever let him in on its deepest secrets?" asked Jacobs.

"Eventually. I just hope it happens soon. I miss my family."

Chapter 54

Jada opened the cabin door and immediately felt the breeze as Malcolm and Reggie raced inside. "Reggie Jackson Mayhew, you just got out of the hospital. Stop that running right now."

"Oh, wow," said Erica as she held Adanne in her carrier. "This place is great. How many bedrooms does it have?"

"Four," Jada replied as she set down her suitcase. She went to the door and shouted to Darryl. "Bring the groceries in first, honey. We need to get the refrigerated items put away."

"Darryl is such a responsible young man," said Erica.

Jada smiled at that. She was a very lucky woman. She turned to see her eldest son carrying a cooler in one hand and a grocery bag in the other. "Just put those in the kitchen."

Reggie came back to the living room, slowing down as his mother glared at him. "Mama, this is going to be great."

"Reggie, I want you to sit here in the living room with your sister while the rest of us bring in our things. No TV until everything is in, hear me?"

"Yes, Mama."

Jada snatched up Malcolm as he got ready to jump on the couch. "Malcolm, the *no rough housing rule* still applies. Your brother still has stitches that need to heal. You come outside with me and help bring stuff in."

"But, Mama, I'm too little."

"Don't try that one on me, young man," she said barely able to contain a smile. "There are plenty of small things to bring in, like Adanne's diaper bag and those toys you insisted you needed."

"Okay, Mama." He walked out slumping, and then peered over his shoulder at her with his sad big brown eyes.

After all the suitcases, boxes and bags had made it to their proper places, Jada dismissed Reggie from baby duty. Besides, Adanne had started to fuss, as it was time for her next meal.

"I'll hold her while you fix her bottle," said Erica. She unfastened Adanne's harness and picked her up as she began to wail. "Oh, no, what's wrong?" Erica brought Adanne to her shoulder, patting her back.

"Once she's into her *I'm starving* mode, there's no comforting her, I'm afraid," said Jada.

Preparing formula as quickly as she could, Jada hoped it would be ready before the coyotes decided Adanne's howls were some sort of mating call. Once the formula reached the correct temperature, she held her arms out for her youngest.

"She is so precious," said Erica.

"Make you want to have one of your own?" Jada raised her eyebrow, half-teasing, half-serious.

"Ben and I talked about it before...." Erica's voice trailed off and her face dropped with sadness.

"Before Emerson? Honey, the one thing none of us can do is let our bad experiences keep us from living," said Jada. "The 'what ifs' in this life keep us from enjoying what's real."

"I know, but it's hard not to think about it."

"Think about it for a moment, decide it's not going to get you down, and then hang on to the good stuff for dear life."

"You're a wise woman, Jada Mayhew."

Jada laughed and pulled the bottle from Adanne's mouth. "Time for burping little miss thing."

"Is that how you and Tyrone have kept it together for so long?"

"You bet it is," said Jada. "I know people see us as the perfect couple, but we've had our rough patches just like everybody else."

"Have you ever...." Erica paused, readjusting herself in her chair.

"Go ahead, girl. Spit it out."

"This is kind of embarrassing," said Erica. "During your time with Tyrone, have you ever been tempted...you know...?"

"You mean have I ever found a man attractive enough to think about fooling around?"

Erica's face became beet red and she lowered her eyes.

"Look at me, Erica."

Erica obeyed, her eyes glistening with tears.

"Honey, I don't mean to make you feel bad. You wouldn't be the first person to have such doubts about your relationship when your natural instincts kick in. The thing you have to ask yourself is why am I attracted to this other person?"

"Is it love or lust?"

"Exactly. You just went through a very traumatic experience so it's making you doubt yourself," said Jada, bringing Adanne up to her shoulder for another burp. "When you think about this other person, do you just think about sex or do you think about forever?"

"I hadn't thought of it that way," said Erica as she wiped a tear from her cheek.

"Don't beat yourself up for your thoughts, honey," said Jada. "You need time to work through this and as hard as it may be for Ben to wait, seems to me he's willing to do so."

"You're right," said Erica. She practically jumped out of her seat. "I think I'll call Ben and let him know we got here safely."

"Sounds like a good idea." Jada smiled at her.

After Erica had left the room and Jada was alone with her daughter, she brought Adanne back down to feeding position and said, "I hope you were listening, little one. Some day you'll be coming to me with the same questions."

Chapter 55

"Jared, what's wrong?" asked Daphne as he entered her office. His disheveled appearance and dark rimmed eyes concerned her.

"I thought when they found Mom and I started this therapy, everything would get better," he said. "But it didn't. I told Detective Mayhew the nightmares were better, but I lied to him so he wouldn't worry. He has enough to worry about."

"So the nightmares have gotten worse?"

"Yes," he said as he wrung his hands. "They're worse than ever."

"In what way?" she asked.

"I have them all night long," he said, eyes widening. "I don't want to go to sleep anymore, because if I do I'll dream."

"Jared, look at it this way. Your mind is in a battle. Part of it wants to protect itself against a memory it perceives as too horrible to think of consciously. On the other hand, your conscious mind wants to remember no matter what the consequences."

Jared stared at her for a moment. "This whole thing has been so destructive. Not just for my family. Whoever's behind this killed the psychic, and then shot Detective Mayhew's son and terrorized his family."

"Yes, those things are destructive if we allow them to be," said Daphne, noting the confused expression on Jared's face. "Another thing you must remember. These events were set in motion the day your mother died. These are things neither you nor I can control."

"I guess not," he said.

"If you're having trouble sleeping, I can get one of the doctors to prescribe something for you."

"I'll think about it," he said.

"You know we've been going at this for several days," she said, concerned he may be pushing himself too hard. "Maybe you need a break."

"No!" he shouted. "I can't stop now. I'm too close to finding out what really happened."

"It's okay," she said, trying to soothe him. "We'll keep working. I just want to know your options."

"Alright then," he said, lying down on the couch, "let's get started."

"Remember, relaxation is the key. Close your eyes and breathe in deeply and exhale." She repeated these instructions several times until his breathing became steady.

"Now continue to breathe deeply and find your special place. Tell me when you're there."

Jared's face relaxed. He moved his head a couple of times, cocking it a few times as though looking for something.

"Where are you Jared?" she asked.

"I'm on the beach, but I don't see the house yet."

"Take your time," she said in a soothing voice. "Just enjoy the beauty of where you are now. When you are ready, walk in the direction you feel will take you to the door. Inhale. Exhale. Can you tell me what you see on the beach?"

"Miles and miles of white sand," he said with a smile. "Beautiful turquoise blue water and foamy waves. Birds. Lots of palm trees. It's beautiful here."

"I'm sure it is," she said. She decided it was time to push a little. "Jared, are we going to the beach house again?"

"Yeah, but it doesn't seem quite as inviting today," he answered.

"In what way?" she asked.

"I'm not sure," he answered. "It's scarier for some reason. I guess I'm afraid to know the real truth."

"Are you too afraid to move on?"

"Yes, but I can't be afraid," he said, frowning. "If I don't find the truth, other people could get hurt or worse. Someone else could die."

"Would it help if I am there with you?" she asked. "If you let me in, I'll walk with you and hold your hand."

"I'd like that," he said.

"Can you see me?"

"Yes. You're wearing a flowered sun dress and your hair is up in a ponytail."

"Good, so I'm coming toward you now." She saw him reach out with his left hand. "Here's my hand. Let's go to the beach house."

She watched as his left hand closed as though grasping her hand. A few beads of sweat formed on his brow and upper lip.

"Don't worry, Jared. I'm right here," she said, trying to reassure him.

"There it is," he said. "Can you go in with me?"

"I can go into the house and down the hall with you," she said. "However, when we reach the door to your memories, you must enter on your own."

"Whew." Jared let out a short nervous sound with his breath.

"Are we there?" asked Daphne.

Jared nodded. "I'm going in now. Will you wait for me in the hall?"

"Of course, if that's what you want," she said. "Let me know when you've entered the room and tell me what you see."

"I'm in and it's very dark," began Jared. "I see the railing by the staircase. There's a noise," he said, a look of terror on his face.

"Don't be afraid, Jared. Nothing can hurt you. I won't let it."

"But, but…there's the bat again. No, no!" he screamed. Jared sat bolt upright and jumped off the couch. He looked absolutely panic stricken.

"Jared!" Daphne shouted in surprise. "Jared, are you okay? Talk to me."

"No, I'm not okay," he shouted. "I'll never be okay again!"

Then he ran from the room.

Daphne had never had someone snap himself out of hypnosis like this. She knew it possible, but had never seen it. She ran after him afraid he might hurt himself in his haste. By the time she reached the front door, Jared was in his car screeching down the road.

"What on Earth happened, Daphne?" asked the receptionist.

"I'm not sure, but I have a bad feeling about it. Get Detective Mayhew on the phone for me."

Daphne went into her office and closed the door. So deep in thought, she trembled as she remembered the look on Jared's face. What had he seen that could have caused such a reaction? And, where was he going?

The phone rang causing her to jerk out of her thoughts. When she answered, she found Detective Mayhew on the other end.

"I normally wouldn't do this, but I'm very worried about Jared Matherson," she stated.

"Why, what happened?" he asked.

"I can't give you details, but I can tell you he saw something during hypnosis that terrified him. It was such a strong reaction that he woke out of hypnosis without my help and bolted out of here before I could stop him."

"So you don't know where he's going?" asked Detective Mayhew.

"No, I'm afraid I don't, but I was hoping you could check on him sometime today. Discretely find out if he's okay."

"Of course, I can," he said. "I'll give you a call when I locate him."

"That would be great," said Daphne in relief. "Talk to you soon."

Since Jared had left so abruptly, Daphne still had a half-hour before her next client arrived. She went to the break room for a cup of coffee. As she sipped the sweet cream-filled brew, her thoughts strayed back to Jared and she wondered if this therapy was doing the man more harm than good.

Chapter 56

After Daphne Swan's call this morning, Tyrone and Jacobs had tried desperately to find Jared. Their search was to no avail. He'd tried to display a calm demeanor when he spoke to Jared's aunt, but his call only sparked her concern. She'd told him Jared hadn't been sleeping well and rarely ate. She hadn't seen him since he left for his appointment.

Tyrone sat at his desk wishing Jared would stop the therapy. Maybe Reid Matherson knew what he was talking about when he said to leave Jared alone. Tyrone was beginning to think he shouldn't have recommended the hypnosis. Of course, once the police found his mother's car and remains, Jared's memories could have come flooding back on their own despite all of Reid's efforts to suppress them.

Tyrone still wanted to tie Reid Matherson to the Walsh murder. This case had even less evidence than Wendy Matherson's case. Deep in his gut, he knew someone else had to be helping Reid. There's no way he could have disposed of his wife's body and her car on his own.

"Mayhew," said Jacobs, pulling him from his thoughts. "The Matherson kid's on his way up. He wants to talk to you."

"Jared?"

"No, it's Ryan," said Jacobs. "Samuels says he's pretty anxious. She's bringing him up."

"I wonder what he wants," said Tyrone. "Do you think he's finally ready to tell us the truth about what went on that night?"

"Maybe," said Jacobs. "When I talked to him earlier to ask if he'd seen Jared, he seemed very upset. He loves his brother. Maybe he wants to tell us what happened so Jared can finally have peace of mind."

"Detective Mayhew," said a familiar female voice behind him. "I put Ryan Matherson in Interrogation Room Three."

Tyrone turned to see Officer Anne Samuels. "Okay, thanks Samuels."

Tyrone wrinkled his brow with curiosity. "Ryan was visibly upset when we found the bats. Perhaps he came by to tell us why he doesn't think his father committed these crimes? Or, maybe he wants to know if we found Jared—only one way to find out."

He walked into the interrogation room to find Ryan pacing and wringing his hands in much the same way his father had done days earlier. This seemed very uncharacteristic of the Ryan he'd come to know.

"Oh, thank God," said Ryan. "Detective Mayhew, I need to talk to you about what happened to my mom. It's very complicated. My father didn't kill her. You see she wasn't murdered, not really. It was all an accident, a terrible horrendous accident."

Tyrone saw the tears forming in Ryan's eyes. "Sit down. You need to take a deep breath and tell me what happened. If you don't mind, I want to turn on the cameras so we can record this."

Ryan sat down, giving his ascent for the recording by a nod of his head. Tyrone could hear him breathing deeply, head in hands.

Leaving the room, Tyrone went to the observation room and turned on the recording device.

"Okay, Mr. Matherson," Tyrone stated upon his return. "Why don't you start all over and tell me what you know about your mother's death. You say it wasn't murder, but an accident."

"Well, you see, Jared's nightmares mean something. I'm sure he's seeing things that happened that night. I stopped by Aunt Cindy's before I came here to see if he had come back after his therapy. He wasn't there. Aunt Cindy said that since he started the hypnosis, he's become more and more depressed. He's not eating. He's not sleeping. I just can't watch him go through this any longer and I can't let my dad take the fall."

"Did Jared see what happened?" asked Tyrone.

"Well, yeah," Ryan said hesitating.

"Take your time," said Tyrone, seeing the tension in Ryan's neck. "It's been ten years; a few more minutes won't hurt anything."

"I think it could," said Ryan. "I'm afraid for Jared. He's my baby brother. I don't want anything to happen to him."

"I have brothers and a baby sister myself, so I know where you're comin' from. But your mother deserves justice, so if you know anything that could put this case to rest, I need to hear it."

"She fell down the stairs...," said Ryan, but before he could say another word, the door burst open.

Lieutenant Terhune burst into the room. "Sorry about this, but we have a situation. Jared Matherson's in the lobby and he insists upon speaking with you, Mayhew."

"Why don't they just bring him up here?" asked Tyrone.

"I told you there's a situation," said the lieutenant. Tyrone got the hint this time and leapt from his chair.

Ryan Matherson stood up·shaking. "If it has to do with my brother, I have a right to know what's going on."

The lieutenant looked at Tyrone and then back at Ryan, sighing. "I'm sorry son, it's not good, and I want you to stay calm."

"How can I stay calm when you won't tell me what's happening," shouted Ryan.

"Chill out, man," said Tyrone. "The lieutenant here is just tryin' to keep things under control."

"Jared came in with a sawed off shot gun wired to his neck. The barrel is pointing at his chin and his finger is on the trigger. He's threatening suicide if Detective Mayhew doesn't come down to talk with him."

"Oh, my God!" Ryan said, tears streaming down his face. "This is what I was afraid of, Detective. That's why I came here today."

"We don't have time to listen to your story now," said Tyrone. "I've got to get down there and talk him out of this."

"I want to go with you," insisted Ryan.

"No," said the lieutenant. "It's too dangerous."

"He's not going to hurt me, and he might listen to me," said Ryan. "He and I have always been very close. I can reason with him."

"It might be worth a try, Lieutenant," suggested Tyrone. He knew very often that family members were able to convince relatives who threatened suicide to reconsider.

Lieutenant Terhune looked at each of them, and then agreed. "Alright. You can go down only as long as you stay out of the way and only speak to him when we direct you to do so. Is that clear?"

"Yes," said Ryan. "Now let's go before he does something stupid."

Chapter 57

Tyrone, Ryan and the lieutenant went to the elevator, no one saying a word in the short ride to the lobby. Tyrone could not help but wonder what had brought on Jared's desire to kill himself. What could he say to the boy to change his mind? He would just have to wait until Jared told him why he wanted to talk.

Tyrone looked at Ryan's terrified face, watching him take shallow breaths. He feared Ryan might pass out.

"Ryan," said Tyrone as the elevator descended. "Is there anything you can tell me that might help me diffuse the situation?"

"Yeah," he said as the elevator doors slid open. "Tell him it wasn't his fault. It was an accident."

Ryan moved towards the lobby at a quick pace. It was all Tyrone could do to keep up with him, leaving the lieutenant behind in their wake. When Ryan stopped abruptly, Tyrone nearly ran him over. He saw Ryan gaze in horror at his brother. Jared paced in a circle with his finger on the trigger surrounded by police officers. Jared had left no chance for anyone to tackle him and wrestle the gun away. Not with the method he'd used to wire the gun to his neck.

"You stay right here," Tyrone said to Ryan.

Lieutenant Terhune had caught up at this point. Tyrone took his weapon and handed it to the lieutenant. "I'm goin' over to see if I can calm him down. The way that thing is wired, he won't be able to shoot me with it."

"But I think he'll listen to me," Ryan implored.

"He asked for me," said Tyrone, trying not to be cruel. "Listen to my conversation with him. If I tell him his brother Ryan is here, then you approach slowly, very slowly. If you rush over there, it might startle him and he might accidentally pull the trigger. Understand?"

"Yes," said Ryan, his voice choking. "I don't want my brother to die."

"We don't want him to die either," said the lieutenant.

"Where the hell is Detective Mayhew?" screamed Jared.

Tyrone turned, walking toward him. "Hey, Jared, I'm right here. Sometimes it takes a couple of minutes for that danged elevator to move."

"Finally," Jared said in an irritated tone. "I need to talk to you. I need to tell you something important."

"I gathered as much," said Tyrone. "But, I don't know why you felt you had to come in here with a gun strapped to your neck. Why don't you take your finger off the trigger and we can get you out of that contraption."

"Not going to happen," said Jared.

"I don't understand," said Tyrone. "You trust me don't you?"

"I know you don't understand," Jared said, laughing half-heartedly. "Nobody could. I didn't even understand until today."

"What happened today?" asked Tyrone.

"I went to see Daphne this morning. You know, the one who's been hypnotizing me, trying to help me remember."

"I know who you mean. She called me to let me know you ran off and she was very concerned about you," said Tyrone. "Did you have some sort of memory during your session that upset you? Do you want to tell me about it?"

"Oh, yeah. It's a big one, too," said Jared, almost hysterical. He started to pace again then he caught sight of Ryan. "Hey bro!" he said, waving with his left hand. "Do *you* remember what happened to Mom?" he shouted.

Ryan looked at Lieutenant Terhune. The lieutenant reminded him to approach slowly and to join Tyrone.

"Hey, Jared," said Ryan, visibly shaking. "What's all this? We can talk about this without the gun. It doesn't have to be like this."

"You know, Ryan, don't you?" Jared began, biting his lip. "Thing is, I always trusted you. *You* always looked after me. *You* made sure nobody picked on me, made sure I ate dinner when Dad worked late. But you let me go on all these years thinking Mom just up and left us. *You* helped them brainwash me. You're just like Dad."

"Jared, please. We all wanted to protect you. Dad thought it was better for you not to remember. He told me they'd put you away. In order to stay together, we needed to keep it our family secret."

Jared whirled in a circle, shaking his head. Tyrone, terrified Jared would accidentally pull the trigger, put his hand on Ryan's shoulder and held his index finger to his mouth. He didn't want him to talk until he gave permission to proceed.

"Jared," said Tyrone. "I'm confused here. You said you wanted to talk to me. I think Ryan should shut up for a while so you can tell me what it is you remember."

He stopped moving and looked Tyrone in the eye. "You're

184 · M. E. May

absolutely correct, Detective Mayhew. I came here to talk to *you*, because *you* deserve to know the truth. Ryan and the rest of my worthless family had plenty of time to talk to me. They knew I was suffering, but didn't give a damn about anybody but themselves. My mother didn't even get a decent burial."

"I can see how upset you are," said Tyrone. "Just look at me and tell me what you came to say."

"I know who killed my mother," said Jared in a calm, scary tone.

"It was an accident," Ryan insisted.

"No it wasn't!" Jared screamed.

"Shut up or you'll have to leave," Tyrone snapped at Ryan. Ryan nodded and took a step back as he sobbed hysterically.

"So, if it wasn't an accident," said Tyrone. "Who killed your mother? Why would you want to die because of it?"

"Isn't it obvious, Detective Mayhew?" asked Jared, tears streaming down his cheeks. "I killed her. I murdered my own mother."

Tyrone took a quick look back at Ryan, who had fallen to his knees, holding his face in his hands. He couldn't believe what he'd just heard. *Jared?* How could it be Jared? He was only nine-years-old at the time.

"Is this something you remembered during your hypnosis?" Tyrone asked. "Are you sure it's a real memory?"

Jared nodded. "Yes, Detective, it finally worked. It took nearly two weeks, but we broke down the barriers my family so skillfully erected. Of course, I didn't tell Daphne everything I saw. I just couldn't. I had to go somewhere and think about it."

"So what happened?" asked Tyrone. "What did you remember?"

"I was nine-years-old and still afraid of the dark," Jared said and sniffed as his nose began to run from crying. "Stupid, huh?"

"Nah. Lots of people are afraid of the dark, even when they're adults," said Tyrone.

"There had been some break-ins in the neighborhood. I heard some noise downstairs and thought there was a robber," said Jared, staring blankly as though he was somewhere else. "Instead of waking my dad, I got my baseball bat and waited around the corner at the top of the stairs. When the robber got to the top, I swung my bat as hard as I could and down the stairs she went."

"You didn't know it was her. Ryan's right, it was an accident," said Tyrone.

"What difference does it make?" Jared responded angrily. "It wasn't a robber, it was *my mother*. I hit her leg; she lost her balance and fell backwards down the stairs. I screamed for my dad and he came running."

"Then what happened?"

"Dad went downstairs and I was still screaming. When Dad checked her, he said she was dead. By then Ryan and Tanner were out of bed. Ryan tried to get me to move away from the stairs, but all I could do was look at her and scream."

"It was a case of mistaken identity. You tried to protect your family," pleaded Tyrone. "It could have happened to anyone."

"But, it happened to me," said Jared, pounding his chest with his free hand and screwing up his face in pain. He was clearly agitated again, pacing and crying. "No wonder I couldn't remember. No wonder it was so easy for everybody to convince me I'd had a nightmare, that it wasn't real. I didn't want it to be real."

"Jared, I know you don't think so right now, but you can get through this," said Tyrone. "We can find people who can help you. Please take your finger off the trigger and let me take that thing off your neck."

Jared stopped pacing and looked at Tyrone. "Have you ever had to kill someone in your job?"

"Fortunately, I've never had to fire my weapon while on duty," stated Tyrone.

"Were you ever in the military?" asked Jared. "Did you ever kill an enemy?"

"No," said Tyrone, feeling more uneasy now.

Jared's demeanor had changed. He'd stopped crying and was a little too calm for Tyrone's taste.

"Then you can't really understand how I feel, can you?" said Jared. His expression was so sad, almost resigned. "At least if you ever decide to kill someone, it will be an enemy. This was my *mother*."

Before Tyrone could say another word, Jared Matherson pulled the trigger.

Tyrone stood there in disbelief unable to move as he watched Jared crumple to the ground. Officers were running towards Jared. One officer checked for his pulse then shook his head. He thought he heard Ryan Matherson screaming, begging to go to his brother. It was surreal. This wonderful young man who looked so much like his mother had accidentally caused her death. Then for some strange reason, his father thought it best to brainwash the boy and make his other under aged sons accomplices.

Unfortunately, the mind never forgets such traumas and Jared's was no exception. Eventually, no matter how ensconced his memories had become, they would reveal themselves. All those nightmares over the past ten years were his memories trying to sneak out in the middle of the night.

Turning, Tyrone saw two officers restraining a very distraught Ryan Matherson. All the voices and sounds jumbled into incomprehensible noise. His lieutenant led Tyrone to the elevator. He was in a daze, barely noticing anyone in particular in the crowd.

Still in shock, his thoughts wandered. How could Jared's father justify what he'd done? What was he thinking? Jared was a minor. He'd thought Wendy was an intruder. He was only nine for heaven's sake.

Still in a daze and not sure how he got to his desk, Tyrone looked up to see Jacobs hurrying towards him.

"Are you okay?" asked Jacobs.

"Not too good, buddy," he answered, tears of anger pooling in his eyes. "I've got to talk to the father and the other brother to get their stories. There's no point in them keeping their little secret any longer."

He related how Ryan had come in to tell him what really happened the night his mother disappeared, but Jared's arrival had interrupted them.

"Damn it!" spouted Jacobs. "What the fuck made them think a cover up was even necessary?"

"Don't know, Jacobs. But I sure as hell intend to find out."

Chapter 58

Two hours later, Tyrone sat across the table from Reid Matherson and his attorney. Tyrone had sent a patrol car to pick Reid up at work. As much as he disliked Reid, he didn't want him to hear the news of Jared's death on the radio or television. That was no way for any father to hear about the death of his child.

In his talk with Ryan after the suicide, he'd discovered someone helped Reid cover up Wendy's death, but he didn't know who it was. He'd overheard his dad talking to someone he called Sarge a few times, but he'd never met anyone by that name. Was Sarge Reid's accomplice? Was he so threatened by Jared's memories that he became desperate enough to kill?

"Mr. Matherson, I have some very disturbing news," said Tyrone, hesitating. He'd almost lost one of his boys. How do you tell a man his son just committed suicide?

"About two hours ago your son, Jared, came to the police station asking for me. As you may know, Jared has been seeing a hypnotherapist to help him remember the night his mother disappeared. He came to tell me he had remembered how his mother died."

"Oh God no," said Reid, clamping his hands to his head and looking defeated. "He was only nine. It was an accident. He thought she was a burglar. You can't throw him in jail."

Tyrone almost felt sorry for the guy. "I'm afraid that's not an issue. When Jared came here, he had a sawed-off shotgun strapped to his neck. After he confessed, he shot himself."

Reid gasped, his flesh turning pale. He held his hand over his heart and looked at his attorney.

"I'm sorry, Mr. Matherson. Jared is dead."

"No!" Reid shouted, looking from Tyrone to his lawyer. He pounded the table with his fist. "You're lying!"

"I wish I were," said Tyrone. "I liked Jared. He was a great kid."

"This is your fault," screeched Reid, the color rushing back to his face. He stood and pointed his finger at Tyrone. "You shouldn't have reopened this case. You should have left it alone. You murdered my son!"

"Reid, stop," advised his attorney, taking Reid's arm and pulling him back into his chair.

"Let me tell you something, Mr. Matherson," said Tyrone, all thoughts of sympathy vanishing. Then, keeping his demeanor calm when all he wanted to do was beat the hell out of this man, he continued. "None of this would have happened had you reported this properly. It was an accident. He was nine. You could have gotten therapy for him instead of coverin' it up and brainwashing the boy."

Reid began to wail in anguish. However, Tyrone wasn't finished with him.

"Now, I want you to tell me how everything went down so I have your spin on it. Sergeant Jacobs and I have already talked to Ryan, but Tanner clammed up."

"If Ryan told you the story, then that should suffice," said the attorney.

"There's one more thing," Tyrone said, looking the attorney in the eye. "Ryan told us there's a friend of Reid's involved. Someone who helped cover it up. Who is Sarge, Mr. Matherson?"

Reid's face was red and soaked with tears of grief. He pursed his lips and shook his head sitting back in his chair with arms crossed. Tyrone could see he had no intention of giving up his accomplice.

"You might want to have a nice long talk with your client," said Tyrone. "We're pretty sure this friend is the one who killed Serena Walsh. Mr. Matherson is already facing charges of attempting to murder a police officer and assault with a deadly weapon for shooting my six-year-old son. If somebody else did this, he needs to give him up."

"Are you listening to Detective Mayhew, Reid?" asked his attorney. Reid continued his closed stance, tears streaming down his tense, angry face. "I can probably get a deal with the D. A., if you cooperate."

"Of course, the charges for murderin' your wife will be dropped, but we'll be addin' illegal disposal of a corpse and interferin' with a police investigation. Like your attorney said, give up your conspirator and I'm sure the prosecutor will be willing to negotiate a reduced sentence on the other charges. I'll go now so the two of you can talk."

As Tyrone was about to place his hand on the doorknob, Reid spoke up. "Wait."

Tyrone turned and walked back toward the table.

Reid looked at his attorney. "Why should I take the fall for this guy? I never asked him to hurt anyone. That was his idea."

The attorney turned his gaze to Tyrone. "If the prosecutor is willing to cut us a deal, Reid will tell you everything he knows."

"What about my elder sons?" asked Reid.

"Ryan was only twelve at the time. He obeyed you because he didn't want Jared to go to an institution. He also came to me voluntarily to tell me what happened. That will go a long way with the judge and prosecutor."

"And Tanner?"

"Your attorney will need to do some talkin' with the prosecutor. Tanner was sixteen at the time. Many boys that age are tried as adults. I'm sure Tanner trusted you to do what was best so I hope the prosecutor will take that into consideration. Of course, if he tells his version of the events, he might be shown some leniency."

"Thank you, Detective Mayhew," said the attorney in a dismissive tone. "Now if you'll arrange for me to talk to the D. A. we'll get this under way."

Jacobs was on the other side of the door catching Tyrone by surprise. "You tryin' to give me a heart attack, jackass?"

"Real nice," said Jacobs. "I wanted to find out how it was going."

Tyrone wasn't fooled. He knew Jacobs was worried about him. It's not every day you watch a youngster blow his own brains out.

"Matherson's ready to deal. He doesn't want to go down with his co-conspirator," said Tyrone. "Once we've got this Sarge in custody, I'll be able to bring my family home."

"I know it's only been a few hours, but I miss Erica already," said Jacobs. "Are you sure he'll give the guy up?"

"I'm sure he'll do it now," said Tyrone. "In a sick twisted way, this whole thing was designed to protect Jared. At least that's what Reid had convinced himself it was."

"Let's go see who's available at the D. A.'s office," said Jacobs.

"The faster we get his statement, the quicker we can put this all behind us."

Chapter 59

Prosecutor, Natalie Ralston, wasn't able to get all the permissions needed to make the deal with Reid Matherson until the following morning. Tyrone had made arrangements for her to meet with him, Reid and Reid's attorney at 10:00 a.m.

Tyrone was waiting in the lobby of the jail when he saw Natalie approach in her dark blue suit, lavender shirt and heels—the ultimate professional. They went through all the jailhouse formalities and were led to the visitor's room.

There sat Reid looking ten years older with his attorney looking grim. After the formal introductions, they all sat down and Natalie opened her briefcase and extracted a document.

"Mr. Matherson, I understand you want to give us information on someone who helped you conceal your wife's death and who may have committed the murder of Serena Walsh and who injured Detective Mayhew's son," said Natalie.

"That's correct," said the attorney as Reid continued to stare blankly at the table.

"I've spoken with my superiors and this is what we can do," said Natalie as she opened her file. "If you tell us everything, including the identity of your accomplice, we will charge you with illegal disposal of a corpse and obstruction of justice. You will serve six months in jail and then be placed on probation for two years. Are these terms agreeable?"

Tyrone watched as Reid's attorney advised him. He couldn't imagine why Reid thought burying his wife's body instead of calling the proper authorities was a good solution. Then to involve your eldest sons in a cover up on the premise of protecting his youngest son, the man was an idiot. He'd be a fool not to take this deal.

Reid finally looked up from the table with red rimmed eyes, speaking directly to Natalie. "What's going to happen to my sons?"

"Tanner realized he needed to cooperate and told us his version of the story," said Natalie. "We've decided that as a minor and under your influence, he wasn't thinking as an adult, but as a child. He will be charged with the illegal disposal of a corpse and obstruction with time served and a year's probation. That means he has to stay in the state of Indiana during his probationary period."

"But he's going to school in Ohio," said Reid.

"A small price to pay," said Tyrone. "Don't you think so, Mr. Matherson?"

"What will happen to Ryan?" asked Reid.

"He was only twelve," said Natalie, frowning at Reid. "We won't be charging him."

Reid breathed a sigh and his face relaxed. "Okay, I'll tell you everything."

Natalie pulled a small digital recorder from her briefcase. She recorded all the usual and then asked Reid to tell her what happened.

"It was about 2:00 in the morning when a loud noise and the sound of Jared screaming woke me. When I got into the hallway, I saw Jared standing at the top of the stairs trembling with a baseball bat in his hand and Wendy was at the bottom of the stairs.

"I went down to her. Her eyes were open and her neck was twisted in an unnatural way. I tried to find her pulse and couldn't. Jared was still screaming and the other boys came out. I told Ryan to take Jared to his room and told Tanner to bring a tarp from the garage. I could still hear Jared screaming," Reid said, tears flowing now.

"I ran upstairs and told Jared it was going to be okay. Then I gave him one of Wendy's sleeping pills and told Ryan to stay with him. I had to protect him. I thought if I got rid of Wendy's body it would all be forgotten."

Reid wiped his eyes on his sleeve and went on. "I had Tanner help me put Wendy in the trunk of her car, which I drove while he drove my car to the reservoir. I dug her grave, Tanner had been involved enough."

Natalie interrupted his tale. "So we know you and Tanner disposed of your wife's body and then you reported her missing two days later, correct?"

"Yes," said Reid.

"Who helped you keep your secret, Mr. Matherson?" asked Natalie. "Who is this *Sarge*?"

Reid gulped and closed his eyes. "I served in Viet Nam at the end of the conflict. Of course, that didn't mean we weren't getting shot at. I saved his life so he owed me."

Tyrone shook his head in frustration. "We don't need your life's story. We need a name."

"It was Percy Grimes."

Chapter 60

Tyrone nearly fell out of his chair. He stared at Reid for what seemed like hours. The shock of hearing him actually say that Grimes helped cover this up threw him into a temporary state of shock.

Suddenly everything made sense. The lack of follow up, witness interviews, no CSI sent to process the house—it all tied together now. Tyrone had been a rookie in the department and was trying to fit in. How could he have missed this? How could he let this guy pull the wool over his eyes?

Cindy Woods and her brother never trusted Grimes. Serena Walsh had tried to tell Tyrone that Grimes wasn't treating her evidence with respect.

Tyrone rose from his chair and looked around the room. "I've got to go back to the station and call Cincinnati P. D. and have him picked up."

"He might not be there," said Reid.

"What do you mean?" shouted Mayhew, no longer able to keep his cool.

"He said he was going to scare the psychic and you, but didn't say anything about anyone getting hurt," said Reid. "I know him. He's desperate. I don't think he'll stop now."

Tyrone kept the table between them, but got right into Reid's face. "You mean you think my family is still in danger?"

"That's exactly what I mean."

Tyrone decided he'd heard enough. He flew through the jail and retrieved his things. He ran to the station and found Jacobs.

Panting, Tyrone said, "We've got to go."

Jacobs looking nonplussed said, "Catch your breath. Where are we going?"

"Brown County."

"What's going on?" said Lieutenant Terhune as he approached their desks. "I just got a call from the jail saying you ran out of there like a bat out of hell."

"Lieutenant," said Tyrone, taking in a deep breath to slow his heart rate. "Matherson just told me who helped him cover up his actions. It's Percy Grimes."

"What?" said the lieutenant.

Jacobs ran his fingers through his hair and paced. "A cop? One of our own?"

"Seems Matherson saved his ass in Nam so he decided to help him out," said Tyrone. "Lieutenant, Jacobs and I need to go to the cabin to make sure Jada, Erica and the kids are okay."

"Give her a call and make sure she's okay," said the Lieutenant. "We'll get somebody from the sheriff's department to keep an eye on them."

"But, Lieutenant...."

Terhune didn't let Tyrone finish. "I understand that you're concerned, but we need to find out where Grimes is and try to pick him up before he does anything else. Put your wife and Barnes on alert and we'll ask the Sheriff to put a guy out at the cabin."

"Yes, sir," said Tyrone as respectfully as he could with his head and heart pounding.

He braced himself to call Jada. At least now, they had a name and a face instead of an invisible enemy.

"Hey, honey," said his wife's sweet voice. "Why are you calling me now? You went to work today, didn't you?"

"Yeah, Jada, I'm at work."

"You sound terrible," she said. "Is something going on? You're not blaming yourself for that boy's suicide, are you?"

"I am feelin' bad about Jared, but that's not why I called." He paused for a moment. "Honey, Reid Matherson told us who helped him cover this whole thing up. It was Percy Grimes."

There was momentary silence from her end of the phone. "You mean to tell me, that a former police officer shot my baby?"

He could hear the anger in her voice despite the low tone. "Yes. We're huntin' him down now, but I've got to tell you that we're gonna take extra precautions with you all. The lieutenant is contacting the Sheriff's office now to make arrangements for a car to be out at the cabin to keep an eye on all of you."

"Sheriff Holden has been very kind to us," said Jada. "He doesn't have a lot of deputies. I hate to ask him to put somebody out here to babysit."

"It's just temporary," said Tyrone, trying to assure her. "Reid's convinced that Grimes isn't finished. Reid said he didn't want anyone to be hurt, that Grimes went rogue."

"Tyrone, I love you. Please be careful."

"I love you, too," he said, fighting back a tear. "Let me talk to

Erica."

Tyrone explained the situation to Erica and said Jacobs was sending photos of Grimes to her and to the Sheriff's Office so they could be on the lookout.

"Don't worry, Tyrone," she said. "I won't let anything happen to Jada or the kids."

"Thanks," he said. "Once we get things settled here, Jacobs and I will head down there. Hopefully, we'll have Grimes in custody before the night is through."

Chapter 61

The morning and early afternoon dragged on as Tyrone waited for word on Grimes. He tried to keep busy by typing up his final report on the Wendy Matherson case. He tried to picture Jared in Heaven being held and comforted by his mother. At least that gave Tyrone a little glimmer of hope in the midst of these tragic events.

"When do you think Lieutenant Terhune will let us out of here?" asked Jacobs.

Tyrone's thoughts had taken him so far into the zone he'd nearly forgotten that Jacobs was there. "I don't know. What I do know is I'm worn out from this mess. I miss my family and I want to go see for myself that they're okay."

"Terhune said there's a deputy at the house keeping an eye out and the Sheriff's keeping tabs on them," said Jacobs, furrowing his brow as he closed a file.

"I know, but it doesn't seem like enough. Don't you want to be there, too?"

"Of course, I do. I can't stand the thought of Erica going through another situation like Emerson."

Tyrone looked at the clock on his computer. It was 3:00 pm. He looked up to see Lieutenant Terhune approaching. He stood in anticipation and Jacobs followed suit.

"Okay guys, there's nothing new on Grimes," said Terhune. "Wife says he's been gone for a week, supposedly on a fishing trip with one of his buddies. The buddy is at home and doesn't have any idea where Grimes might be."

"So, what now?" Tyrone asked, shifting his weight.

"It's Friday and I know you're anxious to get down there. You two go ahead and take off. I know you'll feel better once you're with them."

"Thanks, Lieutenant," said Tyrone. He breathed a sigh of relief and turned to Jacobs. "We'll stop and pick up some of our things and then head down."

"One more thing," said the lieutenant. "No speeding. You need to get down there in one piece and without irritating the local law enforcement."

"Yes, sir," said Tyrone. He motioned for Jacobs to follow him.

"If we stop at my place first, I've got a bag all packed," said Jacobs.

"Really?" Tyrone raised an eyebrow in astonishment at him.

"Well, if all this other stuff hadn't happened, I was going to ask you if we could go down and surprise them this weekend."

"And you assumed I would say yes?"

"You said you missed them," said Jacobs, blushing. "I thought I'd talk Erica into going to one of those nice little inns in Nashville with me so you could spend some time with Jada and the kids."

"How thoughtful of you," said Tyrone, smiling and watching his partner squirm. "At least your assumption will save us some time."

"Okay, well my car's on the north side of the parking lot."

"I don't think so," said Tyrone. "I'm drivin'. I know how to get there and your old man methods make me nervous."

"But...."

"I'm drivin'," Tyrone said more sternly. "Now let's get out of here before the traffic gets bad."

Chapter 62

Daphne Swan had canceled her last three appointments. She'd been terribly upset since she'd heard about Jared's suicide. Logically, she knew it wasn't her fault. She couldn't save everyone. However, her human, emotional self couldn't get past the guilt. Therefore, she made an appointment to see her own therapist. As she waited in the reception area, thoughts of Jared's reaction during his last appointment haunted her.

"Daphne," said the receptionist. "Dr. Carson will see you now."

Daphne nodded and walked down the hallway to Dr. Henry Carson's office. He stood as she entered the room. Placing an arm around her shoulders, he guided her to a plush leather chair.

"Hello, Henry. It's been awhile."

"It's been a very long time since you've had a case this rough," he said. "I'm so sorry about Jared Matherson. Shall we get comfortable and talk this through."

She kicked off her shoes and pulled her feet up into the chair, which was big enough for two people. Then the unwanted tears began.

"I'm sorry, Henry. This one really got to me. I thought I was helping him, but he only got worse."

"As hard as it is, let's work on this logically," he said. "This boy's problems began ten years ago when his father let panic rule his judgment."

Daphne grabbed a tissue from the box on the end table and wiped her face. "Well intentioned, but extremely detrimental to his entire family," she said.

Dr. Carson smiled. "Precisely. So, if we look at Jared's initial trauma, we know as therapists that the sooner the trauma is treated, the better the chance of recovery."

"Of course," said Daphne. "It's like rinsing off a wound, then covering it with a bandage. It may be out of sight, but that doesn't mean it's healing."

"And, that wound can be causing the injured a great deal of pain, but we won't know why until we take the bandage away."

Daphne nodded and looked into Henry's kind silver eyes. "By the time I took the bandage off, it was too late. It was so *infected*, he couldn't survive."

"That young man not only felt that sudden, extremely painful realization of what he'd done, he realized his father and brothers had deceived him. Even his beloved brother, Ryan, had lied to him."

"He felt he had nothing to live for," she said, looking at her hands in her lap.

"Plus, on some level, he may have wanted to punish the rest of the family for what they'd put him through. His death released him from all the pain, but inflicted it on all those he left behind."

Daphne looked up at Henry and smiled. She leaned forward and touched his arm. "Thank you, my friend. You always know how to bring me back from the depths."

"It's my pleasure," he said. "Now, go home, take a nice hot bath, read a book with some good cheese and a nice glass of wine. Take care of yourself this weekend."

"Good advice, Dr. Carson," she said, some of her burden feeling lighter. "Next time I call, it will be to plan a dinner with you and your lovely wife."

"Don't forget, this may take some time. One visit may not be enough. Come back and see me if you need to do so," he said. "You must take care of Daphne in order to heal and be able to help others do the same." He rose from his chair and escorted her to the hallway. She turned to give him one last wave before going out the door.

Daphne reached her car and realized she hadn't pulled the keys out of her purse. She was sure they'd dropped to the bottom and was digging for them when someone came up behind her. She felt something hard pressed into the middle of her lower back. She gasped and dropped her purse.

"Don't move or scream," he said in a low gruff voice.

"What do you want?" she asked, heart thumping wildly.

"I want you to come with me," he said. "I have a gun, so be very calm and I won't have to use it."

"Okay," she said, barely able to breathe. She started to lean down to retrieve her purse.

"Leave it," he growled.

"But my money and credit cards are in there."

"I don't want your damned money," he said, grabbing her arm so tightly she thought he'd cut off the circulation. "Walk."

He led her a few feet to an alley. She panicked at the thought of what he might do to her. If robbery wasn't his motive, was he going to rape her? *Kill her?*

Then she saw the black sedan up ahead. He was going to take her somewhere. There was no one around to ask for help. Even if she tried to run, it was too far to get to the street without being caught or shot.

He released her arm and poked her with the gun. She heard a chirp and the trunk opened. Terror stopped her in her tracks.

"Please don't put me in the trunk," she begged. "Why are you doing this to me?"

"Get in," he commanded.

"Please, I beg you. Don't…"

The pain of the gun butt hitting her skull was excruciating. She fell to the ground, dizzy and disoriented. He grabbed her arm and jerked her up to her feet. She felt the sharp pain as her ribcage hit the lip of the trunk. His hands seemed to be everywhere. She wanted to speak, but didn't seem able to do so.

She was lying on something scratchy, her eyes out of focus and having difficulty keeping them open. Her wrists felt strange and she could barely move. The last thing she saw was him smiling at her as he put something over her mouth. Then everything went dark.

Chapter 63

Tyrone hurried from his sister's house with a lumpy duffle bag in hand. He hadn't packed it well and wasn't even sure if he'd grabbed a toothbrush. He was much too anxious to get to the cabin and make sure everyone was okay. He hit the trunk button, flung his bag in, and slammed it shut.

"It's about time you got your sorry butt out here," said Jacobs.

Tyrone scowled at him.

"I was just pulling your leg," said Jacobs.

"I wish you'd learn the appropriate time to use that lousy sense of humor of yours."

"Well, you're no Chris Rock, yourself," said Jacobs. He turned to look out the window.

"I'm sorry," said Tyrone. "I'm just worried that asshole Grimes might get there first."

"Did you tell Ophelia what was going on?"

"No," said Tyrone. "I didn't want to worry her. I just told her we were goin' down to surprise our ladies for the weekend. I think she bought it."

"I don't know, Tyrone," said Jacobs, looking him up and down. "She's a pretty smart woman. I bet she'll be calling the judge before we even get to the end of her street."

"Yeah, I know," said Tyrone. "Get your seat belt on so we can get goin'."

"Yes, Mother," said Jacobs smirking.

By the time they'd reached Interstate 65 on the south side of Indianapolis, Jacobs was quietly snoring. They'd left at the perfect time. Tyrone was happy they'd beat the rush hour traffic out of the city by at least fifteen minutes. He listened to Jacobs's rhythmic breathing as he daydreamed about having his wife safely in his arms.

The landscape along most of Interstate 65 was dull. Although he'd promised the lieutenant not to break the speeding laws, he found himself doing almost ninety several times. It was easy to do with all the flat farmland. That is until he reached Brown County. Here it became hilly and lush. He knew why his sister and brother-in-law had decided to purchase a place down here as a getaway. It was peaceful and beautiful and he wanted it to remain that way.

Jacobs woke when his cell phone rang. Tyrone heard him say, "Are you serious?"

Tyrone caught Jacobs' eye and knew something was seriously wrong. Tyrone asked, "What's goin' on?"

Jacobs waved him off as he continued to listen. "Got it, Lieutenant. I'll tell him." He put the cell in his pocket and turned to Tyrone.

"Lieutenant Terhune says that Daphne Swan is missing."

"Are you f'in' kiddin' me?" asked Tyrone. "How do they know for sure?"

"She went to see a shrink friend of hers early this afternoon. When he left the office, he noticed her car was still there. Her purse was on the ground."

"Grimes!"

Chapter 64

"Mama, Aunt Ophelia is the best, isn't she," said Reggie. "She took care of everybody when I was in the hospital, she let us use her cabin, and she said we could stay with her while they're fixing the house." He loved his Aunt Ophelia. She didn't have any children of her own yet and had always spoiled Reggie and his brothers.

"Yes, young man," said his mother. "Your daddy's sister is a very special person."

"You're really lucky to have such a great family," said Erica as she drove the minivan up the gravel lane.

"Do you like Aunt Ophelia, Erica?" asked Reggie, looking at her in anticipation.

"Yes," answered Erica. "I think she is super nice."

"Do you have brothers and sisters, Erica?" asked Malcolm.

"I have a brother, but he lives way out in Seattle, Washington, near the Pacific Ocean."

"Wow!" said Malcolm. "I never seen the ocean. Have you seen it?"

"I never have seen the ocean," said Jada, correcting him.

"Really, Mama," said Malcolm. "Me, neither."

Jada shook her head and smiled at Erica.

Reggie giggled because his mama was always correcting their grammar. She told him if he wanted to be president someday, he'd better know how to speak properly.

"Once," said Erica in answer to Malcolm's question. "My parents and I went to visit my brother when he first moved there. It's a really pretty place. If you ever get the chance you should go."

"Mama, can we go?" Malcolm asked unable to sit still despite being strapped in his car seat. "You said you never saw the ocean neither."

"That's not what I meant, Malcolm. I was trying to teach you proper grammar," his mother answered. She turned and Reggie pointed at his brother's confused face.

"Maybe we'll go someday," said his mother. "Now sit still. You don't want to distract Erica while she's driving. We're almost there."

"Look Mama," said Reggie tensing at the sight. "Did you see a man walkin' through the trees?"

"No sweetie, I didn't," said Jada. "Maybe it's the sheriff."

"Yeah, goof ball," said Darryl who up to now had been rather quiet. "Who else would be here? If you really saw anybody."

"Don't call me a goof ball!" said Reggie, throwing a small rubber ball at his brother's face. He didn't like it when Darryl tried to make him look stupid.

"Cut it out," Darryl protested. "You're lucky you're all bandaged up or I'd kick your…."

"Darryl Alexander Mayhew," shouted his mother. "I hope you weren't about to say what I thought you were about to say."

"No, Mama," said Darryl with innocence.

"Yeah, right," said Reggie. He knew exactly what Darryl was about to say, because he'd heard it before, *and* he wasn't ready to let go of this conversation.

"Okay, boys, settle down," his mother demanded. "I'm not going to put up with this behavior. You hear me?"

"Yes, Mama," they said in unison then stuck their tongues at one another.

"I saw that," she exclaimed, then looked out the window.

Erica pulled the minivan into the driveway. Jada got out and helped her youngest boys out of the van while Darryl released his sister from her car seat. He gently handed her to his mother.

"Darryl grab that bag for me, please."

"Mama! There's that man again," squealed Reggie. He saw a man approaching—a man with a gun!

"Okay everybody," said the man. "Let's go inside."

Chapter 65

Tyrone gave the road his full attention and sped up. "What time did she go missing?"

"Lieutenant said around 3:15 this afternoon," said Jacobs. "According to this Dr. Carson, they met at about 2:30 p.m., talked for about forty minutes and then she left. He found her car at 5:45 p.m."

"I didn't even think about Daphne," said Tyrone. He slammed his open hands on the steering wheel a couple of times. "Damn it, why didn't I realize he might go after her, too?"

"You planning to take on that responsibility, too?" asked Jacobs. "You aren't responsible for what Grimes is doing. You said that Matherson indicated Grimes was out of control. Your first thoughts and priority was to make sure Erica, Jada and the kids were safe."

Tyrone's head spun with angst. "Where would he have taken her? He crept into Serena Walsh's house in the middle of the night. This guy is losing it."

"Yeah," said Jacobs, looking worried.

Tyrone's gut clenched. He had a sinking feeling that something else was about to go awry.

"We've got to get out to the cabin," said Tyrone.

Tyrone's cell phone rang. He saw "Unknown" in the caller ID. He decided to turn on the speaker so Jacobs could listen in.

"Hello," said Tyrone.

He was greeted with that same ominous electronic voice he'd heard when he went to visit Reggie in the hospital.

"What do you want, Grimes?" asked Tyrone, tensing with fearful anticipation.

"Ah, so you finally cracked the case, or should I say you cracked Reid."

"What do you want?" Tyrone repeated.

"I think it's more a matter of what do *you* want," said Grimes.

"I don't have time for riddles," Tyrone growled. "In case you haven't heard, the Matherson case has been solved. Now that you've proven useless in helpin' Reid protect Jared, you're damn straight he turned on you. You need to turn yourself in."

"I've heard about Jared's suicide, it's all over the news," said Grimes. "I did my part to protect him for ten years. You get involved with him and he doesn't even last a whole month. If you'd done what I asked, he might still be alive."

Tyrone refused to tell him what he wanted to hear. Of course he felt guilty, who wouldn't? He wasn't going to give this bastard the pleasure of knowing how he felt.

"What did you do with Daphne Swan?"

"Oh, did you lose her, too," said Grimes.

"I'm gonna hang up now. I'm done with your games."

"But Daphne and your family aren't. Oh, and there's that nice homicide detective whose been hanging out with them. Barnes, right?"

Tyrone and Ben looked at one another. He knew Ben's heart must be racing, because his was about to jump out of his chest.

"What are you talking about?"

"I'm at the cabin, Detective. The one your sister and the judge own. You know the place where you've been stashing them. I've been watching them for days and now it's time to play."

"If you as much as touch one of my kids or my wife, I'll kill you with my bare hands," snarled Tyrone. His pulse doubled. He was sweating now and his mouth was dry.

"Come and get them, Detective Mayhew," the voice taunted. "By the way, you have a beautiful wife and her guard dog isn't too bad looking either," he said, and then the line went dead.

Tyrone tried to redial the number. It went directly to a generic voicemail. This guy had no intention of answering the phone. He wanted to terrorize Tyrone and it was working.

"Shit," Tyrone yelled, slapping his hand on the steering wheel.

"Tyrone, we've got to get out there," said Jacobs, his voice shaking and his eyes wide as saucers.

Tyrone closed his eyes. "I have to focus. I have to treat this as if it was someone else's family. We have to call for back up," he said. He dialed 911.

"911, what is your emergency?" said a confident female voice.

"I need help out at Judge Norman Jackson's cabin in Brown County."

"Do you have an address?"

"No, I just know how to get there. Somebody's holdin' two women and four children hostage up there."

"Alright, sir," she said gently. "I need for you to stay calm. What's your name?"

"Tyrone Mayhew. I'm a Missing Person Detective from

Indianapolis. My sister and her husband own the cabin. It's about fifteen miles east of Nashville, not too far off of State Road 46, in Bracken Place," said Tyrone trying his best not to explode. He had to keep thinking like a cop. "I believe it's cabin 14."

"Okay, I've got the Sheriff's department and a state S.W.A.T. team on their way. They'll find the location, just stay calm, Detective. Where are you now?"

"We just passed Nashville. My partner and I are going out there."

"Please don't do that, sir. Do you know who has them?"

"Yes, his name is Percy Grimes. He's a retired cop who got mixed up in something. I can't explain it all now, it's a long story and we're wasting time. He's wanted for murder in Indianapolis so he won't hesitate to kill again."

"Okay."

There was a pause and Tyrone could hear someone talking to the dispatcher. "I just got the location of the cabin. I know you're anxious to get them out of there, but you need to wait for the sheriff's deputies and S.W.A.T. to arrive."

Tyrone hung up the phone and looked at Jacobs. Tyrone's phone began to ring, but he didn't bother to look at it. He knew it would be the 911 dispatcher trying to call him back.

"Shouldn't you answer that?" asked Jacobs.

"Hell no," he said aloud. "I'm not waitin' for this son-of-a-bitch to kill one of my babies. No way."

Chapter 66

Daphne's eyes fluttered as she desperately tried to wake herself. Where was she? Why couldn't she move?

When she finally opened her eyes, it was dark except for a strange red glow. Then it hit her. That man had put her in the trunk of his car.

She wanted to scream, but there was something keeping her mouth shut. It wasn't a gag, but something stuck to her skin. Her hands tied behind her back, she tried to move her legs apart but found them bound as well.

Terror pulsed through her. How long had she been unconscious? Where was he taking her? She hadn't recognized him; could he be related to one of her patients?

It felt and sounded as though the car had left the paved road and was now on gravel. A few seconds later, the vehicle stopped, the engine went silent, and the red glow ceased plunging her into darkness.

What now? Had they reached their destination? What was he going to do next?

She heard the car door open and slam, and the driver walk away. All was silent except for the crunching of his walk. Then all was quiet.

The waiting in the silence only caused her to think more about what he might do to her. Her head was throbbing from connecting with that gun butt and from the horror of her situation. Thinking was not her best friend at the moment.

Then she heard a male voice. "Hey officer, I'm a bit lost. I was looking for cabin twelve and think I took a wrong turn."

Another male voice responded. "You passed it about a mile down that way. If you turn around and go down the hill...."

Daphne heard a loud thump and a moan. Then she heard two pings and silence until the crunching started again. The red of what must be tail lights came back and she heard more sounds of gravel under her.

Once more the car stopped and the crunching resumed. Then the chirp of the automatic trunk release. When the lid opened, a bright light was shining in her face, making her squint.

"Dr. Swan, I presume," he said, in what she thought was an attempt at humor. He ripped the tape from her mouth. "Glad to see you're awake. Welcome to my party. All of the guests tonight will be here to pay the price for what happened to Jared Matherson. Now, let's get you inside before you catch a nasty cold."

"You knew Jared?" she said, her throat so dry her voice squeaked.

"His daddy and I go way back," he said. "He saved my life. Now shut up or I'll get you a new piece of duct tape for those lovely lips of yours." He pulled out a knife and her eyes bulged as she thought he was about to slit her throat. Instead, he cut whatever was binding her legs together.

He grabbed her roughly by the left arm pulling it so hard it wrenched her right shoulder. She cried out in pain. He pulled her out with no regard to preventing her further injury. Dropping her to the ground like a sack of potatoes, she struggled to catch her breath.

Something sharp had bitten through her trousers, scratching her thigh. Daphne felt something warm and wet soak into the cloth.

She struggled through the pain to try to keep from showing her total terror. "So, what's your name?"

He turned on her fiercely. "I told you to shut up. You'll find out soon enough."

Taking both of Daphne's arms this time; he jerked her up onto her feet. "Get moving," he said. "We'll knock on the door like a couple of lost souls. I'm sure they'll let us in, and then the party can begin."

Daphne did as she was told, stumbling from time-to-time. She could hear the snapping of branches under her feet. When they reached the steps, she stopped momentarily to get her balance. He forcefully pulled her up the steps by her right arm and a pain shot through her shoulder. She tried desperately not to cry out as she was unsure how he would react.

The lights in the cabin were shining brightly through the curtains. They stood at the doorway knocking, but no one answered.

Her captor looked around, and then cursed. "Why doesn't anything go as planned? I guess we'll have to find a way in and wait for our guests."

He pushed her up against the door and told her to stay. He rooted around the flower pots and finally came up with a key.

"People are so stupid," he said, smiling. "Don't they know that's the first place a criminal is going to look?"

They went into the cabin and it took a moment for her eyes to adjust. He pushed her onto the couch. Now she finally got a really good look at her assailant.

He was less than six foot tall, but very muscular for a man of his age. Gray hair and mustache.

Pulling a wide roll of duct tape from a duffle bag, he taped her legs together again. He pushed her by her left shoulder into the back cushion of the couch. This time she couldn't help but cry out, tears rolling down her cheeks.

"You broads just don't listen, do you?"

He took a strip of duct tape and forced it across her mouth so roughly she could feel her lower lip burst against her teeth. She tasted something warm and metallic leaking onto her tongue.

Going back to his duffle bag, he pulled out something she couldn't see. When he turned around, Daphne saw the hypodermic needle. She struggled against her bonds and tried desperately to protest.

"If you'd been a good girl, I wouldn't have to do this," he said. "This is just something to calm your nerves. Don't worry; I'll be able to wake you when the others arrive."

The man didn't bother to use an alcohol swab or even to find exposed skin. He jammed the needle into Daphne's thigh and she could feel the warm release of the drugs into her pain-ridden muscle.

"Nighty, night," he said.

She kept watching him in disbelief, wondering if she'd fallen asleep and this was a horrible nightmare. Then her muscles began to relax and her eyes blurred. Daphne fought desperately to stay awake, but it was no use.

Finally giving in, she closed her eyes wondering if this would be her last slumber.

Chapter 67

"What are we going to do, Tyrone?" asked Ben sounding resigned. "I can't stand it that Erica has been placed in this position."

Tyrone felt a pang of guilt. He'd tried to talk Erica out of coming down here, but she and Jada had insisted. Tyrone parked his car in a wooded area just five hundred feet from the cabin. It was dark and very hard to see through the dense forest of trees.

"I've got some supplies in the trunk," said Tyrone. "He won't be able to handle both of us. Opening the trunk, Tyrone retrieved two Glocks from a lock box and found a couple of small flashlights.

He tried to keep his breathing steady, but terror tore at his chest. It was horrendous enough when he'd heard someone shot Reggie. Now this maniac had his whole family, Erica and Daphne. Waiting wasn't an option. They had to stop Grimes now.

"When we get close to the house, you go to the right and I'll go to the left," said Tyrone. "Try not to use the flashlight unless it's absolutely necessary."

Jacobs nodded and they began to walk toward the cabin.

It was hard to walk quietly with all the dead branches and leaves left from last fall to crunch under foot. No matter how hard they tried, every step disrupted the silence of the woods. Scanning the area, Tyrone saw it. He looked at Jacobs and nodded toward the cabin. Ben nodded back and made his way toward the right-hand side of the place.

There were lights on inside, but all the curtains were drawn. As Tyrone drew nearer, he found it much too quiet. He glanced to his left and saw what looked like a Sheriff's car at the edge of the woods a few feet from the driveway. The car door was open and someone was lying on the ground in what looked like a brown uniform. Tyrone wondered if the man was still alive.

Grimes had obviously disposed of their protection. His heart quickened as his thoughts strayed to the idea that his family could already be dead. This crazy son-of-a-bitch didn't seem to care who he killed at this point. This seemed more like payback than anything.

Tyrone froze. He thought he heard a noise to his left. It was dark now and much harder to see. It couldn't be Jacobs. He couldn't have made his way all the way around yet. He pressed himself to the side of the cabin. He stood listening for a sound, any sound. Nothing.

Tyrone decided he should go around the house and try to get in through the back. He could try a bedroom window.

Again, a sound interrupted his thoughts. He squinted, trying to see through the darkness, holding his breath for fear the perpetrator might hear him.

He jumped as something came rushing from the woods. He stumbled backward catching on the side of the cabin to keep from falling.

To his relief, the sound came from a deer. Tyrone blew out a long breath and wanted to laugh, but knew he must keep his silence. Then a sharp pain on the back of his head sent him down to the ground face first. His gun flew out of his hand. Dizzy and barely able to move, he tried to look at his attacker. The fuzzy image held what looked like a baseball bat. He was wearing black and the darkness would not reveal his face.

"Good to see you, Detective Mayhew. So glad you could come join my little party."

Tyrone tried to push up, but his head was blazing with pain. "Grimes, you son-of-a-bitch," said Tyrone. "I'm going to kill you."

His attacker's laughter was all Tyrone heard before the dizziness took him into another world.

Chapter 68

Tyrone came back to the conscious world in a whirlwind of throbbing pain. His head hurt so badly he could barely open his eyelids. The world was spinning. Opening his eyes part way, he could see a door and a small oak table next to it. Turning his head slightly to the left, there was a rustic brown leather couch. Nausea was pulling him into its grip when he realized there was a fire crackling to his right. This was odd because it was such a balmy July evening.

He looked down and could see a stain across his left shoulder. Blood. *His* blood. Then he started to remember–Ophelia's cabin, the phone call, the deer and then the pain. Jada—where was Jada?

"Where are you, you lousy mother fu...ah geez?" His shouting caused Tyrone's head to pulsate with pain. He grimaced and listened for a response he didn't receive.

"Jada! Jada! Are you okay?" He closed his eyes tightly, trying to convince the pain in his head to stop. He had to find his family. He had to save them. Jacobs, what had happened to Jacobs?

Tyrone took a deep breath and tried to stand. That's when he realized he couldn't stand. His arms only came up a few inches and something cold and hard stopped them. Dizzy and nauseated from the effort, he looked down and saw his wrists handcuffed to the arms of the chair. He tried to move his legs to find them bound to the chair legs by duct tape. Then it started again—the laughter. It was coming from behind him.

"Damn you're a heavy son-of-a-bitch," said the familiar voice. "I thought I was gonna give myself a hernia dragging your ass in here. And getting you in that chair was no easy feat. But, your friend here was much more cooperative."

Tyrone saw a woman fall to the floor to his left. Her auburn hair was matted with congealed blood. When she turned her swollen face toward him, he saw it was Daphne Swan.

"Come here you fuckin' coward," demanded Tyrone. He wanted to stare down the man who had eluded him for so long. The man he once called partner. "Face me!"

The laughter rang once more and Tyrone could hear him walking. "That little tap on the noggin' I gave you may have scrambled your brain a bit. Handy that your boy brought his baseball equipment with him. Hang on a minute; I've got your buddy over here."

Tyrone could hear something being dragged. When Grimes drew nearer, Tyrone could see it was Ben Jacobs. Grimes had taken duct tape and wound it around his body pinning his arms down, and then mummy wrapped his legs with it. Ben also had a wide strip across his mouth. There was blood and Ben's terrified eyes met Tyrone's as Grimes deposited him on the floor a few feet away.

"There, now everyone's present and accounted for," said Grimes. Then he bent over and squinted at Tyrone. "You don't look so good. Need an aspirin?"

Tyrone blinked, shaking his head. "Where's my family?"

"Oh, them. They're not here yet, but I'm sure they have to come back sooner or later," Grimes said sneering.

Tyrone's anger flared. He tried to free himself from his bonds, only managing to cut his wrists on the metal cuffs. "If you touch my family, I'll tear you apart!"

Grimes pulled Tyrone's Glock from his jacket pocket. He taunted Tyrone with it, bringing it close to his face. "I don't think so, my friend. I noticed it's fully loaded with enough ammo to dispose of all of you and the doc here. If I need more, I've got Jacobs' gun, too."

Tyrone tried again to free himself. He wasn't going to let this asshole murder his family and his friends. He was so full of anger he caused the chair to hop a couple of times trying to get to Grimes.

"Stop right now," growled Grimes who pointed the gun at Tyrone's face. "You won't be much good to your family if I shoot you, now will you?"

Tyrone stopped struggling, the back of his head throbbing for the effort. *Think like a cop, think like a cop,* he told himself. He had to outsmart Grimes.

"So were you surprised to find out that I helped Reid cover up Wendy's little accident," Grimes said, taking a more relaxed, nonchalant stance.

"I guess I should have known when I found out how badly you botched the initial investigation," said Tyrone.

"Me? I seem to remember you being there, too."

"Yeah, I was there. Fresh, trustin', never even considerin' you might be lyin' to me," said Tyrone.

"Excuses, excuses."

"Why'd you grab Daphne?" asked Tyrone. "She was only tryin' to help Jared."

"Some help she was," Grimes snorted. "She helped him to an early grave."

"She didn't kill him, the cover up did," said Tyrone. "What was in it for you anyway?"

"Simple. Loyalty," said Grimes.

"Come on," spat Tyrone. "You're plannin' to kill me so why not just give me the whole story."

"I don't suppose it would hurt. It will pass the time while we wait for the others," said Grimes. "Besides, confession is good for the soul, right doc?"

Tyrone could hear her crying. She couldn't speak because her mouth, like Jacobs, was sealed with duct tape.

Grimes went over to her and kicked her in the stomach. She pulled into a tighter fetal position and groaned.

"Stop blubbering, bitch. I'm sick of it already."

"I'm sorry I got you mixed up in this, Daphne," said Tyrone. He felt so worthless right now.

"How touching," said Grimes. Then he walked over to the fireplace removing the photo of Tyrone's family which Ophelia kept on the mantle. "Nice family. Looks like someone took it a couple of years ago. Looks like Reggie is about four and the youngest boy is just a baby."

"Yeah, it was," said Tyrone, trying to stay calm and buy some time. Surely, the 911 dispatcher had someone coming soon. He just hoped they'd get here before his family did.

"Sorry about shooting the boy," said Grimes looking sincere. "I just wanted to shoot out a few windows and scare the crap out of you. I'd hoped you would stop if your family was in danger."

"Like I told you before, it was too late to stop. You're a cop. You knew once the body was found, there wasn't anything I could do even if I'd wanted to."

"That's what you keep saying, but I was able to turn this into a cold case ten years ago. You couldn't just leave it at finding the car, could you? No, you brought out the dogs on the word of a physic, of all people."

"But she was right," said Tyrone. "There wasn't any reason to kill her after we found the body. Did you think she'd be seeing you in her visions next?"

"Turns out that she did see me, but that wasn't the reason. Unfortunately for her, she wouldn't stay away from Jared, just like this bitch," he said, visibly angry. "She encouraged him to continue to seek the truth and look what it got him. She needed to be stopped."

"So you're tryin' to tell me your only concern was for Jared." Tyrone laughed and shook his head. "You didn't care what happened to Jared as long as she didn't implicate you."

Grimes lowered his gun and drew back his left fist, and then drove it into Tyrone's right cheek. Tyrone's head throbbed with blinding pain again. He spit out two teeth before the blackness took him once more.

Chapter 69

Tyrone's head swayed as a blur of light teased his vision. For a moment, he wondered if his neck broke when Grimes hit him because he couldn't quite hold up his head. Soon his pounding brain started to function more clearly and he knew he wouldn't be moving at all if his neck snapped. He could barely open his right eye for the swelling in his cheek. The metallic taste of blood filled his mouth.

He turned his head looking for the culprit. What he saw and heard was a terrified Daphne now sitting in a chair, duct tape removed from her mouth, and pleading for Grimes to understand.

"Please," she said. "I liked Jared. I only wanted to help him."

Tyrone could see Grimes bending slightly and cocking his head as though he was looking at something curious.

"You heard Detective Mayhew. He's taking responsibility for your predicament." Grimes stood up straight. "Of course, you chose to help him, so I can't let you off the hook that easy."

"Your argument's with me," said Tyrone, wincing. "Not her, not Jacobs, and not my family."

"Look who's awake again, Doc," said Grimes. "Now, I'll continue with my story; however, any more smartass remarks and I'll put a bullet through Dr. Swan's head." He put the gun against Daphne's temple. "Understood?"

Tyrone nodded his head slowly. He glanced at Jacobs who still lay on the floor. His eyes were closed.

Apparently, Grimes saw him glance at Jacobs. "Oh, don't worry about your pal. After I hit you, he got a little squirmy so I drugged him. I only gave him enough to keep him out for about fifteen minutes or so. It was very convenient to have a sister-in-law who was a nurse."

"I thought...you planned...to continue your little story," said Tyrone, having difficulty speaking.

"Ah, yes, well I hadn't seen Reid for about thirty years when they assigned me to his wife's case. We served in Nam together." Grimes paused and paced for a few seconds waving Tyrone's gun around, finger near the trigger. "We were in the same platoon and saw a lot of shit over there. It wasn't as it is today. Nobody back home cared about us. Well, nobody except maybe our moms."

Tyrone thought he saw some headlights coming up the drive. He quickly engaged Grimes, hoping he wouldn't see them. "Lots of guys went through that. Matherson said he saved your life."

"He sure did," said Grimes, pointing the gun at Tyrone's chest. "We were trudging through an area so full of trees and plants, we could hardly see. Reid saw a flash and knocked me down. Next thing I saw was a bullet lodged in the tree behind me. It looked like it would have gone right through my throat."

"So, how'd you get involved with the cover up?"

"I owed the guy," said Grimes. "The first time we went out to his house to question him, I realized who he was. I asked him to meet me at a bar outside of the city to talk privately. He confessed what he'd done and I told him he shouldn't have moved the body.

"Of course, he was all concerned that Jared would be incarcerated or sent to a loony bin for what he'd done. For some reason, Reid thought it would be better to make the kid think he was dreaming. I never had any kids, so what did I know about what was best. So, I told him I'd take care of it. I left Indianapolis because I didn't want anyone to figure out what I'd done."

"How could you be sure nobody would find the car?"

"They'd opened the dam that week to let more water into the reservoir. Then they designated the area a bird sanctuary. How was I to know the birds would change their minds and move out? Now it's open for fishing."

"But it was an accident," said Tyrone, his emphasis causing his swollen cheek to send a stabs of pain to his eye. He paused, closing both eyes to get through it. "There wasn't any reason to cover it up."

"They'd already buried the body and dumped the car. It was too late. It was bad enough Wendy was dead. Those kids needed their father."

"But what about Jared?" Daphne asked weakly. "Deep down, he remembered no matter how much brainwashing his father and brothers did. He suffered for it every day of his life. He would have remembered it sooner or later, even without my help."

He walked over to her, and then put the gun to her temple again. "You shrinks think you know everything, don't you?" He moved around her, still holding the gun to her head. She looked at Tyrone, tears flowing as Grimes bent down next to her other ear. "I don't give a shit about your professional opinion. Keep your mouth shut and you'll live longer. Are we clear, Doc?"

"Yes," she said, nodding and closing her eyes momentarily.

"Where were we," he said to Tyrone as he lowered the gun and started to pace again. "Oh, yes. Well, I did what I could to help Reid. It was his decision how to handle his kid. Besides…."

Grimes stopped his confession with the slam of a door and Tyrone's heart skipped a beat. Grimes slipped over to the window and peeked round the curtain. He smiled as he turned to look at Tyrone.

"Don't do it," Tyrone pleaded. "I'm the one you want. Don't kill my family." Tyrone saw he wasn't going to get any sympathy from Grimes. He could hear his wife's voice.

"Darryl, you get Adanne out of her car seat and I'll get Malcolm," she shouted.

Pure terror ran through Tyrone as he started shouting. "Jada, don't come in here! Run!"

Grimes ran over to him and kicked the side of the chair sending it toppling over. Tyrone hit the right side of his head again. Desperate, the adrenaline rush of his fear kept him conscious. He wriggled, trying to loosen the duct tape so he could slide his bonds over the end of the chair leg. Grimes advanced on him. He placed the gun against Tyrone's left temple and Tyrone stopped moving.

"One more move and I'll let you watch me fuck her before I kill her. Now lay still." Grimes moved over to the door, waiting with the gun pointed at Tyrone.

Tyrone looked at Daphne and began to cry and beg quietly, "Please, please let them go. They don't know you're involved. They can't tell anyone about you."

"I said, shut up," Grimes sneered, his face red with fury. Grimes had just walked up behind Daphne when Tyrone heard, "Police, don't move."

Grimes grabbed Daphne from the chair and placed her in front of him like a shield. "Get out of here or I'll blow her fucking head off."

"Detective Grimes," said one of the officers. "This cabin is surrounded by State S.W.A.T. officers and deputies from the sheriff's department. It's time to put the weapon down and give it up."

"I didn't come this far, just to give up," Grimes snarled. "If I'm going down I'm taking at least these two with me."

Tyrone looked up and saw Grimes' evil grin staring down at him. Then he looked towards Jacobs who was directly behind Grimes still lying there drugged. If he was going down, he'd rather look at his best friend than at that monster.

Jacobs glanced up at Grimes then winked at Tyrone.

Grimes was backing up towards Jacobs, his left arm gripping Daphne across the neck. Had he forgotten about Ben?

As soon as Grimes was about to step on him, Jacobs rolled forward as hard as he could and Grimes fell backwards. When he did this, Daphne fell forward and landed on the floor next to Tyrone.

As Grimes hit the floor, his gun flew out of his hand and S.W.A.T. was on top of him in seconds. Two of them yanked Grimes up by his arms and had him cuffed in no time.

Tyrone heard the officer who had been trying to get Grimes to surrender saying, "Perpetrator is in custody. Three victims with injuries so we need paramedics in here ASAP." Then he stopped Grimes and said to his colleague. "Search his pockets for cuff keys."

One of the officers was tearing away the duct tape from Tyrone's legs when the door burst open. In ran Jada falling to her knees beside him.

"Mrs. Mayhew, you should wait for the EMT's."

"I'm a nurse," she said. "I can take care of him until they get here."

"I didn't realize," he said. "You find those keys yet, Sparks?"

"Yep," Sparks said. He tossed them over just before taking Grimes outside.

The officer unlocked the handcuffs and pulled the chair away. Then he went over to Daphne and started to remove her bonds while Erica checked on Ben.

Erica pulled the tape from Ben's mouth. "Are you okay?"

"Yeah," he said. "I'm still a little groggy from something he shot me up with to keep me quiet. I'm not hurt as badly as Tyrone is. He took a whack to the head with a baseball bat."

"He drugged me too when we first got here," said Daphne. "He kept it in his duffle bag on the other side of the front door."

Once the EMT's arrived, the S.W.A.T. leader informed them of the drugs used on both Daphne and Ben so they'd be aware in case they wanted to use something that would react with it.

"Pulse and heart rate are a little low, but good," said one of the EMT's when examining Ben.

"You guys should be taking care of Tyrone. Even his hard head can't take the number of blows he's had tonight," said Ben.

"This guy will be fine," said the EMT as he handed Erica a pair of scissors. "Can you cut him out of all this tape so we can check on his friend?"

"Of course," said Erica.

Tyrone looked up with his one good eye. He could see Jada looking very worried as an EMT started to take his pulse.

"Boy am I glad to see you," said Tyrone, his voice muffled by the swelling on the right side of his face.

"Honey," said Jada. "You're going to be alright. Just stay still. You may have a concussion."

"I love you baby," he said, tears streaming down his bloody face. "He was gonna to kill all of us. I had to stop him, I had to…."

"Hush now," she whispered and stroked his uninjured cheek. "It's all over now and we're going to be fine."

"Did I hear them say you're a nurse?" asked the EMT.

Jada nodded, not taking her eyes away from her husband's injured face.

"Here's an ice pack, some gauze and saline solution to rinse out his wounds. I need to get the board. We don't want to take a chance of moving him without a neck brace and board after this last fall."

"Don't you worry," she said. "I'll be glad to help out." Jada squeezed the ice pack to bring it to life and gently placed it on his wretched, swollen cheek. She then poured water over his head to rinse away the dried blood and attempt to cleanse his wounds.

"Where are the kids?" asked Tyrone, grimacing in pain, but glad for his wife's sweet touch.

"They're at the sheriff's house with his wife," she said. "We'd been invited to go there for dinner this evening."

Then he remembered the deputy. "Jada, there's an officer down outside. Did you see him?"

She smiled that sad smile she used on patients when the news wasn't good. He let out a sigh and waited for her answer.

"He didn't make it, Tyrone," she said lightly brushing her fingers over the left side of his head. "Now you stop worrying and do what I tell you."

"Yes ma'am," he said then closed his eyes.

Chapter 70
Four Weeks Later

"Wow that smells good," exclaimed Ben as he walked out onto Tyrone's patio. "You do know how to cook a steak to perfection."

"Damn straight, I do."

"Tyrone, the kids might be listening!" said Jada as she brought out the salad followed by Erica carrying a platter full of corn on the cob."

"Sorry," he said sheepishly. "Jacobs here always brings out the worst in me."

"Whatever!" said Ben. "Happy anniversary, man. Of course, I don't know how this lovely woman's put up with you this long."

Jada laughed and the love he saw in her eyes almost made Tyrone melt on the spot. Instead, he gave his full attention to his cooking and turned the steaks.

Erica came over and gave Tyrone a big hug. "You're looking better. Will you be back to work soon?"

"Doc wants me to take off a few more weeks. You know the routine, gotta see the shrink," Tyrone answered. "Being in the hospital in an induced coma, wastin' three weeks of my life really sucked, so it will be good to have the time to spend with my family."

Jada came up behind him and put her arm in his. "It may have sucked, but it was necessary. You took at least three nasty blows to the head and your brain swelled to dangerous proportions. Believe me; it would have sucked more to be awake through all that."

He smiled at his wonderful wife and kissed her on the forehead. "I'm just glad I recovered in time for this auspicious occasion. Ten years with this wonderful woman. It seems like only yesterday I asked her to marry me, and she's just as beautiful as the day I met her."

"At least one of you is still pretty." Jacobs' comment earned him a punch in the arm from Erica. He looked at her in surprise.

Tyrone chuckled then turned his attention to Erica. "Sounds like we'll both be back to work by October."

"Yeah, Freeman and the lovely Natalie will be taking off on a cruise and that would leave the homicide division way understaffed. Not sure why he wants to go on a cruise," said Erica. "From what I hear, he gets seasick relaxing in a bathtub."

They all laughed. The boys came out to join the adults. Darryl was carrying a bowl of potato salad. Tyrone noticed the boy had grown six inches taller over the summer. How did time fly by so quickly?

While the ladies got the rest of the crew settled around the table, Ben held the platter on which Tyrone began to place the steaks and hot dogs. The younger two boys hadn't advanced to the steak stage yet.

"How'd we get so lucky to have two superbly brilliant women in our lives?" asked Tyrone.

"Not sure. Here we went to the cabin to rescue them and they wound up rescuing us," said Ben. "Erica says Jada was the one who devised the plan."

"Really," said Tyrone. "She didn't tell me that."

"Jada suggested that a few of the State S.W.A.T. Team and the sheriff hide in the back of the van while she drove up with Erica in the front seat. Then Jada parked so Grimes couldn't see the sliding side door. She shouted as if she was talking to the kids. They saw Grimes peek around the curtain, and when he moved the curtain back and they heard you shouting, the officers took the opportunity to sneak around back. They knew he'd be waiting at the front door for Jada to come in."

"I still can't believe it was Grimes," said Tyrone. "He fooled me ten years ago, and when this case reopened, he fooled me again by acting like a retired old man who didn't want to be involved. How could I be so stupid?"

"Don't be so hard on yourself," said Ben. "Except for a few lumps on your head, it's all good. Daphne Swan had a few cuts and contusions and a cracked rib, but she didn't let Grimes' actions keep her down. From what Jada told me, her sessions with Reggie have him back on track."

"Yeah, she's been great with him," said Tyrone. "Now he's as rowdy as ever. Except for the scar, you'd never know it happened."

"And you," said Ben, "you're looking pretty good. Two new teeth implanted and only a couple of scars."

"Well, I'll be much better when Grimes is convicted and put away for the rest of his natural life," said Tyrone placing the last piece of meat on the platter.

"You're not the only one," said Ben.

"I see you and Erica have gotten closer. Anything I should know?" asked Tyrone with a big toothy grin.

"We finally had our romantic weekend in Nashville. It was two weeks later than planned, but it was great. She's looking forward to going back to work and she's decided to move in with me."

"Well done, my man."

"Come on Daddy," said Malcolm, tugging on his father's pant leg. "We're starving!"

Tyrone smiled down at his youngest son, a sense of pride warming him. He was so overwhelmed with gratitude that his family was healthy and safe. He looked at Ben and grinned.

"Okay, ya'll," exclaimed Tyrone. "Let's eat!"

# # #

About the Author

Michele May, whose pen name is M. E. May, was born in Indianapolis, Indiana, and lived in central Indiana until she met her husband and moved to the suburbs of Chicago Illinois, in 2003. Although, she has physically moved away, her heart still resides in her hometown. She has a son, a daughter, and four wonderful grandsons still living in central Indiana.

Michele studied Social and Behavioral Sciences at Indiana University, where she learned how the mind and social circumstances influence behavior. While at the university, she also discovered her talent for writing. Her interest in the psychology of humans sparked the curiosity to ask why they commit such heinous acts upon one another. Other interests in such areas as criminology and forensics have moved her to put her vast imagination to work writing fiction that is as accurate as possible.

Michele is an active member of Mystery Writers of America Midwest Chapter, Sisters in Crime Chicagoland, Speed City Sisters in Crime in Indianapolis, and the Chicago Writers Association and its affiliate InPrint.

Her *Circle City Mystery Series* is appropriately named as these stories take place in her home town of Indianapolis. The first novel in the series, *Perfidy*, won the 2013 Lovey Award for Best First Novel, and the second book in the series, *Inconspicuous*, was released in July 2013.